The House on Chambers Road

C. J. McGroarty

Literary Wanderlust | Denver, Colorado

The House on Chambers Road is a work of fiction. Names, characters, places and incidents are either the product of the author's imagination or are used fictitiously, and any resemblance to actual persons, living or dead, business establishments, event or locales is entirely coincidental.

Copyright © 2025 by C.J. McGroarty

All rights reserved. No part of this publication may be reproduced, distributed, stored in a retrieval system, or transmitted in any form or by any means, including photocopying, recording, or other electronic or mechanical methods, without the prior written permission of the publisher, except in the case of brief quotations embodied in critical reviews and certain other noncommercial uses permitted by copyright law.

Published in the United States by Literary Wanderlust LLC, Denver, Colorado. www.LiteraryWanderlust.com

ISBN print: 978-1-956615-49-4
ISBN digital: 978-1-956615-51-7

Printed in the United States of America

DEDICATION

For Jim, my North Star

For Meredith, my beautiful daughter

PROLOGUE

1792, Jones Estate, Simms, a village outside of Philadelphia

Abigail and Alice stood side by side in the dark bedchamber where their father lay dying. The lamp on the table flickered shadows across his haggard face. His breathing came quick and shallow.

"Do you suppose death will free him of his burden... whatever it was?" Abigail whispered.

"I think it is the only thing that shall free him," Alice said. She reached down to touch the slender brush clenched in her father's hand, its fine bristles stiffened with old green paint. "He would not relinquish this. I suppose it's doing no harm. But come. I must head for home."

Abigail took up the lamp and followed her sister down the stairs. The candle brought a dim luster to the knot of dark hair at the back of Alice's head. The same dark color as Abigail's. The color that had once been their father's.

"Are you certain you cannot stay another night?" Abigail

asked.

"Would that I could. But I promised Marcus I would return this evening. And with Flynn just out of his fever, I best not tarry."

Alice lifted her cloak from its hook at the bottom of the stairs and settled it around her shoulders. "Do send word as soon as..." She pressed a hand to Abigail's arm.

"I'll have Sam ride to you at first light. He and Charles have the grave ready, out near the west field."

With a glance about the shadowy hall, Alice tugged on her gloves and gave a sad little smile. "Father loved this house so. It shall feel empty without him."

Abigail watched from the doorway as Alice stepped out into the dusk. The big clock at the bottom of the stairs began to chime.

CHAPTER ONE

I was driving to an appointment with a new client on the outskirts of Simms the morning I first saw the house.

It was a bright, blustery April day, and as I coasted down Chambers Road in my late husband's vintage Chevy, I felt a little nervous, this being my first appointment after returning to work. Only two months had passed since I scattered Ray's ashes over a hillside down in Virginia, and I was wondering how I would cope with talk of Shaker cabinets and farmhouse sinks while the fog of my grief hung heavy around me. I wasn't sure I was ready.

Then suddenly I wasn't driving anymore. I was standing on a lawn, gazing up at the chalky white façade of a Georgian country house, and a voice was asking, "May I help you?"

I turned and saw a woman, her mouth pulled down in a frown, a binder in her hand, and at that moment I felt I'd awakened from a dream.

"Oh, I'm not sure," I said.

The woman pointed behind her to a driveway and a bronze

sedan with two passengers inside. "I have clients here to see the house."

In front of the sedan, Ray's sky blue Malibu idled, the driver's door wide open. I must have climbed out and left the engine running. But how could I—?

"I'm afraid showings are by appointment only," the woman said. She paused, as if waiting for a reply. "If you'd like to move your car."

"No, I don't need an appointment. I'm Libby Casey. I have a period design business in town and..." Even as I fumbled to make my excuses, my gaze was pulled back toward the house, where something in a second-story window was flickering.

I made my apologies and hurried over the grass toward my car, the wind whipping my hair against my cheeks, bringing me back to myself. Only then did it sink in that the woman was a realtor and the house was up for sale, although there was no sale sign on the lawn. I slid into the Malibu and turned around in front of a two-bay carriage house and then coasted back to the street.

As I continued on my way down Chambers Road, I tried to piece together the odd bits of what had just happened. I'd been driving along under the blinking sun and...a blank, a glitch in time, and then the odd pull of the house.

Maybe it had caught my eye as I was passing, and in a sudden fit of distraction, I pulled off the road for a better look. I'd been so easily distracted since Ray died, my mind sliding from one thing to another, untethered. Still, it wasn't like me to stop on my way to an appointment and risk being late.

I pulled into my client's driveway and gathered up my purse and laptop. After the appointment, I would go back to Chambers Road and get another look at the house. Even through the haze of my confusion, I'd seen it was a fine example of a country Georgian. And I had always loved the charms of eighteenth-century style.

When I got back to Chambers Road two hours later, I sat idling on the grassy shoulder in front of the Reardon School for the Blind, which was hidden far back behind a frontage of tall hedge and shrubbery across the street. I rolled the window down halfway and gazed out at the house. Behind the post and rail fence and the wide carpet of lawn, it loomed bright in the midday sun, solid and implacable, like the keeper of some secret wisdom. The stucco was dingy here and there, and a black shutter hung loose on a first-floor window. But the dentil cornice that rimmed the roofline was intact, its white teeth set out in a perfect row. Under the cornice, the panes of a second-story window winked.

The flickering I'd seen before, like a light flashing Morse code.

With the street deserted, I sat there a while longer. The massive old sycamore down by the road towered over the lawn, its limbs casting shadows in every direction. High above the house, a pair of hawks flew in lazy circles. It was quiet here, and undisturbed, as if time had stopped. As if the centuries had passed and nothing had changed.

Last night I dreamt I went to Manderley again.

Those words came to me unbidden, though it was years since I'd read Daphne du Maurier's *Rebecca*.

My watch pinged noon. I had promised Harry I would stop at Ming Garden for takeout. I pulled away from the shoulder, feeling certain in my bones that I was not done with the house, and that it was not done with me.

—

When I got back to town, Harry was on the sidewalk in front of the 1930s storefront that housed our business, March & Casey Period Design and Restoration. He was talking with a man I didn't recognize.

"And here she is now," he said as I approached. "Libby Casey, this is Keith Janus. He stopped in about getting some work done over in Morley."

I mustered a smile, distracted by the paper bag I was hugging to my middle, the warmth of the containers inside seeping through my jacket, the scent of Chinese takeout fuming up. Shrimp and pepper fry. The sun glinted off Keith Janus's short coffee-colored hair as he extended his hand to greet me. A perfunctory greeting, as if he had things to do and was eager to go get them done.

A moment later, he walked off down Main Street. Harry and I went in and shut the door against a gust of wind.

"He says he's in environmental law, so he gets *my* vote. Could be a fun project," Harry said. "Mid-century place, lots of wood and windows, I imagine. I'm hoping we can go up there next week."

"Mid-century...sounds right up your alley." I fought back a yawn. "By the way, is that a new haircut?"

He swiped a hand through his auburn waves. "Not too *shawt* on the sides?" Harry had left Boston long ago, but Boston hadn't left him. "Mitch thought so, but he said he won't divorce me."

"What I want to know is where are you hiding the gray? You're fifty-two. You ought to have at least a little."

Lately, if I looked closely enough, I could see a thread or two of silver hiding in the dark mahogany of my own hair, and I was ten years younger than Harry.

I took the bag of takeout back to the battered old dry sink I had trash-picked years ago and which now served as our kitchenette. Pulling two plates from the cabinet, I dished out the Chinese. Suddenly, the scent of it fell flat, and I found myself searching for my appetite. That was how it had been through the long ordeal of Ray's illness and death. The idea of food was more appealing than the eating of it.

What I really needed was tea, my comfort drink. I switched

on the electric kettle.

Over lunch, as Harry and I talked about the job in our new client's stone colonial, my mind kept drifting back to the house on Chambers Road. The black shutter hanging down, the winking window, the huge, towering sycamore.

"You feeling okay, kiddo?" he said.

"Sorry, just a little preoccupied."

After a dozen years as my business partner and friend, Harry was good at reading me.

I told him about the Georgian, leaving out the odd glitch in time still scratching at the back of my brain. No point in making him worry about my mental state. He had a mother with dementia and that seemed burden enough.

"The old Jones estate," he said. "Now there's a place that's right up *your* alley. I've never made time to go out and take a look, although I heard a few years back that the owners signed an easement to prevent development there. Apparently, they had no children, and the place meant a lot to them."

"So, there's more land there than meets the eye," I said.

"More than an acre or two."

Then the phone rang, and we left it at that.

—

At home that night, I went upstairs to my office and searched online for information about the house on Chambers Road. My search yielded little, only an old black-and-white photograph on the Simms Historical Society website, looking much like the house did today: the dark shutters; the lawn; the sycamore, smaller back then. Under it, a caption, "Jones Estate 1910, Simms, PA" and a few sentences about the Joneses of Wales, who settled the property in the mid-eighteenth century and lived there for five generations.

A vague memory shook loose in my mind, but in the next moment, it was gone.

My dog, Buck, a shaggy brown mix of Border Collie and

something else, huffed in the doorway.

"I know, sweet boy. It's late," I said to his inquiring copper stare. "Come on. Time for bed."

We crossed the hall into the master bedroom, where Sugar Plum, my tortoiseshell tabby, was already asleep in the upholstered chair in the corner. Buck jumped up and settled himself on the bed. I shook a pill from the little brown jar in my night table drawer and swallowed it back with a gulp of water from the travel cup I kept on the table.

Alone in the dark again.

Sealed in my vault.

I lay back and reached for Ray's hand. Where were those beautiful hands I had loved so much, with the nimble fingers and freckle dust? Moldering into the dirt on that Virginia hillside.

No, Libby. Don't think about that. Just don't.

Buck was snoring softly on the quilt. I got up and went back to my computer across the hall. If nothing else, the mysterious Georgian would give me a reprieve from the vault. I searched a little more but turned up only the latest real estate transaction—a sale of the property four years ago, in 2014—and its current status as being on the market again.

With the pill's effects kicking in, I closed my laptop and went back to bed.

Relax, breathe, let sleep come over you.

"Ray," I whispered. "I'm sorry."

CHAPTER TWO

Spring passed into summer, and summer became fall, and as the fog of my grief began ever so slowly to lift, I sometimes found myself driving by the Jones estate, now inhabited by new owners. I would sit and idle a while on the grassy shoulder, just watching. Odd, but it always felt as if the house had been expecting me.

And then there were the dreams. Or were they nightmares? I woke up from one such dream, cold and shivering. I'd been outside the Georgian in a pouring rain, pounding with a knocker at the red front doors, *Rap! Rap! Rap!* It had felt so real that I reached up to my hair to see if it was wet. In another of these dreams, I was standing in a doorway, staring into a room where a man sat in the shadows by a lit fireplace. And when I called to him, he wouldn't answer, wouldn't even look my way.

I kept it all to myself—the visits to the house, the dreams—until one night I finally told Diana, my best friend, as we sat in her kitchen drinking wine.

"I don't know what to make of it," I said. "Maybe it's just a phase I'm going through."

"I'm sure it's everything weighing on your mind," Diana said, sympathy in her hazel eyes. She pushed a plate of her homemade quiche squares across the table. "Here, eat. Put some flesh on those bones. You're positively wasted."

When I declined, she tugged on her ash blond bangs, her habit when she was thinking something through. "Grief affects everyone differently, Lib. When my uncle died, my Aunt Cathy would go to the park every day and sit on a bench for two hours at a time. It was just her way."

Diana was nothing if not sensible, almost to a fault—the more rational the explanation, the better, as far as she was concerned. But her rational explanation didn't quite satisfy the formless questions in the back of my mind.

She flashed one of her trademark grins. "I think you need a new hobby. Get your mind someplace else so you don't dwell too much. Want to help out next week at the Harvest Food Fest? Mary Stott's making her apple strudel again."

At least she hadn't suggested I give counseling another try. I had seen a grief therapist for a month after Ray died, but I stopped going to her because I didn't have anything new to say. I didn't know how else to describe my sorrow. *I'm bereft. I miss his hands. I'm sealed in a vault.*

And the one thing I had really needed to tell her, I couldn't. Couldn't tell anyone.

—

Over the winter and following spring, I went less often to Chambers Road. Harry and I were gathering steam on a few big projects, and I threw myself into refinishing some end tables I'd found at a flea market. It wasn't the new hobby Diana had suggested, but it helped. Yet through it all, the house tapped a dull beat at the back of my mind, and the dreams, though fewer, still haunted me.

Then, that summer, the Jones place went up for sale again.

"Don't you think that's odd?" I asked Harry when he gave me the news one Friday afternoon. He had just returned from the hardware store, where he heard about the listing from Cassie Hughes. Cassie owned the bookstore in town, Cassie's Pen and Page, and knew everything about everything in Simms. "Why would it be on the market again after little more than a year?"

"Cassie heard they wanted permission to build some kind of outbuilding on the grounds and were turned down." Harry pulled a screwdriver out of the brown bag from the hardware store. "Obviously, they didn't understand the meaning of the word 'easement.' But who knows? People move into a place like that and find out it's not their cup of tea after all."

"Thank God for the easement. Without it, well, we both know what would have happened by now."

I sank into my thoughts. The Jones estate up for sale again. An easement always devalued a property and reduced the market. Maybe I could take a look, see what was hidden behind those blood-red doors I had pounded on in my dreams, the ones I now reimagined as a bright sunny yellow. There were bound to be sooty hearths and deep windowsills and seasoned old floorboards. Yes, eighteenth-century style had its charms.

But how could I even think about that? I had promised Ray I would stay on Poplar Street and look after our Victorian. Queenie, we'd named it for its Queen Anne Revival style. I'd told him I would carry on in the place where we'd shared our life. Our almost magical life, until—"Nickel for your thoughts, Casey?"

I looked over and saw Harry leaning against his desk, tapping the screwdriver against his palm. The sleeves of his burgundy shirt were rolled up, and his charcoal trousers draped loosely on his legs, cinched with a plain black belt. Classic, that was Harry's style, and he had always worn it well.

"Oh, I was just thinking about, well, would you think I was crazy if I said I might want to take a look around the Jones place?" When he didn't reply right away, I said, "You would, wouldn't you?"

He stopped tapping the screwdriver and studied me, his wheels turning.

"You have that Jimmy Stewart look," I said. "Am I about to get some old-fashioned, fatherly advice?"

"Do you want some?"

"I'm not sure. If you're going to tell me it's too soon—"

"Nah. You're a grown woman and you can make up your own mind about where you want to live. But there would seem to be a lot of homework to do before you make this kind of decision. And let's face it, Lib, you've been through a lot. And while you've been getting up to speed lately, you still seem to be working on it."

He winked, pushed off the desk, and drifted toward the back room. "I've got some hinges to tighten. I'm here if you need me."

It had been eighteen months since…there it was again. *Since Ray died.* Yes, I was still a little at loose ends, and still exhausted. But Ray's affairs were settled, and the generous life insurance payout was still untouched because I hadn't been able to bring myself to spend a penny of it. I could afford to buy the Georgian if I wanted to. Buy it, fix it up, start fresh. If I could let myself move on.

—

A few nights later, Diana and I were back in her kitchen, talking about the Jones place again and my idea to take a tour.

"It feels like the stars have aligned," I said, "and it might be the change I need. And I just feel that there's something about the place. Like I belong there."

Diana narrowed her eyes. "You're not mentally transferring, are you? I mean, you're finally starting to get beyond…everything, and I don't want to see you take on something that might need more than you can give it."

"Harry's words, more or less."

"And you'd be leaving Queenie behind. You and Ray worked so hard to fix that place up."

"And I'm glad we did. Really, I am. And I'll always love it." I stared down into my wineglass and saw my own reflection. "But not all the memories there are good ones. Maybe it's time."

—

And so, on a hot, humid August day, I took a tour of the house with Marilyn Farini, a real estate agent in town.

"Isn't that just the neatest thing?" she said when she noticed me staring at the black iron knocker as we went in. A lion's head with a ring through its nose, very dark and sober, the kind of thing you might expect the face of Jacob Marley to materialize out of. "I'm told it's original to the house."

I traced the wild mane and the big ring and wondered whether this was the knocker I had pounded with in my dreams. It should have been hot to the touch, with the midday sun beating down on it. But instead, it felt oddly cool.

In the center hall, Marilyn closed the doors behind us. "Ahh, that AC feels good," she said. She wiped a wave of dyed-black hair back from her forehead. "All new HVAC was installed four years ago, by the way. That'll save you a bundle."

I glanced about the empty hall, making a quick assessment. Dentil crown molding, wainscoting more than halfway up plaster walls, a high ceiling—nine feet at least—all done in cream with a hint of yellow. Pine plank floorboards, pocked and scraped with age, probably not original.

"A house like this doesn't come along very often," Marilyn said.

"No, it certainly doesn't," I said, still lost in the hall's features. The cheap brass sconces on the walls could be switched out for iron or bronze easily enough.

Marilyn dropped her purse to the floor. "Shall we have a look around?"

"If you don't mind, Marilyn, I'd like to walk through the first time on my own."

I knew Marilyn through the Simms Business and Professional Association, and I didn't think she would balk at my request. Which she didn't, offering instead to wait on the folding chair in the kitchen, the only piece of furniture in the house, she said.

I stepped into the first room on the right. *My office*, I thought. Tall windows, eastern and southern exposure, lots of light. Fireplace with a carved mantelpiece and a closet on either side. I opened both of the closets. Nothing inside but dusty shelves. Maybe I could break through one of them and connect my office to the room next door.

That room, I discovered, was just right for a living room. Fireplace with blank walls for shelving on either side, plenty of floor space for a sofa and chairs. A little darker than the office, but I would be in it only—

Slow down, Libby. It isn't time to move in yet.

I crossed the hall to the dining room, which had probably been two separate rooms before someone made it into one big room and built a new fireplace into the outside wall. A doorway at the back end led to the kitchen.

Marilyn looked up from her phone. "How's it going so far?" she asked. She got up and swept her hand around the room. "Now this, I think, you're going to like. The Hempels redid it last year."

And they'd done a pretty fair job, I thought. Farmhouse sink under the double back window, subway tile backsplash, white Shaker cabinets that contrasted well with the dark plank floors. They'd even thought to put the butcher block island on casters. I would have chosen soapstone for the countertops, but the caramel-colored quartz was pleasant enough.

A huge fireplace on the west wall, ancient and blackened with soot, anchored the space.

"And what's this?" I asked, crossing to a door beside the fireplace. I opened it to a narrow staircase that climbed four steps to a landing, turned right and continued upward.

Marilyn came over to join me. She peered up the stairs. "It doesn't look like it's been used in a long time, does it?"

"An old sleeping quarters, maybe." I glanced at my watch. It was after one o'clock, and I'd told Harry I would be back before two for a client appointment.

"I can look there later," I said. "I better check out the rest of the house."

Marilyn went back to her chair while I climbed to the second floor, where I found three bedrooms, all with fireplaces, including a master bedroom with a run-down 1970s ensuite that I now imagined in a gleaming white 1920s style, plus a smaller room with no fireplace. On the third floor, identical rooms flanked either side of a short hallway. I poked my head into one and then the other. Dormer windows, radiators, modest fireplaces.

I turned to go downstairs but found myself lingering in the hall instead. The house suddenly seemed so...hushed, as if it was holding its breath, watching, waiting, refusing to let me go. A moment later, I turned back toward one of the little rooms, feeling like I needed to see it again.

Then my watch pinged. 1:30.

I pulled myself away and went to find Marilyn. "I'll need to come through again, if that's okay," I said. "I want to get Harry's opinion. And I want to walk around the property a bit."

"Just let me know when. But don't wait too long. I understand someone else is coming through next week."

As we said goodbye out on the driveway, I asked her if she knew why the Hempels had left so soon, especially after doing the big kitchen reno.

"Apparently, they missed their family down in North Carolina." Marilyn shrugged. "But I've been in this business long enough to know that people come and go for all sorts of reasons."

With Marilyn gone, I stood beside Ray's Malibu, staring up

at the house. *People come and go for all sorts of reasons.* Yes, for all sorts of complicated reasons.

I was about to get into my car when I caught a flash of white about thirty yards down the road. A woman with brilliant white hair standing in the Reardon School driveway with some sort of stick in her hand. She looked my way for a long moment, perfectly still. As I raised a hand in greeting, a gust of wind blew up, flapping my loose linen trousers around my legs and making the sycamore's leaves quake. *How odd*, I thought. There hadn't been a breath of air all day. By the time I turned back to the woman, she was gone.

A week later, after two more tours, I made up my mind to buy the Jones estate. The opportunity had passed me by once; I didn't want it to happen again. And as I had told Diana, the time felt right for a change. I put in a bid—a low one I hadn't thought would pass muster—and it was readily accepted. Then I put the Victorian on the market.

The morning I signed Queenie away, I took a last look around, walked out on the wraparound porch, and wept. Ray, wherever he was, would have to forgive me for breaking my promise. For that and all the rest.

CHAPTER THREE

October 1758

"Bravo!"

Hugh Jones turned from where he'd been watching Johann Vogel hammer the last cedar shake into the roof of the new house. Miranda was standing on the dirt behind him, dressed in her shift and long blue bed coat. Her feet were bare.

"Bravo!" she sang again, clapping her hands.

With her hair falling loose over her shoulders, throwing off glints of gold, Hugh thought she looked for all the world like the Venus painted by that Italian master.

"My dear sweet," he said. He swept an arm toward the house. "It's quite fine, is it not?"

"Fine as a cathedral." Miranda went and took up his hand. "But what is this?" she said, staring at the object held in his fist.

"An iron knocker for the door. A gift from Johann in gratitude for our continued patronage. Made in his brother's smithy."

"A lion!" Miranda gave a tinkle of joy. "How wonderful!"

"It will make quite the impression, don't you think? But tell me. Are you faring better since this morning?"

"Better, yes." She laid a hand to her swollen belly. "The babe has settled."

Johann descended the ladder that was tilting against the roofline's dentil cornice. Once on firm earth, he gazed up at the roof and said, "Is good, yah?"

"Quite good," Hugh said, but in his next breath amended his words, for "good" did not seem grand enough praise. "Most superior." He went and gave the big Dutchman a fond clap on the back. "We shall see you and the boys in the spring, then. And don't forget that crate of peaches I set out for you. A little something extra for your trouble. They're the last of the crop and sweet as the devil."

Johann nodded and went about collecting his tools and tossing them into his wagon.

Hugh led Miranda back to the little square abode that had been their home for the last four years. Once the inside of the new attached house was finished, this single room with its enormous fireplace would do duty as their kitchen.

He pushed through the side door and ushered Miranda in. "Sit, sweet wife. Priscilla can make some mint tea to celebrate."

"Wife." Miranda's lips curled upward. "My Welshman has given me a title."

"Perhaps one day it shall become official. Out under the sycamore. What do you say?"

Since that night Hugh had bundled Miranda into a wagon in Philadelphia and driven her away from the clutches of her brutish father. Neither of them had felt in a hurry to marry. Hugh had been four and twenty, Miranda nineteen, and it had seemed enough that they were together at last. They would tend to the details later. Four years on, with one child born and another on the way, they had still not gotten round to marriage, although to the rest of the world, they made a pretense of being man and wife. Hugh thought it best, and no one was the wiser.

Miranda's chair scraped against the floorboards as Hugh pulled it out from the dining table. *Her* chair now, the one she'd made a habit of sitting in, and the one he'd made a habit of pulling out for her.

"You deserve the highest of titles," he said. "After all, you'll be lady of our fine new house come next fall."

Footsteps pounded the stairs leading down from the sleeping quarters. Priscilla appeared at the bottom and closed the door.

"He was determined not to shut his blessed eyes," she announced. She brushed back a lock of copper hair that had loosened from its knot. "But all's quiet now."

Priscilla had a felicitous touch when it came to two-year-old James Martin, and Hugh thought that made her as much an aunt as a housemaid.

"My son is never keen to take his nap, is he?" Miranda said. "I hope the new babe proves an easier burden." She twitched, groaned, and smoothed a hand over her belly. "Although that has not been the case of late."

"Perhaps a rest after tea," Hugh said, watching her keenly.

Miranda shook her head. "I want to make a drawing of our lovely house while the light is still good. I will just need a chair put out for me."

"Very well," Hugh conceded. There would be no convincing her otherwise. "Meanwhile, I need to get that new door bolted onto the springhouse. Then I'm off to Niall's to load up some barrels."

The iron pot arm squeaked as Priscilla pushed the kettle over the fire.

"Prissy," Hugh said. "If you must leave before I return, get safe and hasty back to the village, and we shall see you Monday."

When Miranda groaned again, Hugh sent her a look of concern. "Are you certain you are able for drawing?"

She sent him back the same concerned look to mock him and then broke into a laugh, her pain forgotten. "It is nothing, my sweet. Truly. And I won't sit out long."

She blew him a kiss, and he reached out a hand to catch it.

Fortune had smiled on him when he met Miranda. She was indeed his Venus, his angel, his charm. Hefting his haversack from the floor to his shoulder, he sent up a silent prayer of gratitude and walked out into the mild day.

—

It was a short walk through the woods to the clearing where the spring bubbled up and sent a cool rush of water streaming west. A peaceful place, and mostly quiet, shadowed by the tangle of trees that had already littered half their leaves onto the footpath. So many fine trees, *his* fine trees. But were they truly his? Sam Grey Feather said the trees belonged to the earth, the *Mother*, as he called it, and to no one else. As Hugh gazed up into the oaks and maples and pines stretching to the heavens, he was inclined to agree.

Sam. As wise a man as Hugh had ever met, and as loyal a friend.

He stepped up to where the stone springhouse straddled the stream and spent a moment admiring it. Three years ago, it had taken the whole summer to build, months of digging and hauling, laying the stone, mixing the mortar, nailing the roof. He had once helped old Coop Burton build a little stone cottage on the next farm over back home in Holywell. But the springhouse was the first thing he'd ever built with his hands alone.

"There is love in your labor," Miranda had said, dressing the blisters on his hands after a hard day's work. "And I cannot wait to behold its yield."

He had forbidden her from taking even one peek at the springhouse until it was finished. When he finally led her out to see it, she leaped down the embankment, stood on the entry planks, and kissed the hastily fashioned wood door.

"It's all quite lovely!" she exclaimed. Then she opened the door, turned to Hugh, and beckoned him to follow her. It was there, in the cool, damp interior with the stream murmuring through, that the seed of James Martin had been planted. Miranda had always been sure of it.

Now, as he went to remove the old door from its hinges, he thought back to that moment of heat and pleasure that would always come to him in this place, and he was sure of it too.

One day, perhaps, he would tell his son of his humble genesis. That he'd sprouted from a seed planted in a springhouse.

And what story would he tell the new babe?

The new babe. A seed of a different sort, harder in the womb than James Martin had been. Tonight, Hugh would light a candle to Arianrhod, one of his mother's ancient Welsh deities, and ask her to keep Miranda from harm.

CHAPTER FOUR

One night, about a week after I moved into the house, I lay awake, the moon glowing silver through the slats in the blinds, Buck snoring softly beside me. It was the middle of November, and the long Indian summer had finally waned, leaving a nip in the air. I huddled deeper under the covers. I should have turned up the thermostat before bed, or lit a blaze in the fireplace—a charming fireplace with a carved blue mantelpiece, one I hoped I could make good use of.

I sat up and looked at the clock on the night table. 1:54. Too late for a fire now, and too late to take a pill. Diana was coming in the morning to help me set up my home office, and I would need a clear head.

That's when I heard it for the first time.

Elizabeth!

A man's voice, a whisper. I held still and listened, my heart beginning to tap. The wind had picked up throughout the night, and the branches of the oak outside my bedroom window were probably sweeping against the roof. The tree was desperate for a good pruning. I looked over at Buck. He hadn't stirred a paw.

I switched on the bedside lamp. The room still felt a little foreign after only a week in the house, and it took me a moment to feel satisfied that everything was in its place, undisturbed, as it should be. I got out of bed, went to the window, and parted the drapes. The oak was frosted with moonlight, its half-bare branches tossing in the wind.

The move, like all moves, had been stressful, and more than a year and a half after Ray's death, sleep was still...well, the mind can play tricks when it's tired.

Elizabeth. My name, although only my mother had ever called me that. When she died six years ago, the name fell out of use, and now it sounded strange to my ears. Yet that is what I imagined the tossing oak had whispered.

Down in the driveway, a shadow moved in the moonlight. A fox, trotting toward the backyard with its thick tail hanging down. I let the drapes fall, went to the hallway, and peered into the darkness. The grandfather clock downstairs began to chime. *One...two...*I imagined the pendulum swinging its lazy arc inside the case like the sway of a hypnotist's watch. Side to side, side to side. On some other night, it might have helped put me under, but on this night, I was irretrievably awake.

With the house quiet again, I went back to bed. Buck half-opened his eyes, then closed them.

"It was nothing," I whispered. Then I switched off the lamp, fell back on the pillow, and waited once more for sleep.

—

After breakfast the next morning, I took Buck for a walk and then went to the little room off the kitchen to do some laundry. This room was another project waiting to be started, its linoleum floor scuffed and yellowed, the large pane of glass in the side yard door cracked near the top. I would need to replace the glass, sooner rather than later, so that the little crack didn't become a big one.

I shoved a load of clothing into the washer and pulled another from the dryer. Pajamas, underwear, socks, heaped in there all night and now rumpled as tissues at the bottom of a purse. As I folded them and placed them in the laundry basket, water drained into the washer, and *click*, the first cycle began.

Wash cycles, rinse cycles. *Life cycles*. What cycle was *I* in now? The widow cycle, although it felt much too early for that.

Pushing the basket aside, I went back to the cup of decaf I'd left cooling on the kitchen counter. Decaf for the insomnia, not that it was helping. Then I called a tree surgeon, a Mr. Tom Barrett, whose name and number Cassie Hughes had recently given me on a Post-it note. He offered to come out that afternoon to look at the oak. Better to get it trimmed soon, to eliminate any sounds that might whisper out of the night.

A moment later, I was heading to unlock the front doors for Diana when I suddenly changed course and started climbing the stairs. I needed something up on the third floor. That was the thought at the back of my mind as I stepped into the hall and went to one of the little rooms where I'd put things left over from the move. There was something here I needed.

I stood in the doorway and stared in at the yellow diamonds the sun made on the floorboards as it streamed through the dormer windows. What was I doing here? When Buck huffed behind me, I pulled my eyes away.

"We have work to do, don't we?" I asked, and I led him back downstairs.

But part of me stayed behind, up on the third floor. A few molecules of my being seemed to still have business there. If only I could remember what it was.

—

Diana arrived just as I finished hanging Andrew Wyeth's *Wind from the Sea* over the office fireplace.

"Did you start without me?" She poked her head through the doorway, a vinyl grocery bag dangling from her hand.

Sugar Plum stirred from where she'd been sleeping in a ray of sun. With a leisurely stretch, the cat rose to all fours, yawned, and wandered away.

"Just the print," I said. I stepped down from my ladder, scrutinized the Wyeth, and adjusted the frame. "Does it look straight to you?"

Diana set down her bag. "Perfectly, and I would expect nothing less. I like. And before we go any further, you're still in for the last day of the farmers' market tomorrow, right? I'm on the hunt for a few more gourds. And here." She pulled a spray of stems beaded with orange berries out of the bag. "Nothing says November like firethorn."

I laid the firethorn on the windowsill. "Your contributions are much appreciated. So, what else is hiding in there?" I peered into the bag. Stacks of plastic containers huddled around two bottles of wine. "This is all lunch? You've been spending way too much time in the kitchen."

"Don't get too excited. Some of it's from yesterday's special at the café. It was either lunch or garbage. There's enough for dinner too, if you're game. Cal's meeting Phil at McGraw's tonight to catch up on a little man-talk."

"Sold," I said. I reached for the bag to take it to the kitchen, but Diana grabbed it first.

"Here, let me." Before trailing off, she studied my face. "You look a little wiped out, sweetie. Another bad sleep?"

I shrugged. "Still working on it."

When she returned, we maneuvered the furniture into place, unpacked a few boxes, and unrolled the Oriental rug over the middle of the floor.

"Next the drapes and then we're finished," I said.

As I crossed the hall to get the drapes from the dining room table where I'd left them, Buck barked from the kitchen.

"Hey, boy!" I called. "What's going on?"

Buck hardly ever barked. When he did, it usually had something to do with Sugar Plum, my little agent provocateur.

I found the dog standing outside the laundry room.

"What's she up to now?" I poked my head in, expecting to see the cat. A jumble of the clothing I had folded and put in the laundry basket lay scattered on the floor.

"What did you do?" I asked. Buck gazed up, all innocent, and watched as I bent to scoop up the clothes. "Is this some kind of new trick?"

No longer interested, he turned and wandered away.

—

Diana and I finally settled into the kitchen for lunch. Autumn salad, one of her seasonal specialties at Cozy Cottage Café. Romaine and arugula mixed with roasted squash, dried cranberries, goat cheese, and pistachios, and topped with her signature cider vinaigrette. There was almost nothing my friend couldn't mix, chop, or concoct into a delicious meal. And with my appetite slowly returning, her tasty dishes were regaining their lost appeal.

While she tonged the salad onto plates, I poured steaming water from the electric kettle over the tea bags in two mugs. A billow of cinnamon and clove fumed up warm and pleasant. I drew in a breath of it. *Ahh…*comfort.

"By the way," Diana said, sinking onto a chair. She pulled at her chin-length bob. "Are these highlights too blond? I had Jill try something less ashy this time."

"I like it. Very cheery." I raised my mug and tapped it against hers. "Sláinte." *Sláinte.* I hadn't said that since Ray. He and I would make that toast at dinner every night…An unassailable ritual. Sometimes he would wink. Only Ray ever winked at me, and so it became something intimate between us, the dark blue eye, like wet slate, snapping like a camera shutter, recording me—

"Hey, you," Diana piped up across the table. "Where'd you go?"

"Here and there."

"See anything you want to tell me about?"

I shook my head.

"I think it's about time for something new." Diana's voice lifted with a note of encouragement. "I know your birthday isn't for two months yet, but party plans are underway." She bit a piece of squash from her fork, chewed, and chased it with a swallow of tea.

"Not that again. I don't need a party, Dee. Like I said before, a forty-third birthday isn't a milestone, and who cares anyway?"

She frowned. "I care, that's who. You missed your fortieth...you know, with everything that was going on. And the forty-first and -second, I might add. You wouldn't even let Cal and me buy you dinner last time." When I didn't respond, she said, "Do I have to make the whale analogy again?"

"Yes, I know. It's time to come up for air."

"Look, we'll keep it small, I promise. Just a dinner party. And I won't put plankton on the menu." She flashed her Diana Pruett grin.

I didn't want to disappoint her. Diana, above all others, had not given up on dragging me back to the land of the living. "You're being pushy again, you know that?"

"I'll take that as a yes," she said, trying to fork up a pistachio. "It'll be a birthday dinner to celebrate a new start in your new house."

—

While Diana was off running errands, I went back to work in the office and waited for Mr. Barrett to arrive. An architecture text, a leftover from my college days, was leaning against the bookcase where I'd propped it yesterday. I had intended to leaf through it to revisit the Georgian style, but I hadn't gotten very far.

I shoved the book back on the shelf, happy all over again that I had followed up my architecture degree with a master's in period interior design. Working on a smaller scale felt comfortable, and I had always loved the styles and objects of the past. Drafting I had never loved. Too much of it made my eyes cross.

A loud clang startled me. The door knocker.

Mr. Barrett, bearded and bespectacled, was a half hour ahead of time but made no mention of it when I opened the door. *Never be too late or too early.* The ghost of my mother, Annabelle. Sometimes I couldn't tune her out.

Wasting no time, Mr. Barrett assessed the oak, gave me an estimate for a trim, and got into his pickup and motored away.

An hour later, as I finished tucking supplies into my desk drawers, rain began spitting against the windows. I switched on the banker's lamp and took a moment to admire the space. Everything in its place now, all the hard edges softened in the low light. Buck had found a spot to doze in the middle of the newly laid rug, and now he roused himself and regarded me with a blink.

Clap!

"What was that?" I asked.

I followed the dog as he trotted off toward the back of the house. In the kitchen, he stopped and looked about. Maybe the screen door had flapped open—the wind was picking up again—but when I checked it, it was locked tight. Not quite satisfied, I walked through the first floor, on the lookout for anything that might have fallen. Buck trailed me for a while and then got bored and wandered away.

Finding nothing amiss, I figured another window shutter must have blown loose from its rusty hinges. But I didn't care enough to go out in the rain to verify.

I went back into the kitchen and poured some food into Buck's bowl. The rain was steady now, coaxing a faint waft of soot and damp from the big, blackened fireplace. I had worked in enough old buildings to know that they always exhale their past. Wood, smoke, earth, rot, and who knows, even sweat and tears. Communiques sent across time, like the light from stars.

A glimmer of what happened long ago.

I turned on the ceiling lights, and the kitchen blazed to life. *Clack, clack, clack.* The pelting of rain on the roof nearly drowned out the chime of the grandfather clock as it struck four. I slid Diana's gyro-style chicken and spanakopita into the oven to warm.

When the front door banged open, Buck abandoned what was left of his food and trotted off to investigate.

"Get out the corkscrew!" Diana bellowed from the hall. "I'm having a wine emergency!"

Sodden and dripping, she appeared in the kitchen, escorted by Buck. She fussed with a mat of bedraggled hair and sighed.

"No umbrella?" I asked.

Diana shrugged off her barn jacket and held it up. "If only. Where should I put this drowned rat?"

"Pop it in the dryer, why don't you?"

She disappeared into the laundry room and then called out with mild alarm, "Hey, what's with the clothes all over the floor?"

"Not again." I looked at Buck, who was scrounging in his almost empty bowl, then went to join Diana in the laundry room.

"It used to be clean. I'm not so sure now," she said, plucking up a few socks.

"Buck, I think."

"Maybe it's the move. Does he seem more anxious than usual?" She tossed the last sock into the basket.

"Not really."

But could she be right? Was this some kind of cry for attention? Buck's heart had been as broken as mine after Ray died. For weeks he moped around the house, watching, waiting, resting his head on one of Ray's old undershirts I'd spread for him on the floor, sleeping on Ray's side of the bed. Now, here we were in a new house, everything still so strange to him, so unfamiliar.

Diana tossed her jacket into the dryer. "Corky used to drag one of my slippers around the house after we moved into Ashford Street. I'd have to hunt all over the place for the darn thing. Then, when I finally decided to let him keep it, he didn't want it anymore."

"The peculiar habits of pets," I said, heaving the laundry basket to my hip. "Get some wine. I'll run this upstairs."

CHAPTER FIVE

The next day, a light rain was falling as Diana and I arrived at Whitman Park and the big wooden pavilion that housed the farmer's market. While Diana drifted off to hunt for gourds, I wandered idly among the dozen or so damp shoppers rummaging for bargains.

A collection of small pumpkins on a vendor's table caught my eye. I drifted over to get a better look. Thanksgiving was eleven days away, and despite the fact that I'd just moved into a new house, I still wanted to host the dinner. It was a tradition I didn't want to break—I hosted on the odd years, Harry on the even. Now, with six people coming and a woefully naked dining-room mantelpiece, a few pumpkins were just what I needed. And maybe some of those large pinecones in the box beside them, uncommonly large—

A tap on my shoulder. "Libby?"

I turned and met the bright pewter gaze of Cassie Hughes.

Cassie squeezed my shoulder, then let her hand fall. "I'm so glad I ran into you. How are you doing?"

"Busy." I knew what would come next. A question about when I would stop in to see her at the bookstore, as I had promised to do not long ago. "And you, Cassie?"

"Just wonderful, and we need to make that coffee date we were talking about." She blinked and the fringe of white bangs over her eyes jumped. "It's been too long."

A coffee date with Cassie. Pleasant enough, but it would require two hours out of my schedule and a well of stamina I wasn't sure I had. Cassie was a talker, a living, breathing ticker tape of observations, most of them interesting, but still.

She leaned in. "Did you ever have a chance to call Susannah Kunkel at the historical society? I gave you her number, remember?" Cassie was also a giver of numbers—to wit, Mr. Barrett.

"I have it," I said. But where had I put it?

"It's her personal cell number, so I'm sure she'll pick up. I know she'd love to talk to you about your new *old* house, and so would I. Such an interesting place, all that history and who knows *what else*."

What else? She said this with a sly look, sly looks being part of Cassie's repertoire of faces. Before I could ask what she meant, Diana sidled up with her shopping bag of gourds.

"Hey, Cassie," she said, offering a grin that might have been friendly. Diana had more than one in her own repertoire, and hers could be hard to read. "Looking for discounts?"

"Found them," she said, hoisting a cloth bag printed with a bookshelf and the words *Cassie's Pen and Page* in purple lettering. "I'm on my way out."

As Cassie drifted off, Diana leaned toward my ear. "What's she trying to get you to do now?"

"She wants to have coffee, and she thinks I should talk to Susannah Kunkel."

"Then you better do both of those. Our girl Cass won't give up until you do."

Twenty dollars got me a box of the big pinecones and seven

pumpkins. Mixed with some fall foliage, they would cheer up the mantelpiece nicely. Maybe I could talk Diana out of some more firethorn too.

"Ready?" she said, and we walked out into the November drizzle, the scent of autumn heavy around us.

—

The rain had stopped by the time I dropped Diana off and made my way home. Buck was waiting in the kitchen as I maneuvered through the door with my boxes of pinecones and pumpkins. His copper stare tracked me as I set the boxes on the floor and pushed them aside.

"Give me a minute, Mister," I said.

He walked over to where his leash hung from a hook beside the pantry. His idea of a good walk didn't include a leash, but I carried it all the same.

Outside, we made our way toward the woods in the back of the property. Buck bounded through drifts of dead leaves, stopped to sniff a scent at the base of a big maple, and then galloped ahead. The outdoor spaces here were new territory for both of us, and my dog took pleasure in getting to know them. When I caught up with him, he was standing by the fence that enclosed the remains of an old garden, peering in through the crusty pickets. It had already become one of his regular stops along our route. He pawed at the ground by the gate.

"Anything interesting?" I asked.

Almost as large as a neighborhood basketball court, the garden had long been abandoned, its wooden bedframes rotting to dust under snarls of withered weeds. It felt desolate in the way gardens do when left to time and the forces of nature. But it had once been green and vibrant. A kitchen garden, I assumed, for surely the Joneses would have kept one through the years for growing their herbs and vegetables. Hard to say whether this was where the original garden would have been. But it made sense. The ground was good and flat, and sunny for hours of the day. Next year, perhaps, I would bring it back from the dead. Tomatoes and basil and sweet peas.

"Let's go," I said, urging Buck on.

We followed the footpath through the trees until we came to the old stone springhouse. Another of the dog's regular stops. Wedged into an embankment where a stream once ran, the springhouse, like the garden, had been left to decay, although here and there was evidence of repairs to the crumbling mortar and the shake roof. There must have been a door once, oak or pine, but it was long gone.

Buck leaped down the embankment and disappeared into the springhouse's dark interior. I waited in the quiet, a canopy of bare branches arching overhead, the moldering leaf rot and damp of the woods all around me. Another communique from the past here in this ancient place, where generations of oaks and pines had lived and died and sunk into the soil, circled over by silent hawks.

"Buck!" My fingers were growing numb.

I descended the embankment. Buck poked his head through the springhouse door, something black clenched between his teeth. He dropped it at my feet and stepped back.

A dead bird? I kicked it gently. Not a bird but a...what, a glove?

Buck nosed at it once and then bounded away to root in the old streambed.

I picked it up and brushed away a few bits of dirt. A man's glove, by the size of it, made of thick leather and a foot long, with a cuff at the end of the shaft. An old style, not the kind of glove a man would wear these days. I peered into the empty springhouse. Had someone wandered onto the property and left it? They must have done so last night. If it had been here yesterday during our walk, Buck surely would have found it. My dog, like St. Anthony, was the patron saint of lost things.

I shoved the glove into my coat pocket and whistled to Buck, who sprang from the brush, out of breath.

"C'mon," I said, scanning the woods. "Time to go."

—

In the kitchen, I turned the dead bolt and tossed the glove onto the table. First things first. I found Cassie's Post-it note tacked inside my daily calendar and left a voicemail for Susannah Kunkel. Then I fixed dinner, a spinach and cheese omelet paired with Diana's leftover autumn salad. The damp chill had left me feeling famished.

Settled in at the table, I laid the glove flat and examined it. A few nicks and scrapes scarred the leather, and there was some wear on the palm, but other than that, it was in decent condition. A quality reproduction, maybe, part of a costume bought online from one of those vintage clothing sites that promise to turn you into a pirate or a pinup girl.

Turning it over, I noticed that the cuff was embellished with three stitched figures done up in loops and flourishes, a little frayed and faded but still intact. I traced the trails of thread with my finger. Letters, someone's initials, I assumed, but not easy to read. The middle one, was it a *P*?

I slid my phone across the table and began searching the history of gloves. I paused on an image of a leather glove with a cuffed shaft much like this one. A man's eighteenth-century gauntlet, worn mostly for work and often made of calf or doeskin.

I didn't think the glove could be more than two hundred years old, so I returned to my original thought that it was a reproduction, initialed as a gift, maybe for one of those passionate reenactors. That didn't explain what it was doing in my springhouse. I snapped a photo with my phone and texted it to Diana with a note. Maybe she would have a useful theory. A few minutes later, she replied: *Count Dracula, your glove is missing. Fill me in tomorrow.* An emoji of a vampire ended the text.

Not so useful.

I loaded the dishwasher and pushed the kitchen chairs into place as I did every night, a habit instilled in me by my fastidious mother. The glove lay on the table like the dead bird I had taken it for. No wiser to its mysteries, I left it there and went to do some work in the office.

Later, Buck followed me upstairs to bed. I'd hung a big photograph of Ray in the hallway, one of my favorites, and I paused now to admire it once again. A young, healthy Ray stood on a pitcher's mound in his uniform, a fringe of brown curls hanging down from under his cap. He was staring at the ball in his hand as if he and the ball were the only two things in the world. A holy man with his talisman.

My holy man.

Ray, doing what he'd done best, what he'd always said he was made to do. A next generation Sandy Koufax, they'd called him, heir to the same tricky curveball, until a shoulder injury put an early end to his major league career, and to the dream in his heart. That was long before I knew him. I pulled myself away from Ray and went to get ready for bed.

A half hour went by and then another as I lay against my pillow, reading, waiting to grow sleepy. At midnight, I switched off the lamp.

Relax, breathe, let sleep come over you.

I had thought after Ray died, I would be able to sleep again. In those final months of his life, I'd lain each night on a cot in the master bedroom, half awake, listening for him in case he might need something. A drink of water, more medicine, a simple reassurance that I was still there.

"Get someone in at night," Diana had said, squinting at the shadows under my eyes, "or you'll be no good to anyone."

When I finally took her advice and started sleeping in one of the bedrooms across the hall, a night nurse at Ray's bedside, I found I lay awake anyway, listening despite myself, trying in vain to tune out the occasional pained moan, the nurse's whisper as she quietly attended to him.

A year and a half later, I was listening still—not for my husband, of course, but for some other voice, one that would tell me Ray was at peace, and I should be too, despite what I'd done.

What I'd done. It was the thing I had never been able to tell anyone. The thing that still chafed my heart raw.

Those final weeks near the end, Ray lay wasting in this same bed where I lay now. Each day another day of suffering. "It's okay to let go," I would whisper, never sure if he'd heard me. But still he clung to this world, a shell, a husk, his beautiful hands bony as claws. Hands that had once touched me, pleased me, felt all my secret places.

What was he holding on for? Me? Us? What if he could stop in the next hour, the next minute? That was the thought which spun on a constant loop through my exhausted brain. What if he could be free?

When the nurse called in sick one evening and the agency couldn't get a replacement, I took it as a sign. It was time. I sat beside the bed that night, reading to him quietly, stopping now and then to feed him juice from a cup. In my stomach churned a stew of anger, pity, pain. *Why do you have to suffer, Ray? Why is this happening to you?*

A minute before midnight, I poured some liquid morphine into the cup of juice, my hand trembling, my heart tapping quick as a cat's. Too much morphine. Much too much. As the clock downstairs in the parlor began to strike, I raised his head, put the cup to his lips, and poured it into him.

Ten...eleven...twelve. Twelve, Ray's lucky number.

Hot tears spilled down my cheeks. I held his hand and waited. I couldn't take it back now. It was done. Seconds went by, a minute. *Please, Ray! Please!* And then came that final grating rasp of his breath.

I could still hear it sometimes. I heard it now.

I opened my eyes to the darkness. "Ray, I'm sorry," I whispered, still wondering whether it was his suffering or mine I had done it for. "Please, please forgive me."

CHAPTER SIX

December 1758

Hugh pulled on his new gauntlets and made a show of admiring them.

"They are more than handsome," he said, smiling over at Miranda, who was watching him from the bed under the low ceiling of the sleeping quarters, her hazel eyes dull with exhaustion, her lips turned up in approval.

"A gift for your twenty-eighth birthday," she said. "A handsome gift for the most handsome of men."

Twenty-eight, Hugh thought. How had he so quickly gotten to such an age, and how in all those years had he never had a pair of fine gauntlets?

"I suppose Niall supplied the leather," he said.

"Yes, and Hattie refused to take a single guinea for stitching them. What do you say to those initials?"

Hugh inspected the neat threads of script that graced the cuffs. "Expertly done, I must say. Your cousin knows her way around a needle."

"You can thank her yourself. She'll be here at three o'clock, remember?"

"With that remedy she promised you. And how goes it this morning? Your head still aching?"

From the corner near the fireplace came a faint mewling. One of the twins was waking up.

"Oh, dear," Miranda said, a darkness passing over her features, one that Hugh had seen too often since Abigail and Alice were born. "Always hungry, aren't they?" She fell back on the straw mattress. "And to think they are yet only four weeks old."

Hugh went to the pair of oak cradles where the babes lay swaddled against the cold. The face of the hungry one twisted into a look of discontent. Whether Abigail or Alice, he couldn't be sure. His daughters appeared identical in all ways. He brushed back the soft dark curl behind the babe's ear and saw the little pink mark, like a pale blot of ink. Abby.

He removed the gloves, dropped them to the dresser, and carried Abby to the bed. "Here, someone needs you." He laid the bleating babe down beside Miranda.

Miranda smiled upon the child, her darkness now passed, and gathered her in with a soft *coo*.

The delivery had come early and hard, and weeks later she was still fatigued, at times even aloof, as if she could not be bothered to form a maternal relation with the babes. Hattie had told him not to fret—the twins were small but healthy, and Miranda's dark clouds not uncommon for a woman who had just birthed a child. And Hattie was the one to know such things. She had helped many women in this part of the county birth their children.

"You know," Miranda said, smoothing Abby's dark curls. "This one is going to be good with business affairs, just like her father."

"One of your premonitions, is it?"

"Yes, and do not try to dissuade me."

"Since when have I ever been able to dissuade you of anything, my sweet?" Hugh smiled down at Miranda, Abby at her breast. "Now, I had better be off to find Sam so we can deliver those barrels."

"Be sure to take your gloves, Mr. Jones," Miranda said.

"I should like to take them everywhere. I'll treasure them now and always." As Hugh took the gloves from the dresser and turned to go, he remembered the paper he had scrawled with lines of verse from one of Miranda's books. *Serenely sweet you gild the silent grove, my friend, my goddess, and my guide.* It was their habit to leave small remembrances for each other about the house. This one he had tucked among her stockings.

"There is treasure to hunt for in the dresser," he said, wanting her to find it soon, for it would improve her spirits.

"Very well, my Welshman," she said with a yawn. "But you spoil me."

As he descended the narrow staircase, Hugh raised the gloves to his nose and drew in a whiff of the new black leather. A fine gift, indeed. And he would give a fine one to Miranda in return. Finer than anything she might imagine. Such an object was already in his possession, but he would save it and find her something more modest for now. Some colors for her palette, perhaps. She had lately told him she wanted to start painting again.

—

When Hugh reached the barn, Sam Grey Feather was standing beside the wagon in his buckskins and his coat of napped leather. A string of hide held back his black hair, revealing prominent cheekbones.

"Have I kept you waiting?" Hugh asked.

"You have given me time with my pipe." Sam lifted the long stem of his bone pipe to his lips and puffed a cloud of smoke into the air. Then he tapped out the ashes and slid the pipe into a pouch hanging from the waist of his buckskins.

"You and your pipe," Hugh said with a smile. "You shall be smoking it on your very last day."

He climbed into the wagon and his friend did the same, a familiar bulge pushing through Sam's buckskins as he lowered himself to the seat board: the blade he kept strapped to his calf. He never traveled without it, and Hugh could not blame him. Sam had known trouble once or twice, although he had not bidden it.

They drove onto the lane that ran east through the woods, Gwydion and Virgil settling into an easy pace. Rum barrels rattled in the wagon bed with every rut in the earth. The last shipment of hides Niall sent to the Indies had been a good enough trade to bring a dozen large barrels north to Pennsylvania.

"I do hope you will join us for dinner at Christmas," Hugh said. "The ancient gods of my ancestors promise to be in attendance. You might get along with them."

Sam offered him a crooked grin. "The gods you brought with you from across the sea." His eyes turned back to the lane. "So much has been brought here from across the sea. It is as my father told me before he moved west. The land will become filled with it."

"Aye, and I cannot but think you carry some wound in your heart about that," Hugh said, hearing the truth and regret in Sam's words. "I wouldn't blame you if you did."

"My heart carries many wounds, Hugh Jones. But if you and your gods had not come here, I would not have you as my friend and brother."

"Nor I you. Friend, brother, and crop foreman worth his weight in gold, I might add. If you ever leave, I shall weep like a woman for the loss."

Two hawks circled in the gray sky above the lane. Sam tilted his head to follow their flight. "My mother said I have been given two spirits. The spirit of my father's Lenape blood and the spirit of the white man's blood that ran in her veins. It has made me a forked road to travel."

Hugh thought of the spirits running through his own veins. His mother's heathen forebears and his father's tattered Methodism. Perhaps it was always so. Perhaps every man, every woman, was a patch of disputed ground beset by skirmishes in the blood.

The hawks winged away, and Sam turned back to Hugh. "But I have made my choice. Those five acres you gave me in the south field will be my home through many suns and moons to come."

"And how goes it on your little plot?" Hugh asked, lifted by Sam's promise to stay.

"The rooster thinks much of himself, as a rooster is made to do. But those gauntlets..." Sam nodded toward Hugh's grip on the reins. "I have not seen them before. You must tell me their story."

CHAPTER SEVEN

That night I dreamed again of the man sitting in the dark by his fire. And when I called to him, he did something he had never done before. He looked my way and then scraped back his chair as if to stand up. I opened my eyes, half in and half out of the dream, the chair's scrape lingering in my head.

But it wasn't in my head. It was in my—

Buck leaped to the floor and trotted to the hall. My heart began to hammer. Had someone broken in? A prowler climbing through a window? The dog's paws thumped on the stairs.

I switched on the lamp. Two a.m. *Crap!* Where was my phone?

Another scrape across a floor. I slipped out from beneath the covers. Downstairs, Buck barked and then went quiet.

The baseball bat! I stood up and yanked it out from under the bed, a hidden weapon I'd never thought I would need. Another bark. I hurried into the hallway and down the stairs with the bat in my grip, heart pounding so wildly I could hardly breathe. I had to find my phone!

At the bottom, I reached for the switch on the wall, quaking now with fear. The hall light flared, and for one frantic moment, I stood with the bat at my shoulder, ready to swing.

Buck's head poked through the dining room doorway.

"There you are!" I said, scarcely able to speak the words. When he turned back toward the kitchen, I followed, thrumming now with fear and adrenaline.

Buck won't let anyone hurt me. Buck, don't let anyone hurt me!

"Who's there?" I yelled into the kitchen. My palm hit the dimmer switch hard.

In the flash of the lights, there was only Buck, dancing in place at the table. My chair, the one I'd made a habit of sitting in, was pulled out. I'd tucked in the chairs after dinner. I knew I had. But this one had been dragged away, scraped along the floor.

"Come here, boy," I said, the bat still raised, my heart still pounding. Buck paced over and sat back. "Did you see someone?"

On the table, my phone. I went and grabbed it and dialed 911.

Several minutes later, the knocker clanged. Only then did I move from the kitchen. Buck followed me to the front doors, the baseball bat still in my hand.

"Good evening, ma'am," a police officer with graying hair and a round black face greeted me. Behind him, the quiet night obscured the lawn and the road and the sycamore. "I'm Officer Small. You called about a possible prowler?" His eyes went to the bat. "Mind if I come in?"

"Please do," I said. "It was a noise, back in the kitchen, just a few minutes ago." I pointed down the hall. "It was the chair. I'll show you."

In the kitchen, I leaned the bat against the wall, suddenly feeling conspicuous in my flannel sheep pajamas. "I pushed all the chairs in tonight," I said. "I do that every night. That's how

I knew something was wrong."

A panic caused by a chair out of place. Did that sound foolish?

Officer Small's face remained blank. "So, you heard the chair move across the floor, is that it?"

I nodded. "Even my dog heard it."

While I waited in the kitchen with Buck, Officer Small spent the next ten minutes wandering about the house, opening closets, checking all the locks. The basement was his last stop, and when he finally ascended and clicked shut the door, he offered the hint of a smile. "Well, everything seems locked up tight here. No signs of forced entry. Do you think the noise you heard could've been something else?"

For a moment, I was ready to concede—the refrigerator ice machine, maybe—but I shook my head. "My dog went right to the chair. I'm sure it was that."

Officer Small gazed down at Buck and then at the bat leaning against the wall. "It's always best to call us right away if you think something's wrong," he said. "That bat's not going to save you, ya got that?" He pulled up the bat, turned it over in his hands, and smiled when he saw the Ted Williams signature across the shaft. "This looks like a pretty nice souvenir. Signed by the slugger himself, eh?"

Owned by him once, too, and his gift to my husband. But I didn't bother telling him that.

He dropped the bat back to the wall. At the front doors, he said, "I'm going to check around the perimeter one more time. If you hear me out there, don't be alarmed." He gave a cursory glance around the hallway. "This place looks pretty old. Maybe you got a ghost." Then he winked and was gone.

A ghost. No, I wouldn't let that idea worm its way into my brain. I wasn't even sure I believed in ghosts. I had occasionally heard noises in a few of the older places Harry and I worked in— thumps or creaks. But I'd learned to pass them off as something else, or to just ignore them.

Back in the kitchen, Buck was lapping at his water bowl. "Time to go up," I said, shoving away thoughts of ghosts.

As I pushed the chair back into place, my eyes fell on the empty tabletop. *The glove.* I'd left it there before going up to bed. Now it was gone.

—

In an exhausted fog, I washed my face and pulled on some clothes. I'd gotten only three hours of sleep with my brain a tangle of threads: the glove and the chair and Officer Small. I considered calling in sick. But Harry and I had to review the Myers project. And I needed to talk to someone about what happened last night. Circumspect Harry seemed like the perfect someone. Besides, Diana would be busy at the café.

Downstairs, I put on a pot of the Ethiopian blend that had been sitting in my freezer unused. Today, regular coffee, not decaf. The full throttle, as Ray used to call it. After dropping two slices of whole grain into the toaster, I scoured the kitchen for the missing glove and then did the same in the dining room and living room. I held out hope that Buck had dragged it off to somewhere, like Corky with Diana's slipper, and that he would soon bring it back. But even if he did, that wouldn't explain how the chair got pulled out from the table.

The acrid smell of burning bread jarred me from my search. The old toaster didn't so much toast bread as cremate it.

"Curses on you," I said, waving at the smoke signals rising from the slots. This morning was going no better than last night. I dropped in two new pieces of bread and poured some coffee.

Maybe you got a ghost.

More than one, Officer Small. But until last night, they'd all been in my head or in my dreams or…somewhere else.

A yeasty scent reminded me to rescue the toast. Then my cell chimed on the kitchen table. Diana Pruett.

"A little bonkers here, sweetie, but I have a few minutes," she said as soon as I picked up. Dishes clanked, and water ran in the background. "So, that glove you found. I'm all ears."

I'd just started filling her in when a loud grinding noise erupted on the other end. Diana's coffee grinder chewing up beans. "You sound busy," I shouted. "Maybe we ought to talk later."

"Oh, drat. Hold on," she said. A moment later, the grinder went quiet. "Sorry, the morning started out iffy and hasn't improved. The glove, you know it probably belongs to some kid." More running water. "A goth or something likes to dress up in black and hide out in your woods with his friends and smoke a little pot or maybe get busy with his girlfriend. That springhouse is just the kind of creepy place they'd go for."

"Yes, but there's more. It—"

Someone called Diana's name. "Look, sweetie. Mini crisis here. I need to go. We'll talk."

My grandfather clock chimed nine. Late to work. I buttered the cold toast and wrapped it up to go.

Twenty minutes later, I pushed through the door of March & Casey, and a bell tinkled overhead. Harry's idea to get the bell. *An old-fashioned touch*, he called it. The aroma of brewing coffee permeated the office.

"Hey there," Harry called from behind the room divider that hid the dry sink from view. "Want some joe?"

A cup clinked into a saucer. The cups and saucers were Harry's idea too, overflow from a large trove of vintage china he and Mitch had collected over the years. Another old-fashioned touch.

"Had a cup at home," I said, joining him. "I think I better switch to tea."

Harry's blue-green gaze settled on me for longer than a moment.

"Your eyes are the exact color of the Aegean Sea," I said. "Did I ever tell you that?"

"Yes, and better the Aegean Sea than the Charles River."

"Anyway, they're staring." I switched on the kettle and

dropped a pillow of English Breakfast into my favorite cup, the yellow one speckled with tiny pink roses.

"You look like you might have had a rough weekend."

"Let's say things have been a little...strange."

As we stood taking the first sips of our hot drinks, I related my account of the glove, the chair, and Officer Small.

"And he didn't find anything amiss?" Harry said.

"Nothing. You know, I'm beginning to feel like Ingrid Bergman in that movie where weird little things start to happen. What was the name—?"

"*Gaslight.*" Old movies were Harry's specialty.

"But then it turns out her husband is trying to drive her crazy, right? Of course, it can't be my—" I stopped short of *husband*. "I don't know what to think."

We ferried our cups to our desks.

"Well, no one's trying to drive you crazy," Harry said. "Anyway, it's too early to push the panic button."

He sat down, but I leaned back against my desk, too jittery to confine myself to a chair. Maybe the Ethiopian at breakfast hadn't been the best choice. Too much of a jolt after so many months of decaf. "So, what's the alternative to the panic button?"

Harry shrugged. "You're in a new place. Let the dust settle." He relaxed back in his chair. "When my father died, my mother swore he was still there in the house, moving things, a dish or the car keys. I think it gave her comfort that maybe he wanted to hang around, be close to her."

"But you don't think Ray could be—?"

The landline rang. Harry held up a finger and answered it. "March and Casey, Harry March here. Oh, yes, Mr. Myers. What can I do for you?"

As Harry chatted with Mr. Myers, I poured myself another cup of tea and lingered back at the dry sink, nibbling my cold toast. Could my deceased husband really be with me in my new house?

Better be nice, Libby Casey, or I'll come back to haunt you.

Ray's attempt at humor one day as he lay on the sofa in sweatpants that had grown too baggy and a face that looked older than his fifty-two years. We'd been arguing about whether to make a trip to the doctor for the second time in a week after he developed a nagging cough. I thought we should, and he thought we shouldn't.

I went back to my desk. Ray would have every right to haunt me. But surely, he would have shown up in our Victorian rather than my new Georgian. Queenie, where his heart was, where we'd had our too brief idyll. *Gather ye rosebuds while ye may.*

No, there had been no sign of my deceased husband anywhere, as far as I could tell.

Harry hung up. "He's eager to see the numbers. I'll go up there tomorrow."

"I went over the job last night, so we can check them now, just to be sure."

—

That evening, I searched again for the glove, holding out hope it would reappear, that Buck had dragged it back from wherever he might have put it. But my search yielded nothing. In a voicemail on the landline, Susannah Kunkel said she would have time in the morning to chat. I called her back, and we made plans to meet at the historical society at nine o'clock. Harry would be at the Myers place, and I would be free until noon.

I fed the animals, took Buck for a walk, and made a quick meal. As I sipped a second glass of cabernet, I gave in to the mellowing effects of the wine. Forget the glove, forget the chair. Tonight, I would sleep.

My cell phone pinged with a text. Diana. *Let's catch up tomorrow. Dog tired here.*

Buck rose to all fours in his bed by the fireplace. "Are you dog tired too?" I asked, and he followed me upstairs.

In my room, I fiddled with the floor lamp, a little woozy with the wine, and finally managed to switch it on. "Eureka!" I declared. Buck was already over by the bed, staring with great focus at my pillow. No, at something *on* my pillow. Something black.

The glove.

"Buck, did you—" No, there was something too neat, too purposeful about it. The fingers stretched out, the shaft flat and smooth.

My already light head grew lighter. Then the air blinked. That day I first saw the house. The flicker at the window.

Breathe, Libby. Breathe.

What had Cassie said yesterday at the farmer's market? *Such an interesting place, all that history, and who knows what else?* What else?

I pulled my phone from my back pocket. I couldn't call the police, not so soon, not for this. What would I say? A glove I found yesterday disappeared and now it's shown up on my pillow. I would get a reputation. The police would talk among themselves. *She's a little off in the head, so pay her no mind.*

And Diana was too dog-tired to talk.

I inched toward the bed. I had to get the glove off my pillow, but I didn't want to touch it now. It seemed like a thing possessed. Buck went around to the other side of the bed, jumped up, and settled in. If he could be brave, so could I. It was just a piece of leather, after all.

Steeling my nerve, I snatched it off the pillow. It felt oddly warm, as if someone had just taken it off. *I should throw it away*, I thought. *Toss it into the kitchen fireplace and burn it.* But instead, I shoved it into the night table drawer. I would take it with me tomorrow and show it to Susannah. Maybe she could tell me something about this house I needed to know.

I shook out a pill and got ready for bed. Then I switched out my pillow with the one next to it and left the light on while I waited to fall asleep.

CHAPTER EIGHT

The next morning, I pulled into the lot behind the old bungalow that housed the Simms Historical Society, grabbed the plastic bag from beside me, and got out of the Prius, my other car. Sunlight glinted fire off the windshield, but the day was winter cold.

I hurried around to the front of the building and climbed the steps to the porch. It had been a few years since my last visit, and I couldn't help but admire all over again the bungalow's classic styling. The low-slung overhang, the wide front door, the generous windows. Quite beautiful once, I imagined. And it might still be if someone would paint and sweep and replace the three missing balusters in the railing.

I shut the front door behind me.

"With you in a minute!" Susannah called. A few moments later, she descended the staircase at the back of the bungalow. "So, Libby dear," she said, dropping from the last step. She tucked back a lock of white hair. "Let's get a cup of tea and we'll talk about the Jones estate."

Back in a little alcove, we fixed our tea. With the heat kept low to avoid large utility bills, the place was chilly. I was grateful when I could finally wrap my hands around my mug of hot Lipton's.

We settled into a room across the hall that might have been a bedroom once. An array of books and papers lay strewn on a big round table.

"When Cassie told me you bought the Jones place, I was happy to hear it," Susannah said, setting down her tea and dropping into a chair. "I think it makes for better custodianship when someone has a stake in the town, don't you?"

"I'm certainly going to do my best to look after it." I took a seat beside her and set aside the plastic bag containing the glove. I would wait for the right moment to introduce it. "I confess that I know very little about it. I'd hoped to do some research before I moved in, but everything happened pretty quickly."

"As I'm sure you know, it's one of only a few colonial Georgians still left around here. It's remarkable in a number of ways, not the least of which is that the Jones family lived there through five generations."

"I saw that on the website. They became an established family in Simms, I would think. People must have known them."

"In fact, a Jones descendant still lives in the area. Over in Brigham, if I'm remembering right. Don't recall her name and don't know if she's still alive. I've lost track." Susannah sipped from her mug and set it aside. "But yes, they would have been known well in Simms. Mind you, Carroll County would have had only about three hundred residents at the time Hugh Peter set up house."

Hugh Peter. The initials on the glove. I had taken the middle one for a *P.* "So, Hugh Peter was the first Jones here?"

"He built that house you're in. Some of the tax records are here if you want to see them."

For the next few minutes, we examined the pages of an old ledger scrawled with ancient cursive. I clutched my warm mug. Susannah seemed impervious to the bungalow's chill.

"Here, in 1760, is where you see a jump in taxation." She tapped at a page. "That's when Hugh finished the big house." She peered at me over her wire rims, eyes forget-me-not blue against her ruddy complexion. "That little wing off the west side, that's what, your kitchen? That was the first true dwelling, built by the former resident. Hugh and a brother moved into it in 1752. A few years later, the brother moved down the road."

"And Hugh eventually built the bigger house beside it."

"Yes. Not unusual in those days." Susannah closed the old ledger with care. "Our collection on the Joneses isn't large, unfortunately. You might check in with the Carroll County folks. I know they have a few things over there." She eyed the assortment on the table. "What else might you want to peruse?"

We looked through the odds and ends she emptied gingerly from manila envelopes—an old county map, a yellowed piece of newsprint, a subdivision document from the nineteenth century.

"I was over there years ago, when Ross and Ruthie Phillips were living there," Susannah said. "I would say it's hardly changed much since Hugh built it. Of course, the property's much smaller than the original one-hundred-eighty acres. What do you have now? Twenty, isn't that what the easement included?"

"Eighteen. Mostly woods."

"Kitchen garden still there? Ross stopped puttering in it some years before he and Ruthie moved out."

"Yes, I want to revive it one day." I let a beat go by, impatient to get to the root of something more useful. "Do you know much about the Joneses? What they were like?"

"Well, I have a few of them right here," she said. She slid five old photos from yet another envelope. "I keep meaning to frame a few of these and hang them up. Time gets away, and one or two of our volunteers have moved on."

The inscrutable faces of the Jones family stared up from the tabletop like suspects in a lineup. Victorians, by the look of them.

"And Hugh Peter," I said. "Are there any images of him around?"

Maybe one in which he's wearing a black glove?

"Word has it there's a painting somewhere, hung in the house for many a year." Susannah swept the photographs into a pile. "Money for a portrait wouldn't have been a problem for Hugh. He seemed to make a good living on the flax and peaches. I read somewhere that he and the brother—Niall, as I recall—were trading hides for rum from the Indies for a while. Niall operated a tannery."

"Rum running? That sounds dangerous. Was it legal?"

"Oh, yes, all on the up and up. They sold it to taverns around the area, I imagine. That and the steady crop business must have brought in enough income to pay for that home of yours and all the outbuildings, carriage house, barn, springhouse—"

"Yes, the springhouse. It's not in great shape, but it's still there. My dog Buck and I pass it on our walks." I reached for the plastic bag. "And, well, I found this in there the other day, or rather Buck did." I pulled out the glove and smoothed it onto the table. "An old glove. You see, it has initials on the cuff. I thought it was very odd. I mean, that it would suddenly appear in my springhouse."

Susannah leaned forward and examined the glove through her wire rims. "You've got yourself a nice gauntlet there."

"I don't know whether it's authentic or a reproduction. My friend thinks maybe kids left it. But I think it's too much of a coincidence now that you mention 'Hugh Peter.'" I pointed to the middle initial on the cuff. "I think this is a *P*."

She squinted at the faded threads. "I have a magnifying glass out in the drawer, my old lady's extra eye. Hold on a minute, I'll get it. Maybe we can make a little progress."

When she returned, we examined the stitching, trading the glass between us, finally deciding that the first letter was an *H* and the second, yes, a *P*. With that to go on, it was easy to imagine that the last letter, with its loop at the top and tail at the bottom, was a *J*.

"*HPJ*," I said. "That must be it."

Susannah went quiet. "So, this glove just suddenly appeared?"

"Out of the blue. And there've been other things going on at the house. Things I'm sure I'm not imagining."

"You think the house is haunted?"

"Have you heard any stories over the years?"

"It's an old place, Libby. It's not unusual for people to report strange, what would you call it, activity in an old place. My brother's house up in Vermont had an extra boarder, so he said."

"And Ross and Ruthie Phillips, did they ever report such things?"

"They were private people, and they wouldn't have put the word out about a ghost in the house. You know what happens then. You and your home become a curiosity, people talk, children come by and peer through the hedges." She chuckled, waved a hand, and reached for her tea.

Was she impatient with the subject, or was she being less than forthcoming? I tapped the glove. "It does look like the real thing, doesn't it? And the initials, they must be Hugh's, unless someone else in the family had the same name."

"No other Hugh Peters. His only son was James Martin, died at the Battle of Germantown, I believe. Hugh's other children were girls, twins. I have a family tree here somewhere, but I think it's missing a generation. I'll make copies of whatever you want."

"So, James Martin was a soldier in the Revolution?"

"Left a wife and baby behind." She picked up the glove and handed it to me. "I know someone who might be able to help you with *this*. Her name's Penny Jenkins. She moved out to

Creighton a few years back. Had a whole wardrobe of period clothing she used to show around. I'll call you with her number."

I folded the glove back in the bag and waited while Susannah copied some of the Jones documents and slid them into a folder.

"Just wait and see how things go for you there, Libby. And try not to jump at every little noise," she said, handing me the folder. She offered a gentle smile. "Keep in mind that people sometimes make peace with the ghosts that live among them."

Those words rang in my head as I closed the bungalow door behind me.

CHAPTER NINE

May 1759

Hugh walked about the rooms inside the new house, taking stock of the work completed since March. He had pitched in as much as he could with Johann and his sons, and they had made good progress on the floors, walls, and moldings. But his hope of finishing the construction by autumn had long since vanished. There would be neither time nor coin enough to do it.

He pulled shut the front doors and stepped into the May sun. He had promised Miranda they would move from the confines of their crowded little home after the harvest, and he had not yet informed her otherwise. The thought of doing so now pricked him like a needle. He didn't want to set her back in her paces. Since those first difficult months after the twins' birth, her spirits had revived, but not fully.

He hurried himself along. He would need to make quick tracks if he was to get the rum delivery to the Brown Pony Inn by ten o'clock. The journey would take the better part of an hour, and he didn't want to disappoint Henry, who was a good and steady customer. James Martin would come with him. The boy was three now and needed to escape the house and go abroad to see who or what was out there.

Jasper bugled from the chicken coop behind the house. "Crow all you want, you noisy old cock," Hugh replied. "Just make us more chickens."

What Hugh really wanted, what his mouth watered for, was some thick smoked rashers. Next year, perhaps, he would ask Charlie Evans on the other side of the south field to butcher him a pig. He could make Charlie a trade. A small cask of rum for the rashers and a plump loin. He might even buy his own pig one day.

At the barn, he hitched the wagon to the horses. Then he drove it down to the lane, parked, and went to fetch James Martin. He found him sitting with Miranda on a blanket at the edge of the hay meadow, gnawing at a nub of bread, his honey hair amber in the sun.

"What do you think?" Miranda set aside her pen and held up a square of paper, her fingers stained with ink. "Aristotle has inspired me. His thoughts about acorns and oaks."

Hugh studied the expertly rendered oak branches arching gracefully into the sky. "You are a master, my sweet." This he meant with all his heart, for Miranda's talent was enviable. The lessons she'd had in the city years ago were the one good thing her father did for her.

"And now I am reminded," he said. "I have a gift for you. New paints for your palette. What do you say? Hattie said Martha Little Cloud will make them for a bushel of fruit. You can take up your brushes again."

"Oh, my sweet husband! Martha's pigments are the very best. And her polished beads. Might we get a few of those as well? I shall sew them on my bonnet."

"A wonderful idea." Hugh lifted James Martin from the blanket. "And now, young hemp, you and I have traveling to do."

"And I have garden labors while the girls are sleeping. A bounty is beginning to grow." Miranda stood up, her face still too pale. No, this was not the day to tell her the house would not be ready in September. A few more weeks of fine spring weather would put the color back in her cheeks, and then he would convey the news.

She leaned in to kiss James Martin's cheek. "Bon voyage, mon enfant," she whispered. And when she turned her eyes up to Hugh, they were soft with affection.

—

Hugh pulled the wagon into the dirt lot beside the Brown Pony Inn. Tucked in a clearing off the main road that wound through the southern part of the county, it was one of the cleaner and more respectable establishments in the area, and Henry Wilkins took great pride in keeping it that way.

Hugh hopped down to the dirt just as Henry rose from a bench outside the door.

"Captain Wilkins," he called. Everyone addressed Henry as Captain, although he no longer held any office.

The old publican limped over to greet him. "Hugh, my good man. Just in time." It was what Henry always said when Hugh pulled in with the rum. "I've promised a punch for some of the boys this evening, and I don't want to disappoint them. No Sam today?"

"Busy with crops work."

Hugh lifted James Martin from the wagon seat, and they all went into the tavern. Hints of ale and dust and soot mingled in the air. A pair of patrons sat at a table in the corner, one of them wearing a rather large ring that Hugh thought begged to be noticed. A thick band of silver bearing a round amber stone in the center, worth more than a shilling or two. The remaining dozen or so tables were empty. The big fireplace had been swept clean.

"Ale?" Henry said. "It's nice and cool."

Hugh accepted the offer, and Henry disappeared into the kitchen. When he returned, he set two full mugs and a plate of strawberries on the table where Hugh and James Martin had settled. Henry pushed the plate of berries toward the boy. "Here you are, Jamie boy. The first of Hilda's crop."

"Much obliged, sir," James Martin chirped.

"Good manners on this one," Henry said.

While James Martin nibbled his berries, Hugh and Henry sipped their ale and talked about the business of the tavern, Hugh's crops and the rum, and finally the war out in the territories, the French and their Indian cohort digging in their heels against the English and *their* Indian cohort.

"No bloody end in sight," Henry said. "But what about that new house of yours? Any end in sight there?"

"I'm hoping for a January completion."

"It shall be a fine inheritance one day for this lad." Henry nodded down at James Martin, who was finishing the last of his fruit. "Make me an invitation when all is said and done. I'd like to see it."

With their ale consumed, Hugh helped Henry roll the barrels of rum into the cellar. Then they said their farewells. As Hugh drove the wagon toward home, his son chattering beside him, the warm sun seemed to simmer his thoughts. What Henry had said about the new house, that it would one day become James Martin's. A happy thought indeed, except for one thing: his son was not fully his son, according to the law.

Hugh had been so occupied of late that he had not stopped to consider that his estate was growing and that one day it must pass on. He could not let the matter languish any longer. He and Miranda must marry and make legitimate their bond and their children.

He looked down at his boy, the small hand resting on Hugh's knee as if to find ballast against the jump and sway of the empty wagon. His heart swelled. Such a fine boy. The finest he could hope for.

A wedding under the sycamore and the blue June sky. Yes, with Miranda bare of foot if she so wished, and the children and Priscilla and Hattie gathered round, and Sam too. After that, Hugh would find a solicitor to make his will and testament and set the world to rights for his family.

CHAPTER TEN

After leaving Susannah, I made a quick trip home to walk Buck and then stopped for gas before heading to the office. While the pump ran, I listened to a voicemail from Diana suggesting we meet for an early dinner at McGraw's Pub. *"We can talk about Dracula's glove over spicy pretzels and beer,"* she said.

Spicy pretzels and beer. Good medicine. I texted *Yum!* and confirmed.

Harry was already back and at his computer when I pushed through the office door. "That was quick," I said. I dropped my bag and coat into a chair and drifted back to the dry sink. "How did it go with Dave and Sissy? Good news, I hope."

"They like what we're offering, and they want to move forward. We can file for the permits next week. And guess what?"

I dropped an Irish Breakfast into my favorite cup. "Spit it out. My brain's in neutral."

"Keith Janus came out of the woodwork, left me a message

about finally getting started on his place."

"Keith Janus?"

"The guy up in Morley. The environmental lawyer. He came by last year. You met him out on the pavement, remember?"

"Oh, yes, vaguely. Where's he been all this time?" I switched on the kettle, and it began to hum.

"He tells me his wife filed for divorce a few days after we saw him. With his ownership of the house in question, he backed off. But he claims to have it all sorted out now. What do you think? Can we handle three big projects at once?"

"Four, counting the Jackson job we got last week." The kettle clicked off. I poured the steaming water into my cup. "But we have most of the permits for the other jobs. That leaves us free to work on Janus."

I wanted to tell Harry about my visit with Susannah and the reappearance of the glove. But maybe that was too gloomy a subject. We ought to revel for a while in all the good news. One project moving forward and another that looked promising.

"It's officially lunchtime," he said. "Let's eat and you can tell me about your visit with Sue Kunkel."

"You're doing it again."

"Doing what?"

"Reading my mind."

I filled him in as we ate at our desks. Hugh Peter Jones and his family, the peaches and flax and rum, and finally, the glove. "It's in my purse. I'll show you."

I unearthed the glove and handed it to Harry.

"You're sure you didn't leave it there?" he said, reaching up to take it. "In the bedroom, or maybe Buck—"

"I want to believe it was Buck. But I don't think it was. I hadn't seen it since it disappeared the night before. And like I told you yesterday, I'd looked everywhere."

"It was just lying there on the pillow?"

"Like a hotel chocolate. I showed it to Susannah." I tapped the cuff. "The initials, see?"

"What did she say to all of this?"

"She didn't know what to make of it, but we decided those initials belong to the man who built my house, Hugh Peter Jones. Susannah claims she's never heard tell of anything unusual at the property."

Harry handed me the glove. "You know Susannah. She's not much for gossip. And I'm sure she wouldn't want to scare you."

"Well, it's too late. I'm scared already. I mean, confused or whatever this is." I drew in a cleansing breath, as my yoga instructor used to call it, and let it out again. "Harry, do you think buying that place...well, do you think it was a mistake?"

"It's still too early for the panic button, remember?"

"Why did the last two owners move out so quickly? The Hempels did that expensive kitchen reno but only stayed for a year."

Harry smoothed and folded the waxed bag he'd brought his sandwich in. "Let's take it a step at a time," he said. "How about I come over tonight and have a look around? I don't mean to worry you more than you already are, but do you think there's a way someone might be getting in?"

"Getting in, and what? Playing pranks?" I crossed to my desk and threw the glove onto it. "I've been making sure to lock all the doors. And they would be pretty strange pranks, wouldn't they?"

"Nevertheless, I'll come over tonight." Harry raised his sandwich to take a bite. "You never know."

—

Diana and I sat opposite each other in a booth at McGraw's, digging into the spicy pretzels on the table between us. We had worked our way through nearly the whole bowl and most of our pints of lager while I related the story of the chair and the glove.

"You never changed the locks, did you?" she said.

"No, why?"

"Maybe Harry's right. Maybe someone is getting in. And if

they aren't breaking in, that means they have a key."

"I don't know, Dee. It's all too weird. A glove disappearing and then showing up on my pillow. And a chair moving by itself. Why would someone sneak in and move a chair?"

The fine print in Diana's grin read skeptical. "Is it too early to call in the psychic medium?"

"You're not helping."

"Sorry, sweetie. I don't really believe in that hooey. You know that. But I meant what I said about the locks. Get them changed, even if only for peace of mind. And don't cross that dog off the list of suspects. He always was more clever than he had a right to be."

The waitress arrived with our dinner, took our order for two more pints, and trailed off toward the bar.

"There's one more thing," I said. "I think I heard a voice one night in my room. A man saying my name. My real name, Elizabeth. At the time, I thought it might have been the wind blowing the tree against the roof, but now…"

Diana frowned. "A man said your name?"

"Yes, and I'm not hearing things, if that's what you're thinking."

"O-kay," she said with uncertainty. "How often?"

"Just the once. I'm starting to feel like I'm on one of those reality TV shows. You know, someone moves into the perfect house where strange things start to happen, and six months later has to move out."

"More hooey," Diana countered. "I'd like to know how much they're being paid to peddle that garbage." She gave her bangs a tug. "I don't know, Lib. You seem like, like you didn't catch up to normal after Ray, and you're still not sleeping—"

"Please, Dee. Just go with this, will you? Yes, I'm stressed out. I have been for, well, you know how long. But stress doesn't move things around the house. At least Harry believes me."

Diana slumped against the back of the bench with a wounded look. "I believe you. I mean, I believe something is going on. But you have to admit you were a little mixed up for a while. And I wasn't the only one who thought so. Maybe you should have given the counseling more of a chance."

"Been there, done that."

She dabbed her mouth with her napkin, waiting for a better answer. "Look, as you well know, you're talking here to an official worry wart, so indulge me a little."

I felt myself soften. "Yeah, I well know."

"Whatever you need, I'm here, okay? I want to help. And you wait and see. Things will calm down."

The waitress returned with our fresh pints.

I used this interruption to change the subject. "Take those home, why don't you?" I nodded toward the untouched basket of rolls on the table. "If we eat them now, we'll explode."

"Cal, the human vacuum, will thank us. And before I forget, what should I bring for Thanksgiving?"

For the next few minutes, we talked about the menu and who was bringing what and the new cocktail recipe Diana wanted to try.

"Oh!" I said. "Did I tell you that Maddie can't come up from Virginia this year?" Maddie, Ray's daughter from his first marriage, was twenty-nine, a horse veterinarian, and the picture of her father in all the right ways. "She's on call that weekend."

"How's she doing, by the way?"

"Busy, last time I spoke to her. She said the two vets she went into practice with seem pleased to have her."

Diana gulped from her pint. "How did that kid grow up to be so sweet and so smart? I mean, with that mother of hers."

"She says Wendy is still sober. I wasn't sure which way things would go when Ray died. Wendy always seemed so needy of him. I was afraid she would fall off the wagon."

"At the end of the day, we're the only ones who can save ourselves." Diana poked at a roasted carrot on her plate. "Nobody can do it for us."

"How true," I said, wondering whether I was going to need saving soon and whether I was going to have to do it by myself.

—

By eight o'clock, Harry had come and gone, having found no problems that needed immediate attention. I cleaned up the kitchen, thinking about his suggestion to get new locks on the basement windows. But now I thought it best to replace the windows altogether. They weren't original to the house, and they were ancient and filthy and not even close to insulated. I would get a good deal on new ones from March & Casey's window contractor.

What now? The house was too quiet. What was I supposed to do here alone, in this place that might be, probably was, haunted?

As if my thoughts had just been broadcast to the universe, there came a scratching noise from the basement. But I quickly realized it was only Sugar Plum digging in her litter box. Maybe Susannah knew what she was talking about when she told me not to jump at every little noise. But was there something she *hadn't* talked about?

Buck padded into the kitchen, his bright copper eyes gazing a question into my face. "Come on," I said. "Let's do something fun."

I gathered up the boxes of pinecones and pumpkins from the farmer's market, along with the bundles of firethorn Diana had brought to dinner and deposited them all in the dining room. Then I went back to the kitchen for the CD player. Time for some music therapy.

While Buck settled in beside the fireplace, I set the player on the table and popped it open. A CD was already inside, the last one I must have listened to. *Car Wheels on a Gravel Road.* Lucinda Williams. A gift from Ray years ago, "Just because," he'd said.

I dressed the mantelpiece while Lucinda sang in her

Mississippi twang. *Still, I la-ong for your kiss.* Ray and I made love to that song once, after a few tense days of arguing over some silly thing I couldn't now remember. The sex had been so good, so delicious, we'd called it Lucinda Sex. "I think we might have to retire that jersey, baby," he had drawled into my ear afterward. And we never made love to that song again.

The memory rushed up to meet me—Ray so close, so warm—like a tide at my toes. The feel of his skin on mine, his whisper at my ear.

No, Libby. Leave it. Just leave it.

I switched off the music and let the memory wash back out to sea.

Before going up to bed, I checked the locks on the front and back doors. I would change them as Diana had suggested to cross the intruder theory off the list once and for all. Then I went to get the glove from my purse. I needed to keep it close so I could show it to the woman Susannah told me about, the one with the vintage wardrobe.

In my room, I opened the night table drawer to drop the glove in. But I changed my mind and laid it out on top, smooth and neat as it had been on my pillow. Time for a test.

I hoped it would still be there in the morning.

CHAPTER ELEVEN

The glove was still on the night table.
I wasn't sure what that meant as I got dressed and made breakfast and called Todd, the window contractor, about new basement windows. But I took it as a good sign. The fewer things that moved by themselves in my house, the better. And maybe, just maybe, whatever entity or phantom or being put the glove on my pillow had decided to go away and leave me alone.

Before leaving for work, I went in search of my scarf and found it draped over the living room sofa. As I yanked it up, I noticed that a book was lying on the floor in front of the bookcase.

I went and picked it up. *Grace When the End Is Near*. A collection of essays written by people with terminal illnesses. I'd bought it after Ray and I found out the drug trial had failed. I thought it might help me understand what he was going through, or help me see the bigger picture, or...

I gazed over at the bookcase, all the books tucked neatly in. How had it fallen out? Behind that question, a mounting trail of others. The glove, the chair, the flickering air, me here in this place. How, how, how? But maybe *how* wasn't the right question. Maybe it was *why*?

I turned the book over in my hands. Why *this* book?

One night I'd found Ray reading it in bed. I must have left it lying somewhere.

"Some of these folks here said they'd know when they're ready to go," he said, his soft drawl tinged with sadness. "I'm not sure I'll ever be ready to go, to leave you behind. But sometimes I think I should make my exit tomorrow, while I feel like I'm still with you."

I looped my scarf around my neck. The familiar sorrow—my constant, ever-present Ray sorrow—circled back to me, mixed with a wave of fear and confusion over what was happening in my house. No, it wasn't going to leave me alone, whatever it was, because something was terribly wrong here. Or maybe *I* was the terribly wrong thing here.

Buck came in and stood beside me.

"You know it too, don't you?" I asked.

I tossed the book onto the coffee table. Another test.

—

I hurried up the sidewalk to March & Casey, sunlight slicing through tufts of clouds, my mind swirling with the morning's strange discovery and my stomach still in a knot.

Harry was on the landline when I entered.

"Actually, she just walked in. Let me ask her." He lowered the handset and looked my way. "I've got Keith Janus on the line. He wants to meet at ten, Monday morning at his place. I took a peek at your calendar. Looks clear."

When I turned up my thumb, Harry made the appointment and hung up. "That was a happy surprise," he said. "I was worried we'd have to chase him down."

"And you would be perfect for the job. You're a very charming chaser." I swiveled my chair back and forth, back and forth. Should I tell him about the book?

"We'll go up there on Monday, then how about we close the office Tuesday, take an extra day for the holiday this year?" he suggested. "The Ziegler job will be done tomorrow, and after a walk-through Friday, we'll call that one a wrap."

"I'll need to work from home Friday. Mr. Barrett left me a message yesterday to say he could come then to trim my oak. I think I should be there." *No, don't tell him about the book.* "Can you do the walk-through?"

"You mean I have to fend off that little Yorkie all by myself?"

"Rusty? Don't worry. His bark is way bigger than he is."

"It could hardly be smaller," Harry said.

We worked through the morning and ate lunch at our desks. In the afternoon, Laura Majewski called about the kitchen renovation we'd be starting in her Victorian twin after Christmas, up Poplar Street from where Ray and I had lived. Could I come by after Thanksgiving, she asked, to review the job? Something about misgivings that she would explain when I got there. Whatever it was, I hoped it wouldn't mean reconfiguring the floor plan or changing the cabinet order again. With the work scheduled to begin early January, it was too late for alterations.

"The usual client jitters," I said to Harry as I hung up the phone. Client jitters weren't unusual, especially on big, expensive projects. We'd think the cat was in the bag, and then all of a sudden it would claw its way out again, scratching hard for another escape. "But a new seventy-thousand-dollar kitchen would give anyone the jitters."

Harry grinned across the office. "I'll leave keeping Laura calm to you," he said. "I'm sure you'll handle her perfectly."

—

After a stop at the supermarket, I drove home in the autumn evening. Lights aglow in houses, trees bare against the slate sky, a slight smokiness in the air. My favorite time of year.

The mysteriously moving book was on my mind as I unlocked the back door and set down my grocery bags. I hurried to the living room without taking off my coat and saw it still on the coffee table where I'd left it.

I picked it up, intending to put it back on the shelf. But instead, I dropped down to the sofa and began paging through. In each line, the dying exhaled their innermost thoughts. Struggle, pain, anger, little victories, surprising discoveries, acceptance of death.

Did anyone ever really accept death? Didn't we all want to stretch our lives out to the last possible minute of some very distant day? To hold on, no matter what?

Ray and I had made a pact when the lymphoma was diagnosed, eight years after we were married. He would fight to defeat it, fight as long as he could, and I would support him all the way. It seemed academic at first, the treatment plan, the checkups, the vow not to let the disease win, and then the drug trial that would be our last hope.

Hope. It never really dies. It just becomes something else. Something hard and calcified inside you like an artifact.

I closed my eyes. It was all done now.

A nudge at my knee. Buck.

"Saving me again, are you?" I dropped the book back to the coffee table and followed him to the kitchen. Once the animals were fed, I dug for my own dinner in the bags of groceries. But when I finally sat down to eat my veggie burger with provolone, I had to force myself to chew and swallow.

Diana called as I was cleaning up the kitchen. "I wouldn't normally bug you about this, but I was just wondering, green beans or kale? For Thanksgiving, I mean. I was going to make the beans, but I saw some great-looking Red Russian and it got me thinking."

"Your choice," I chirped. "It'll be good no matter what."

"You always say that. Kale it is, then. How was your day, by the way?"

A book jumped from my bookcase for no reason. "We've got another big job coming. I'll stop by the café tomorrow and tell you about it. It's Thursday, so you'll be there, right?"

"There's nowhere else I could be, sweetie. Leanne fractured her hand yesterday, and that leaves me and only me to do the baking for a month. Not the end of the world."

Thwack. Somewhere close by, something hit the floor.

"Dee, I think I need to go," I said, taking tentative steps through the dining room.

"Everything okay?"

"Yeah, fine. I'll see you tomorrow. Promise."

Out in the hall, I found Buck staring into the living room. I went and flipped the light switch. *Grace When the End Is Near* was back on the floor in front of the bookcase.

"No," I whispered, my face going cold as the blood drained away. "No, no, no!"

If I'd harbored any trace of doubt that my house was haunted, or any trace of hope that the odd occurrences might cease, it all vanished in that moment.

"Stop! Please stop!" I shouted, my eyes still on the book.

What was I going to do? I couldn't sell the place. Not now, not in the near future. I had made an investment, and I didn't want to lose it. I didn't want to deal with another crisis. I didn't want to be defeated again.

I reached for Buck to steady my hand, tears spilling from my eyes. "You stupid fool," I muttered. I'd allowed this house to overpower me, to draw me in with its Georgian charms and the promise of a new start. Now all I could feel was cheated.

CHAPTER TWELVE

August 1759

Miranda and Hattie were crouching over the herb beds, clothed only in their shifts, when Hugh pulled open the garden gate.

"I thought I might find you ladies here," he said. "How goes the harvest?"

"We've got enough thyme for a palace guard," said Hattie from under her straw work hat. "I've read that long ago, the Greeks mixed it with oil and rubbed it on their skin for battle courage." She turned up her broad face and smiled. "Maybe it only made them smell like a roasted loin of pork."

"Or a squash pudding." Miranda stood up, feet bare as usual and pushed back the brim of her own hat. Her face glistened, the day being warm and close. "What say you to squash for dinner, Mr. Jones? We've got enough of that for a palace guard as well."

Hugh went and kissed her moist cheek. "I shall look forward

to any worthy dish you and Prissy might cook up, Mrs. Jones."

"Ah, but not yet Mrs. Jones," Miranda said with a gentle tug of his ear. "Not until Reverend Potts returns from England."

"Yes, a pity we have to wait. But the sycamore will be golden by then, hmm?" Hugh smiled to himself. Miranda under the golden sycamore. A lovely scene indeed. "And here's good news of another sort. Johann says the house will be finished at the New Year. But since the parlor and bedchambers will be completed by November, we can move in then, if we can tolerate noisy labors being done in our midst."

Hattie dropped a clutch of thyme into the basket beside her and walked over to Hugh and Miranda. "Good news indeed," she said. "Your little army will make their final camp, eh?"

"Yes," Miranda said, glancing toward the house with a sudden, odd watchfulness. "Final camp."

Hattie lifted her hat off to fan her face, revealing the threads of gray that had lately come into her brown hair. She was sixteen years older than Miranda, and Hugh thought that a good thing, for Hattie was more mother than cousin to her, Miranda's own mother being gone these many years. She returned the hat to her head. "Now, back to the lavender and poppy."

"So much lavender this year," Miranda said. "I could simply lie down in it all day." She shifted her gaze again to the new house, still watchful, and whispered to Hugh, "But we mustn't speak of armies. The children should not know of such things. Don't you agree?"

Hugh could not have named the feeling stirring inside of him at the sight of Miranda's darting eyes. He only knew that there was something present he hadn't seen before, and it did not sit quite right.

"No armies, then," he said. "Now, I'm off to my own crops. Sam and the crew are waiting."

—

Hugh made his way out to the orchard under a blazing sun, Miranda's curious behavior on his mind. Had another of her premonitions come upon her? Something about the war out in the territories? She sometimes had a feeling about this or a thought about that, and simply couldn't be talked out of it. But that look…

At the foot of the orchard, he unstrapped the canteen across his chest and drank a long swallow of the water he'd carried in from the cistern last night. It was warm but sweet to the taste. Long lines of trees stretched away from him, their limbs heavy with yellow fruit. Thanks to God for the rain they'd had in the last few weeks. It would keep the cistern full for a while and raise the well level. And it would help grow the peaches into the fall.

He pushed the cork back into the canteen, then twisted a peach from a branch and bit into its ripe, juicy flesh. Old Silas Grey had made him and Niall a good bargain when he sold them this orchard and all the acreage around it for little more than ship fare back to England and the cost of some new clothes. Of course, that bargain had taken almost every shilling they had earned as laborers during those two years in Philadelphia. And they'd had to rehabilitate some of the—

"Hugh Jones!"

Hugh looked up to see Sam Grey Feather loping down the tree line in his breeches and shirt, his black hair glossed by the sun. "Sam, just the gent I was looking for." He twisted another peach from a branch and threw it to his friend.

Sam brought it to his nose and took a bite. "Fine fruit, as always."

"Where are the men?" Hugh asked.

"Pulling up weeds in the flax fields. The rain has watered them well." Sam bit into the peach again, taking in nearly half of it.

"I've heard from Tom Potts. He'll be ready to take the harvest in two weeks. There's a ship going out to Ireland. How do the seed pods look?"

"Ready as they can be."

Hugh tossed the pit of his ravaged peach to the ground. "Come, let's get some of the fruit in. Friday, we'll haul a load to the markets." He gazed up at the white sun. "And if this devil of a heat keeps up, we shall lose every drop of water our flesh might hold."

They reached the place where Sam had parked the wagon, pulled some empty wood crates from the back, and dropped them to the ground. Hugh took the canteen from over his shoulder and offered it to Sam.

"By the way, James Martin has asked for you more than once in the last week," he said, watching Sam gulp. "He shall make a rebellion if you don't stop by."

"I have carved a bird for him. I will bring it tomorrow. And Miranda and the twins, they are well?"

Hugh pulled down a branch of the tree next to him, sniffed at a peach, and let the branch spring away. "Miranda, yes. I believe so."

He *wanted* to believe. But did he believe it in his heart, in the center of his being? Would he swear to it on a Holy Bible?

CHAPTER THIRTEEN

That night, another dream, the one where I was at the front doors, banging the knocker, rain pouring down. *Rap! Rap! Rap!* "Let me in! I know you're there," I cried, angry to be left standing in the rain.

Elizabeth!

I opened my eyes. The last few molecules of my dream dispersed.

Elizabeth, take heed!

I tossed back the covers and turned on the light. "Who are you?" I shouted, trying to sound brave. "What do you want?"

Take heed, for you shall be troubled all your days.

"Please, go away! Leave me alone!"

Buck looked up from the quilt. I reached out for his warm, reassuring presence.

What did it mean? *Take heed.*

I got out of bed, yanked on my robe, and hurried downstairs, turning on lights as I went. In the kitchen, still trembling, I poured a shot of cognac. *You shall be troubled all your days.* Was it some kind of curse? Why would this...this entity, this *thing* curse me?

I swallowed back the drink and poured another. It was him, Hugh Peter Jones. The accent. I thought it English at first, but it must have been Welsh. He hated me for being here, and he wanted me gone.

This house had been sold twice in five years—a warning sign right from the start. I should have known.

I couldn't go back to bed. Not now. So, I made a small fire and tipped the Rémy Martin bottle over my empty glass. Another wouldn't hurt. As the cognac trailed warmly down my throat, Buck wandered in and came over to sit beside me.

"What are we going to do now?" I asked. "How will we make it stop?"

—

In the morning, I opened a fresh bag of Sumatran blend and spooned it into the coffeemaker. Then I added an extra scoop. I'd had barely four hours of sleep, and I was exhausted.

Todd arrived at seven thirty to measure for the windows. After he left, I called Susannah's cell phone to remind her about finding Penny Jenkins's number.

At a little before eight, I started out for work. The office was locked when I got there. No Harry. I opened the blinds on the windows and door, craving sunlight, and settled in to do some quick research on ghosts. There were more than a million websites on the subject. Where to start? I scrolled through a few pages and finally clicked on a site called *A Guide to Ghosts and Spirits.*

The array of supernatural entities was dizzying. Apparitions, ectoplasm, mists, orbs, spirals of light, poltergeists.

Poltergeists. According to the website, a poltergeist was capable of moving objects, making noises, producing smells, causing light to—

Harry breezed through the door with a "Hey, kiddo" and

disappeared into the back room to hang up his coat. "Todd come by this morning?"

I clicked out of the website and tried for a cheery note. "Fifteen hundred dollars for new windows installed, which I made him sign for in blood. And he's throwing in re-hitching my loose shutter out front."

Harry reappeared and leaned back against his desk, hand in his pocket Harry-style. "Is there a reason you look like you need a good night's sleep?"

I explained about the voice in the night, and since I hadn't yet told him about *Grace When the End Is Near* falling out of my bookcase, I added that for good measure. In for a dime, in for a dollar. Harry wouldn't judge.

Would he?

"I'm all but sure that cop was right, that I have a ghost in my house," I said. "And I don't think he's very happy with me." That simple admission caused a tear to well and stream down my cheek. I wiped it away. "I was just doing some online research and putting two and two together." Another tear. "I think it's a poltergeist."

Harry came and lowered himself to my desk. "A poltergeist? So...you think it's Jones, the guy who built your house?"

"If I had to guess."

"What do you think he wants?"

"I wish I knew." I pulled a tissue from the box on my desk and dabbed at my eyes. "Maybe he just wants to torment me because he was miserable in life and he still is in death. 'You shall be troubled all your days.' What the hell does that mean?" I looked up at Harry's questioning face and let out a long sigh. "I know this all sounds preposterous. But you know me. You know I'm not crazy."

"Of course not," he said, squeezing my arm and lifting himself from the desk. "Hold on. I'll get us some Peet's."

As Harry drifted off to pour the coffee, our landline rang. I cleared my throat and answered it. Susannah Kunkel calling to say she had contacted Penny Jenkins about the glove.

"You can reach out and take it from there," she said, before giving me Penny's number. A pause, then, "Things are going okay, are they? No more surprises in your springhouse?"

"Nothing else in there so far," I assured her, and said goodbye. Finally, a small bit of progress.

Harry reappeared, set a steaming cup on my desk, and folded his lean frame into his chair. Harry was all grace when he moved.

I filled him in on the call with Susannah. "Maybe I can make some headway," I said.

"We'll celebrate with a little pick-me-up later," he said, and I knew he meant the bottle we kept stashed back in the dry sink. Harry was the one who gave me my first taste of Rémy Martin way back when, and ever since we had kept a supply in the office for special occasions. "Now, what can I do to help you with all this?"

"In another life, you would have been my doting husband. Or maybe you would have taken me for crazy and locked me in the attic."

"How'd you guess?" He flashed a grin that was replaced a moment later with a long stare.

What was swimming beneath the calm Aegean of those eyes?

"I think the important thing is you don't feel like you're in some kind of real trouble there," he said. "Like you're unsafe."

"I don't know how I feel." I trailed off, thinking of Diana's words at McGraw's. *I don't believe in all that hooey.* None of this felt like hooey anymore.

"You're welcome to come stay with Mitch and me for a while if you need to. You can bring Buck and Sugar Plum. Mitch would love that."

"You're the best," I said. "I might take you up on it."

"You know..." Harry paused. "Mitch and I could do Thanksgiving this year. It's not too late."

"No, please. I can do it. It'll be a good distraction, and I need some friendly faces in my house."

—

At noon, I headed up to Cassie's Pen and Page, a five-minute walk from the office. I could have called her to set up our coffee date, but I had books on my mind now, and it was time for a few new ones.

The shop was housed in a charming 1920s brick storefront that sat by itself on a corner, its tall front windows filled with books and photographs and little vintage lamps kept lit at night. Cassie ran it more as a pastime than a living. One of many pastimes that included a crafts consortium, a community podcast, and a small arts foundation, all supported by the sizable alimony from her patent attorney ex-husband, Barry.

What will she start next? A petting zoo? Diana once commented, deep into her second glass of wine.

Three or four people were browsing when I entered, Cassie nowhere to be seen. I asked the young clerk at the wooden checkout counter to go find her.

As I wandered the shelves of books, my mind went back to *Grace When the End Is Near*. I had bought it here at Cassie's. Before it ended up on my floor, I'd hardly given it—

"Ms. Casey?"

I turned. A man with short, dark brown hair was staring back at me. I'd seen him before, but I couldn't manage to pull his name from the stewing muddle of my mind.

"I thought that was you," he said, his voice edged with a little gravel.

"Yes, hello."

An awkward moment passed. Who was he? A burnt orange sweater peeked from under his navy jacket. He smelled like the outdoors, the November chill.

"I'm Keith Janus," he said, smiling. "Maybe you don't remember me. I'm the guy up in Morley?"

"Oh, of course. Mr. Janus. I'm sorry, I—"

"Don't apologize, and please, call me Keith."

"Harry and I will be seeing you Monday, right?"

He nodded. "Looking forward to it. So, you just out doing a little browsing today?"

"I stopped in to see Cassie. She owns this store. What brings you over to Simms?"

"My dentist moved away so I had to find a new one, and she happens to be here in town. I thought I'd stop in to check this place out. I like what I see so far. Very homey."

The longish nose, bronze eyes flecked like mica, faintest shadow of whiskers—I hadn't had a chance to notice any of it that long-ago day in front of March & Casey. And the random strands of silver in his dark hair.

"We're lucky to have it in Simms," I agreed. "A real old-fashioned bookshop."

From the back, the young employee approached with Cassie in his wake.

"There's Cassie now," I said, offering a smile in apology for cutting our conversation short.

Keith Janus raised a hand in farewell. "Enjoy your day, and I'll see you and Harry Monday."

A moment later, Cassie docked beside me. She watched Keith drift into the racks. "I sure hope *he* comes in again," she said.

Men were another of her pastimes.

Cassie blinked under her white bangs. "Do you know him?"

"Not really." Best not to tell her he was a prospective client, or things would get complicated. "He was just remarking on how much he likes what you have here."

Cassie's round face brightened. "Oh, well. I like what he has too, hmm?"

We set a coffee date for Tuesday. I returned to browsing the shelves, made a few selections, and then headed up the street to the café. But when I got there, the place was awash in customers, Diana too busy to talk. So, I ordered some vegetable barley soup to go.

—

The book was still on the coffee table when I got home from work. Its presence seemed to taunt me. *Are you going to pick me up and put me back? Or are you going to wait and see what I do next?*

Buck sidled up and huffed.

"Okay, let's go," I said.

As I shut the back door, Buck disappeared into the twilight. I caught up with him at the garden. He stood at the gate, as usual, staring through the space between two pickets.

"On the hunt?" I peered over the fence.

Something was moving inside the gate. The iron ball and chain that served as a weight to keep it closed. It was swaying.

Back and forth, back and forth, the arc of its movement wound down. There was no wind tonight, but even so, a piece of iron the size of a cannonball, well, it would only move if the gate had been opened. I looked down at Buck. No dog could open a gate that swings out. A gate held shut by a ball and chain.

Probably a raccoon or a possum that had climbed up the fence and jumped over.

A rustling noise at the far side of the garden made me jump. "Come on," I said, and I hurried Buck back to the house.

In the kitchen, I brewed some herbal tea and tunneled into thoughts about the ball and chain and the odd rustling noise, telling myself once again that it had been a raccoon. But I couldn't help thinking that it was him out there, the ghost of Hugh Peter Jones, skulking around in his single gauntlet—

Penny Jenkins. I still needed to call her. Retrieving the Post-it I'd scribbled her number onto, I dialed and left a message. Two minutes later, she called back, suggesting I text her some photos of the inside and outside of the glove. As soon as I hung up, I did as she had instructed.

Just a piece of leather, I told myself again, glove in hand. But was it? I brought it to my nose and breathed its scent. Leather, sweat, dust, and something dark.

Outside the kitchen windows, night fell like a black curtain. Something dark indeed.

CHAPTER FOURTEEN

Tom Barrett arrived at eight in the morning with his tree-trimming truck and his son Scott. While they set to work on the oak, I took Buck for a walk. I drew in long breaths of chilly air as we walked toward the woods, trying to dispel the lingering effects of the sleeping pill I'd taken last night. At the garden, I stopped and peered in. The ball and chain hung perfectly still.

Yes, it had probably been a raccoon.

Buck danced beside me, eager to run for the woods. "Lead the way," I said. But instead of following him, I yanked open the gate and stepped inside, caught by the sudden scent of something sharp and floral, out of place in the dead garden. I closed my eyes and breathed it in. What was it?

Tom Barrett's chainsaw began buzzing in the distance like a giant locust, rending the silent morning, breaking the spell. *Buck*, I remembered. I hurried off to find him.

Back at the house, I poured a cup of coffee then padded to the office in my socks. Sugar Plum lay dozing in the upholstered chair opposite the desk. Maisie Jackson and I had been engaged in a friendly game of phone tag, but this time when I called her back, she answered, and we set a date to meet at my place early in December to review the plans for her attic studio renovation.

At eleven o'clock, I decided to take a break. The chainsaw had gone quiet. Thick flurries were starting to fall. I shoved a load of laundry into the washer—working from home always meant working *at* home—and my eyes caught again on the crack in the back door's big glass pane. Ray once said that taping a crack in glass can keep it from getting worse, so I went to the kitchen to rummage for—

Bang, bang. The door knocker. Tom Barrett, snow flecking his green cap, wanted me to know that he and his son Scott had gotten all the problem limbs down. I thanked him, then closed the door against the chill and listened to his truck motor away.

Of course, now I knew that it hadn't been the limbs speaking to me in the night.

—

By four o'clock the snow had stopped. I gave the animals an early dinner and then leashed Buck for a walk. This time I took us out the front door and down to the street, thinking a change of scenery would do us both good. Chambers Road, never busy, was deserted as we made our way through the light powder on the shoulder.

We'd only gotten about thirty yards down when a human-sounding yelp broke the quiet. Buck's ears twitched. We both turned toward the noise.

It had come from across the road, the Reardon School for the Blind. Something was moving on the driveway. A woman, crumpled in a heap.

"Hello?" I called.

By the time Buck and I got across the road, she was sitting up, her hand tapping over the ground.

"Are you okay?" I asked. A silly question, for the poor soul had obviously fallen.

"Yes, yes, if you could just find my stick, please," she said. An English accent, or so I thought. Surely not Welsh.

I picked a white rod out of the snow-dusted surface of the blacktop and snatched it up. "Here, let me help you."

Commanding Buck to stay put, I bent to offer my hand. It was then I realized I'd seen her before, her white hair and her stick. She was the woman I'd seen standing at the edge of this same driveway in August, on the day I first toured the house. She found my hand and closed her grip around it.

"I knew that was you," she murmured. But who did she think I was? Once upright, she held out her hand for her stick. "Thank you. You're very kind. I must have tripped."

"Are you alone?" I asked. "Are you waiting for someone?"

Her head turned toward the sound of my voice, her sightless eyes seeming to stare through me—or into me. The faux fur collar of her parka skimmed her jawline. "I'm not waiting for anyone, no."

When she didn't explain, I said, "It's a good thing we came along when we did."

"You and your dog." She dropped a tentative hand in Buck's direction.

"His name is Buck, and he's friendly. I'm Libby, by the way. Libby Casey. I just moved in across the road. I think you mistook me for someone else?"

"I'm Emmeline." She finally swiped at Buck's head. The dog looked up expectantly. "I bet this one's smart. So how are you finding the old place?"

"Busy after the move, but things will settle down." It was growing dark now, and colder. My stomach rumbled for dinner. "I'm afraid we need to head back. But what about you? May I help you get somewhere?"

Emmeline turned and took a step back down the driveway, stick out ahead of her. In the distance, the big school loomed, a shadow in the gray evening, glimmers of yellow in the windows.

"Just getting a bit of air. I'll find my way," she said over her shoulder. "Thank you again for your kindness. We'll see each other soon."

Yes, perhaps we would, for surely she worked here, maybe even lived here. But as I led Buck back across the road, I couldn't help wondering why an elderly blind woman would be out wandering alone in the dark on a snowy evening with no apparent purpose. Was her mind starting to go? Should I alert someone at the school? This time she only fell. Next time it could be worse.

—

Penny Jenkins called at one o'clock on Sunday afternoon to give me the news that the glove was a genuine eighteenth-century gauntlet.

Surely it had belonged to Hugh Peter Jones. But what would I do with it now? Maybe Penny would take it off my hands. She might want to add it to her collection. It had value, after all, even if there was only the one.

"I just love the initials," she said. "I think they make it special, personal, and they're quite well done. Anyway, I hope this helps you somehow."

"It does and thank you." No, I wouldn't offer her the glove, not yet.

"Did Susannah tell you about the Jones descendant in the area? Vivian. The last name escapes me. I met her once, a few years ago. When she found out I had a vintage clothing collection, she insisted on giving me two of her grandmother's old hats."

"Susannah said something about her but wasn't sure whether she was even still alive. Do you know?"

"I haven't heard otherwise. But then, I haven't kept up."

"I'd like to talk to her if possible, about my house."

"I could try to find her if you like. My friend Ginny knows her, I think."

"I would really appreciate it."

"Well, I better go. I'm picking up Mother this afternoon, and she doesn't like waiting."

My mother would have liked yours. My last thought as we said goodbye.

After hanging up, I decided I might paint the hall bathroom that afternoon. I even got as far as covering the floor tiles with an old bedsheet and setting out the can of apple green paint, a brush, and a roller.

But before I could get to work, I found myself climbing to the third floor.

I went to the same room I'd gone to the day I followed that first vague summons. The west room, I called it. Boxes and bags lay scattered about, left over from the move, still waiting for me to pick through. A dull gray light washed through the dormer windows. I turned on the floor lamp in the corner, trying to pry from my brain the reason I'd come up here. The radiator under the windows knocked, pushing out its modest warmth. I looked over at the little fireplace on the outside wall. How long had it been since anyone used it? A hundred years or more?

I turned to the row of boxes lining one wall. Old keepsakes and mementos, mostly. The things we drag with us wherever we go but rarely look at. I pulled back the flap on one of the boxes. Photo albums. I'd almost forgotten they were up here. I sat down on the floor and pulled one out, unable to resist.

Letters, postcards, photo albums—the kind of tangible evidence of human interactions that was becoming obsolete in the digital age. A pity, for how would anyone see us, know us, understand our hearts two hundred years from now without something to pick up and hold? Some artifact of our lives that might say who we were?

Something like a leather glove.

I opened the album and paged through. Me, my mother and father, our dog Olly and cat Jingles, Granny Eleanor Casey, a few cousins, birthdays, Christmases, a playground, an amusement park, a prom, and a graduation. I was an only child, so the lens was almost always trained on me. My father was the one who liked to take the pictures, and he was good at it. Tim Casey had a true photographer's eye.

I set the family album aside and dug in the box for another. I knew which one I was looking for. And there he was, my father, nineteen, hair shorn, staring out from the edge of a rice paddy in Vietnam, a place he never talked much about, an improbable smile on his face. I was twelve when he died of a heart attack while delivering mail. His death was an old wound, one which had mostly healed over. But I sometimes thought it an irony that he survived the war only to die years later in a place as quiet and uncontested as a mail truck.

I flipped through the rest of the black-and-white snapshots he'd taken during his tour of duty and finally came to the Polaroids of my parents before I was born, and then more black-and-white shots, of just Annabelle, taken by my father with his 35mm camera. My mother in a way I thought only he must have seen her. The bright eyes and soft, Hedy LaMarr face, her expression like an invitation, wavy dark hair hanging down, swept across one eye. My mother was beautiful. No denying that.

A shadow in the doorway. Sugar Plum.

"Here to keep me company?" I asked. She lumbered in, accepted a pat on the head, and wandered off to nose around the bags and boxes.

On a roll now, I pulled out one more album, labeled on the front with a Post-it note. *Ray & Libby*. I opened it to the two of us staring back from a beach on Ocracoke Island, the sand white under a bright October sun, Ray in cutoffs, shirtless, tattoo on his right shoulder, and me in a gauzy dress, barefoot, my dark hair falling down from under a sun hat. Our first vacation together, and it couldn't have been worse. Mosquitos big as flies, an obnoxious boarder at the bed and breakfast, the ruined kayak trip.

We'd had to drag the kayaks back onto shore in a furious

downpour. "That's okay," I said to Ray, my shirt glued to my skin, hair dripping into my eyes. "I don't really like kayaking anyway." He threw back his head with a throaty laugh and said, "Why didn't you tell me?" And I said, "Because I'm a really good sport." At that, we both nearly collapsed with laughter.

Back home a few weeks later, Ray gave me a T-shirt printed with bright green letters: *I Love Not Kayaking*. Where was that shirt? Suddenly I felt the need to find it.

I got up and dusted myself off. Sugar Plum was pawing with great concentration at the floor in front of the little closet across the room.

"A mouse?" I asked, going over to see.

No, not a mouse but a piece of paper, sticking out from under the closet door. She swiped at it again and then wandered away.

I picked it up. It was about half the size of a sheet of copy paper, but thicker and yellowed with age. A few lines of curving script trailed across it in faded black ink, in some places smudged, like the ink from a fountain pen might be, or the ink from...could it have been a quill?

I opened the closet. The door creaked on its old iron hinges. Except for a few wooden shelves and the crudely plastered walls, the space was as empty as the day I moved in. As empty as my springhouse had been until it wasn't.

I turned off the lamp and scooped up the cat, suddenly nervous and eager to get downstairs. In the kitchen, I sat down at the table with the mysterious paper. *1 May, Beltane* was written in the upper left corner, followed by three numbers, *176*, and a fourth that was too smudged to read. Beltane, a pagan holiday of some sort, as I recalled. Celtic, was it? The date made me think this was a letter. But why was there no person to whom it was addressed?

Only fragments of the following three short sentences were clear and legible: *a grave worry has come upon me...I have not seen before...something to be done about it*. At the end, instead of a signature, there was only a slash of ink.

A grave worry.

I studied the fine mesh of lines running through the paper, probably cloth fibers. I heard once that they sometimes made paper back then with rags. The left edge, I noticed, was frayed ever so slightly, like it had been torn carefully from a binding.

A paper with a date and a message but no salutation or signature, torn from a binding. This wasn't a letter. It was a page from a diary.

—

Before bed, I dug through a dresser drawer and found that T-shirt Ray had given me. I slipped it on. Just under it was one of Ray's T-shirts, unwashed from when he'd last worn it. I pulled it to my nose but try as I might to conjure the natural earthy scent of him, it was gone.

I opened the tidy little varnished box on top of the dresser and drew in the sharp note of wood inside. There he was. This was the smell that hung around him after a day of sawing and nailing in his garage workshop. He had proposed to me after one such day, his work boots covered with sawdust as he thumped into the kitchen and snatched up a piece of the orange bell pepper I'd been chopping. It was a year after Ocracoke. He pulled the box from his pocket and handed it to me. A perfect square of varnished blond cedar, the top domed like a treasure chest.

"What do you think of this?" he drawled.

"Very sweet," I said. "Did you make it from wood scraps?"

"Yeah, but you have to open it."

Inside, a beautiful one-of-a-kind ring lay nestled in upholstery velvet. An emerald in an antique silver setting.

"To go with your eyes, my wife's eyes, forever," he said, then he leaned in and kissed me.

My mother grumbled when I told her the news. "Do you think, well...I hope he's not too old for you, dear." I had settled the matter as I often did such disagreements, with a "No comment."

The difference in our ages, eleven years, had never given Ray or me a moment's hesitation. But for my mother, well, maybe it was the dimming prospect of a grandchild that bothered her. Would Ray want a second round of fatherhood? Or maybe she worried that he would die too many years before I did and leave me alone, as my father had her. How improbable that would have seemed then. That Ray should die too soon.

Before getting into bed, I lowered the right side of my pajama pants and ran my finger over the word written on my upper hip. Ray's name in tidy, navy blue letters with a small red heart underneath. A surprise to Ray a month before we were married. "You can't be the only one with a tattoo," I'd said. And he'd said, "I guess this means you're mine."

I tucked the diary page into the night table. Then I settled into bed, reached over to Buck, and felt his beating heart.

Relax, breathe, let sleep come over you.

CHAPTER FIFTEEN

October 1759

With the children abed upstairs, Miranda and Hugh sat at the table in their little room of a house, sipping the brandy Niall and Hannah had brought as a wedding gift. Embers glowed in the fireplace. Night was closing in.

"Now you are truly Mrs. Jones." Hugh grazed Miranda's neck with a kiss, breathing the scent of her lavender oil.

The ceremony that morning was a fine affair, the sycamore yellow, the sky blue, a small cadre of guests gathered around. Hugh had noticed the Reverend Potter looking askance at the children from time to time, no doubt wondering why he and Miranda had not managed to marry before rather than after they were born. But the old Unitarian kept his peace, as Hugh had thought he would.

Miranda leaned in and returned Hugh's kiss. "And you are truly my husband. But I have been thinking." Her hazel eyes suddenly hardened into flints. "There is something you must help me do." She swallowed the last of her brandy and went to the mantelpiece, where she took down a scrap of folded paper.

"What is it?" Hugh asked.

She brought the paper to him. A single word trailed across it in her neat, rounded script. *Prescott.*

"Your surname?" he said.

"Not mine anymore. Not mine ever again. Come, let's get the shovel. It is time."

"Time for what?"

"For a burial." She waved him out of his chair.

After fetching the shovel from the barn, Hugh met up with her at the kitchen garden where she'd said she would wait. "Where shall we go to dig?" he asked.

"Here." She pushed open the gate and pointed down. "Where we might walk upon this name every time we cross the threshold. Where all the color and sustenance growing out of the earth will make a mockery of it."

Hugh regarded his new wife, her hair lit with the moon, her fair face intent, and he wanted only to oblige her. *My dear, sweet, abiding girl.* She had endured the evils of her cold father for too long, yet it had not hardened her. It was enough that she had escaped him, and now finally she would put him to rest.

"As you wish," Hugh said.

But before he could put his foot to the shovel, Miranda held him back, saying, "I shall go first."

She took the shovel, stabbed it into the earth, and put her foot on the step of the blade. "I am Prescott no more," she whispered. She pushed down with great exertion and broke open the soil. Then she looked up at Hugh in triumph.

When at last they had dropped the paper into its grave and covered it with earth, they walked back to the little house that was now made even smaller by the bigger one looming at its side. Hugh felt that something had come to an end and that something else had begun, although he didn't feel he could put a name to any of it.

That night, he and Miranda came together in their bed, taking their pleasure quietly so as not to wake the children. Afterward, she fell quickly into sleep, but Hugh lay awake, thinking about what she had whispered before she turned away from him.

Un rêve d'amour. A dream of love.

Was love a dream? Yes, a dream and a balm and whatever good there was to be had in this life. He reached out and laid a hand to Miranda's warm shoulder and felt the rhythm of her breathing. They would live in their dream as long as God would allow. And then they would carry it to Heaven.

—

Two days later, Hugh rode into the village to meet with Mr. Hornsby, the solicitor. The old man, hunched with age, poured them tea in his parlor, and they set to work on Hugh's will and testament. At his death, the property and crop business would go to James Martin. Miranda would reside in the house for as long as she wished and would have the right to make decisions about any household concerns until her death or such time as she might remarry.

Hugh shoved away the thought that she might die or marry again and continued on with the provisions. The household goods, the livestock, small cash bequests to Sam Grey Feather and Hattie, if and as such money allowed, and monthly stipends for Abby and Alice held in trust.

"For their use and only theirs," Hugh said. "Please write that in."

Mr. Hornsby raised his quill from the page he was recording on. "You expect the girls to take husbands, do you not?"

"If they wish. But still, I am not in favor of a woman being stripped bare of all she might have to make her way in the world just because she has a husband. My daughters must be able to survive come what may."

"As you desire," Mr. Hornsby said, setting his quill back to the paper. "Pardon my saying that you think a bit freely, Mr. Jones."

"So I have been told," Hugh said.

"And who might serve as trustee?"

"Mistress Caroline Hathaway. My wife's cousin. She is unmarried and therefore eligible for court. If she is unable to serve, then Robert Porter on Fourth Street in the city."

"Porter, yes. I know him." Mr. Hornsby grunted and scribbled the last of the terms.

Hugh signed the page, pulled on his gauntlets, and set out for home, satisfied. All of his family would have what they were due when his time came.

CHAPTER SIXTEEN

Harry and I pulled into Keith Janus's driveway a little early, so we waited in the car to pass the time.

"What do you think?" Harry said, eyeing the house. "Midcentury meets Frank Lloyd Wright?"

I nodded. "Good use of glass, nothing overdone." My travel cup sent up a welcome fume of ginger tea as I lifted it to my lips. "Smaller than I expected, but that's not a bad thing."

"Apparently his wife was the one who picked this out. But she didn't ask for it in the divorce. Something about she decided to move to Arizona."

"I wonder why he keeps it. I mean, if she's the one who wanted it in the first place. Why not sell and move on?"

"Good question. But lucky for us, he didn't." Harry checked his watch. "Should we knock?"

The front door sat off-center amid a façade of windows, tan brick, and dark wood trims. Painted a deep chocolate brown, it was almost invisible in the shadow of the overhang.

"This door looks depressed," I said as Harry searched for the doorbell. "A nice orange might do, don't you think?"

He turned up his thumb and then pressed the bell with it. Thirty seconds later, he pressed it again.

The door whipped open and Keith Janus, in sweatpants and a flannel shirt, socks but no shoes, greeted us with an apology. "Sorry about that. Come in."

He waved us into a wide front hallway floored with oblong slates. "Time got away from me. I was downstairs fixing a toilet."

The rooms on either side of us were completely open, no walls, no doors, the one to the right obviously an office, the one to the left a dining room. Both were brightened by the home's large front windows. At least the light was good, even if there were no walls. I myself liked walls, and so did Harry. We were forever trying to talk our clients out of banging them all down.

Keith must have noticed me pondering. "Alicia was the one who wanted to open this up," he said. "I want to close some of it back up again, or partly, and put in a coat closet. I worked construction summers when I was in college, but walls and closets are a little beyond me."

We moved on to the living room directly in front of us, a kitchen off to the left, a fireplace and stairway to the right, and big windows at the back with French doors that opened to a deck and a sloping hillside.

"It's not worth much right now," Keith said, pointing to the deck. "It's unstable so I never go out there. Why tempt fate?" He turned back to Harry and me. "If you don't mind, I'd like to make it part of the project. Come on, I'll show you the rest."

We wandered off on a tour of the house, discussing the changes and updates he wanted done. The furnishings throughout were sparse, some of them 1960s modern, and most of the hardwood floors were uncarpeted. Had Alicia's last hurrah been to make off with the furniture and rugs?

"Do you need any help with décor?" I asked once our tour had brought us back to the living room. The place positively wept for a little cheering up.

"Actually, you read my mind. I would love to replace some of this stuff with something, I don't know, a little cozier."

We chatted a while longer and then Keith said he needed to get to work, something about a conference call.

As we all said goodbye at the door, he turned to me, his bronze eyes alight, the flecks shimmering. He shook my hand and then Harry's.

"What do you think?" Harry asked as we drove away, but he wasn't talking about the project. "James Garner in mid-career? Slightly slimmer and with shorter hair."

"You mean Keith?" I asked. "Leave it to you to see Hollywood."

"Anyway, this'll be fun."

—

That evening, I retrieved the diary page from the night table and typed it into a Word document. Then I printed it out and slipped it into the folder of Jones materials Susannah had copied for me, leaving the original copy on top of my desk. Before lodging the folder back in its drawer, I took out the family tree and looked at all the generations of Joneses set out in neat, descending order. They were all dead. Dead and gone. Except for one.

I tucked the tree back into the folder and shut the drawer. All I wanted was to live here in my charming old house, pick up the pieces of my life, and move on. But that simple desire had become tangled as a knot.

"I just want to move on!" I called to no one, or someone. "I just want some peace! Can't you give me peace?"

A bang sounded above me, and then another, like a door slamming. Then came the sound of Buck galloping up the stairs.

My pulse began to race. Something was up there, and it wasn't a prowler. I wanted to run, but I couldn't move from where I stood behind my desk.

Do something, Libby!

Finally, I managed to pry my feet from the floorboards, get to the kitchen, and grab my phone. I dialed Diana. No answer. I called Harry.

"Hold tight. Be right over," he said.

When he arrived twenty minutes later, we walked through the house together. First floor, second floor, and up to the third. Buck was sitting outside the west room. The door was closed.

"I didn't shut that door, Harry. I've never shut it."

Harry looked from the door to me.

"That's the room where I found the diary page I told you about today."

"Let's take a look." Harry opened the door and went in, followed by Buck and then me. I turned on the floor lamp.

"Anything out of place?" he asked.

The boxes and bags were just where I'd left them yesterday. I shook my head. "Could we check the closet?"

Harry swung open the closet door. After a quick peek in, he said, "All clear here," and shut it again.

Back downstairs, I poured us both a shot of cognac. "There's something about the third floor. It's like I'm being pulled up there sometimes. And now this. And the garden. I keep smelling something out there, and the other night, I saw..." I shook my head and swallowed back my shot. "I don't know where to go with any of this. It's all becoming a bit much."

Harry turned his glass in a circle on the table. "You know, not all mysteries can be solved, Lib. You might want to think about what to do if you can't solve this one."

"You mean sell the place?"

"Just something to keep in your back pocket for now."

"I was sure when I moved in here...Maybe I was just running away."

He swallowed his drink and wiped his mouth with the back of his hand. "Away from what?"

That thing that keeps twisting inside me. That thing I did.

"Everything," I said.

Harry knew there was more behind that simple yet complicated answer. But he didn't pursue it.

"Anyway, I'm not ready to run again. Not yet."

"What does Diana say to all this?"

"She's not exactly a believer in this kind of thing. But she's been busy at the café, and I haven't had a chance to catch her up on the latest. I'm afraid you're bearing the brunt of it for now. If you want me to shut up about it—"

"You don't have to shut up. I've known you a long time, kiddo. When something's troubling you, it's troubling me." He held up his glass. "One more nip for the road?"

I poured us another shot. Was Rémy Martin going to become my new best friend?

"Let's figure out tonight first," Harry said. "Why don't you follow me home and stay in the guest room?"

"I don't know. It's late and I don't want to be a—"

"It's one night. And you'll sleep better than you would here."

Whether I would sleep better at Harry's, I didn't know. But it would be a relief to get away from the house for a while.

"Okay," I said. "Let me grab some things."

CHAPTER SEVENTEEN

The next morning, I took Buck home from Harry's, went up to the third floor in the light of day, and opened the closet in the west room. Nothing. I shut the door and went downstairs to pack my lunch, wondering what I would do if it happened again tonight. The slamming door.

At Diana's Cozy Cottage Café, I settled into my favorite booth by a window to wait for Cassie—the booth where Ray and I used to dig into a lazy weekend breakfast—and ordered a mocha latte from Rita, the tall, lanky waitress who'd been serving at the café for years. As I took my first sips of coffee, I thought about what Harry had said, that I might not be able to solve the mystery. I couldn't keep running to him like a frightened child every time—

"Sorry I'm late." Cassie's breathless voice made me look up.

She shrugged off her faux fur jacket, tossed it onto the bench beside her, and slid in. Her bright orchid sweater brought out the shimmering pale blue of the gems dangling from her ears.

"They *are* lovely, aren't they?" she said when she caught me staring. She tapped one of the earrings and offered a playful smile. "Blue topaz. The last gift Barry ever gave me." A moment passed. "No, that's not true. The divorce was the last gift."

Rita sailed out of the kitchen and smiled down at Cassie. "Hey there, haven't seen you in a while. What can I get you?"

Cassie cocked her head. "Please tell me you have some of that delicious pumpkin pie cake. I've been thinking about it for days."

"You're in luck. We have one sheet left." Rita winked. "Something to drink?"

I caught Cassie's eye and tapped the mug in front of me. "The mocha latte with orange. You should try it," I said, and Cassie nodded.

We made small talk while we waited for the cake and coffee. Thanksgiving plans, Lottie Garland's house up for sale, the Simms tree lighting coming up that weekend.

When the cake finally arrived, Cassie regarded it wide-eyed, lifted her fork, and dug in. "This always feels like a mortal sin."

"More than one," I said, watching her savor it, tempted to order a piece for myself.

Breakfast rush over, the café grew quiet, only a few customers scattered at the odd booth or table. A bright morning sun washed through the tall window beside us, making Cassie's earrings twinkle. As she whittled away at her cake, I turned the conversation toward my visit with Susannah. She was bound to ask about it. I left out the part about the glove I had taken with me.

"You certainly do own a piece of history now," Cassie said, cooing with satisfaction as she tasted the latte. "And I hope you'll invite me over someday. I'd love to see it." She set down her fork, the cake nearly vanquished. "I knew Ross and Ruthie, of course, but—"

"Ross and Ruthie Phillips, you mean?"

Cassie nodded. "They used to come into the store now and then and leave with an armful of books. Ruthie, poor thing, suffered from rheumatoid arthritis. Once in a while, when she couldn't get out, I would take a few books over to the house, but I never got further than the front hallway."

"Did they ever say what it was like to live there?"

Cassie shrugged. "Ross lived in the house when he was a kid, with his parents and a sister, I think, so I guess it seemed like home. Didn't Susannah tell you? When Ross's father died, Ross inherited the place. That's when he moved back, with Ruthie. They lived there for twenty years before moving on to an assisted living facility."

"Susannah mentioned they were private people."

"They weren't much for social life. Once in a while they came out to some function or other." Cassie leaned forward. "I was talking to Ross at a fundraiser once, and he was a little tipsy, and he told me that he and Ruthie weren't the only two residents in the house that could be accounted for."

"Oh?"

"I thought it was the wine talking. But who knows? Ross, he was always a little...unusual."

"So, what he was saying was, the house is haunted?"

"An old place like that, with so much life lived there, there's bound to be energy, don't you think?" Cassie's pewter eyes studied me. "Have you had any experiences?"

I mulled over a reply while Cassie sipped her mocha. What was it Susannah had said about becoming a curiosity? *People start to talk...children come by and peer through the hedges.* As a person with a business and a reputation to uphold in Simms, I couldn't afford to become a curiosity, or to be thought of as *unusual*. I grabbed my mug and swirled my coffee in circles. "A few noises," I said. "The house settling, maybe. That kind of thing."

"Well, I doubt it's anything, really. But I do know someone who does cleansings."

Of course she did. There was almost no one Cassie didn't know.

"I'd say you could ask Ross himself about the house, but he and Ruthie are gone now," she said. "And I don't know what became of the next owners. I think the name was Johnson. Anyway, I hope you won't keep the place too much to yourself."

The café door opened. A man in a winter jacket hurried in and then turned and held the door for someone. Diana. She exchanged a few words with him as he closed the door against a gust of wind. When she spied Cassie and me across the café, she waved on her way to the kitchen.

"Well," Cassie said, checking her watch. "Books are waiting to be shelved." She got up and pulled on her coat. The blue topaz teardrops winked. "This was so fun. We need to do it more often."

Another customer entering the café lost control of the door to another whooshing gust. It swung back with a bang.

"Good heavens," Cassie said. "It's getting so blustery. I better scoot or I'll be blown to Timbuktu."

Hardly five seconds after she was gone, Diana pushed through the swinging door from the kitchen. "So how did it go?" she asked, dropping to the bench Cassie had just vacated. Two more customers entered the café.

"Good," I said. "You're starting to get busy here, though, so I'll catch you up Thursday. I have a lot to tell you, anyway."

"Sorry I missed your call last night. I fell asleep on the sofa. Anything important?"

The story of the slamming door seemed too complicated a topic with the café filling up. "Not really." I would tell her later.

Diana swiveled her head toward the growing drift of customers and stood up. "Duty calls and so does the autumn casserole." She nodded thoughtfully toward Cassie's empty plate. "You know, I saw her at the hardware store Sunday, and she said she just found out she's diabetic."

"Oh?" I was now regretting that I'd talked Cassie into the mocha. "My Uncle Norman had diabetes. That's what eventually did him in. He couldn't seem to give up the sweets."

"Well, she's a big girl, and who are we to tell her how to live her life? Anyway, Cal and I will see you Thursday with all the goodies and Tara in tow. Turns out my twenty-two-year-old wunderkind will be home from her new job in Chicago after all. Her boss is giving her the whole holiday weekend off."

"What about Kenny?" I asked.

"He's doing Thanksgiving at Taylor's. He's like a puppy dog with that girl. But it'll get him out of my hair for a little while. He's been driving me crazy lately. Want a teenager?" Before heading back to the kitchen, she flashed one of her trademark grins. The trouble-with-Kenny grin that seemed to show itself more and more these days.

I sat alone in the booth. A puddle of brown was all that remained of my mocha. I tipped the mug and let the semisweet sludge spread over my tongue.

"Hmm," I sighed, thinking about cleansings.

—

Buck stood in the middle of the kitchen as I struggled through the back door with two shopping bags of food. He watched me set the bags on the table and then huffed softly at the exact moment I released them. "I know, but hold on," I said, rooting through my purse to find my cell phone. A text from Todd had come in, letting me know the window order would be in next Thursday.

As I put away the last-minute items for Thanksgiving dinner, my mother's voice spoke from her tidy kitchen in the Great Beyond. *If I don't have it now, I just won't have it.* The Ghost of Thanksgiving Past, making a final check of her ingredients before the holiday meal.

My mind turned back to what Cassie said at the café. Could Ross and Ruthie Phillips have been haunted by the ghost that was haunting me? If so, had they simply learned to live with it? Or had it driven them away? No, they lived here for two decades. As for the Johnsons, good luck finding *them* without first names. How many people named Johnson were there? Millions? I did a quick check on my phone. The second most common surname in the U.S. There would be property records at the county, of course. I shoved a quart of half and half into the refrigerator. Maybe I could find the Hempels.

I swung open the back door. Buck rocketed into the yard and began tracking whatever scents the wind was stirring. Then he bounded off toward the woods. A bank of clouds sailed across the afternoon sun, turning the yard to dusk. A true November day, moody, changeable. *The thread of autumn gold worn bare, a note of portent in the air.* Part of a poem I'd had to learn in fifth grade.

I caught up to Buck at the springhouse. This time, when he went in, I followed. I didn't know what I expected to find. Another glove? Or some clue about my haunting, maybe. A breadcrumb to add to the other breadcrumbs. A way back out of the forest.

Inside, stone ledges along the walls were layered with debris and a powdery mortar that had shed from between the stones. Dead leaves littered the dirt floor and clogged the channels where the spring once ran.

"Empty," I said to Buck, who sprang out the door and disappeared.

Yet not quite empty. Something remained here that couldn't be seen. An imprint or a residue, like the scent of the kitchen fireplace on damp days. It hung in the air like a distant whisper.

Back at the house, I rummaged for a quick dinner. I should have brought home a piece of Diana's pumpkin pie cake. I could have smothered all my troubles with pumpkin filling and buttercream frosting and delicious yellow sponge.

But why had Cassie done that? Eaten a piece of cake? She didn't know how lucky she was to have a disease that wouldn't kill her, wouldn't waste her to skin and bones, if she would just watch what she ate. I dropped two pieces of bread into the toaster. A careless disregard, that's what it was. Like throwing away your life as if it meant nothing at all. When I saw her again, maybe that's what I would tell her.

While the bread toasted, I went to my office to see if the diary page was still there. Part of me hoped it would be gone. Whisked out of my life by whoever had left it. But there it was on the desk, staring up at me like it had all the time in the world to wait. I tucked it into the folder in the drawer.

Sugar Plum dropped from the windowsill where she'd been dozing and escorted me back to the kitchen. I poured a glass of cabernet and recalled Harry's words of wisdom again.

Not all mysteries can be solved.

Maybe, maybe not, I thought, buttering the toast I was no longer hungry for. But tonight, I was too tired to think about it.

—

In the morning, I tried to forget about my mysteries and focus on Thanksgiving preparations. It was time to set the table—I always did that a day early so I could admire the plates and stemware and neatly placed napkins before the deep dive into cooking, and before it was all torn apart.

I pulled my gold tablecloth from the sideboard and flicked it open over the long farmhouse dining table. Ray had made the table for me as a wedding gift. Salvaged wood boards, stained dark, with twelve matching chairs. After his baseball career ended, he'd made a good living building furniture, much of it period reproductions. We used to joke that our mutual love for old things would serve us well one day when we ourselves were *vintage*.

I spaced out six place settings of Granny Eleanor's Royal Albert old country roses china, as careful of it now as I'd been whenever I dried each piece in her kitchen after an early Sunday dinner as a girl. I had broken two pieces in the dozen years since she died and left it to me—a salad plate and a teacup—and I'd kept them tucked into the back of the sideboard in a little box, like relics, like the bones of an old saint. *Saint Eleanor.* The yin to my mother's yang.

When I finished setting the table, I went to the two front windows and swept back the linen drapes. Down by the road, a trio of Brewer's blackbirds flurried out of the big sycamore and settled onto the post and rail fence. As I watched them hop and fuss on one of the rails, my eye caught sight of a silver sedan coming into view down the road. It pulled up to the driveway of the Reardon School and parked.

A man in a tweed cap got out of the driver's side, slammed shut the door, and called a greeting to someone down the driveway. A moment later, Emmeline emerged from the towers of shrubby frontage, tapping her way with her stick, her free hand pulling a wheeled valise. She released the valise to the man and let her stick guide her to the car. At the door, she stopped and turned my way, as if she had seen me watching. She couldn't have seen me, of course, but all the same, I stepped behind the drape to hide myself.

As the car pulled away, my thoughts returned to the night Buck and I had found her in a heap on the driveway. The odd things she'd said. Her mental confusion. I hadn't called the school to check on her, as I had meant to. But I promised myself now that I would do it.

CHAPTER EIGHTEEN

December 1759

It was just after dark when Hugh arrived home from Philadelphia. He settled Virgil into the barn with some hay and water, and then hurried toward his new house, eager for a fire and some toast and cheese.

His visit to the city had been a good one. He'd found two more customers for the Jones peaches come August, and only hours ago he had enjoyed a dinner of lamb stew and turnips with old Mercy Wheeler. God bless Mercy, for she and Jeb had been the kindest of landlords when Hugh and Niall boarded with them years ago on Walnut Street, taking naught but a pittance monthly. She had remained among his dearest friends.

He drew in a breath of the crisp night and the mournful lowing of Lass and Brynna and thought of the countryside stretching out around him—the hills and fields and valleys that so reminded him of Wales. He imagined his father's plow back in Holywell, waiting out the winter in the barn, ready for the barley rows.

Home, he thought, struck with the longing that still came to him. But this place was his home now, and he had learned to love it just as well.

Firelight glimmered through the parlor window. Who was sitting up at this hour? He pushed through the front doors into the quiet center hall.

"Daddy."

Hugh turned and saw James Martin sitting cross-legged on a Windsor chair in the parlor, holding the carved wooden bird Sam had made him. His son was almost never without it.

"Well, young man." Hugh stepped into the room, pulled off his gloves, and put a hand to his son's shoulder. "What are you doing in here all by yourself?"

James Martin looked back to the fire. "Prissy said I was to sit here and warm my bones."

Something about the boy's demeanor fell heavy on Hugh. He hadn't offered his usual sweet smile.

"I have brought something special for you," Hugh said. He withdrew a piece of barley sugar from the haversack slung over his arm. "Here, for the best little fellow on God's green earth."

James Martin took the parcel, peeled away its burlap wrapping, and looked up at Hugh with a question in his eyes. He had never seen barley sugar. This piece was in the shape of a pig.

"Go on. Have a lick. See what you think."

James Martin ran his tongue along the cloudy sweet and beamed up at Hugh. "It's quite fine."

A rattling noise came from back in the kitchen.

"Where is Mama?" Hugh said.

"In her chamber. She was sleepy."

"Come along, then."

The boy slid off the chair and followed Hugh to the kitchen, clutching his treat.

"Mr. Jones, you have returned," Priscilla said from beside the hearth, broom in hand. A single lamp on the table held off the night. "How was your journey back?"

"Dry roads all the way. And how fares it here?"

James Martin climbed into a chair at the table and occupied himself with the sugar.

"The babes sleep well. May the Lord bless them," Priscilla said. "Hattie called round with a tonic. Mistress Miranda is abed."

"So I have heard from my son." Hugh opened the haversack and withdrew two large skeins of blue wool. "Here is something you might make into a new shawl. Spun and dyed by Sally Palmer."

"Much obliged, Mr. Jones. It's quite lovely." Priscilla took the wool and gave it a fond squeeze.

Fatigued from his long day in the city, Hugh decided to forgo the toast and cheese and instead go right up to bed. He took a lamp from the mantelpiece and lit it from the one on the table. Then he turned to his son. "Prissy will see you up, young hemp. I will go now and join Mama."

James Martin gazed up with serious eyes, the same hazel color as Miranda's. "Why did Mama scold me today?"

"Scold?" Hugh looked at Priscilla for an explanation. Neither he nor Miranda believed in scolding the children, which had once led Hattie to suggest they read a certain verse in Proverbs. "What happened?" he said.

"Things were a bit at odds." Priscilla laid her wool on the table. "You know the mistress...of late."

"And I trust this affair was settled?"

Priscilla nodded with a certainty that seemed meant to convince him.

"Perhaps Mama was feeling a bit fatigued," Hugh said to his son. "I'm certain she'll feel better tomorrow." He kissed the boy's head, hefted his sack to his shoulder, and went upstairs.

In the bedchamber, he took off his boots and wiggled his

toes. The chamber was chilly, the fire nearly down to embers. Miranda lay dead to the world under the bed linens and blanket. Hattie's sleeping tonic had worked its wonders.

He threw a clutch of kindling and two small logs onto the fire. Then he took the last of the things he'd brought back from the city out of his sack. A jar of lavender oil that Miranda would be sure to fuss over—the batch she and Hattie made in September had run out weeks ago—and two bound volumes tied together with twine. Diaries with roan covers, about the size of a bedside bible, but much less voluminous. A gift from Mercy.

"I've no use for them now that Jeb is gone," she'd said. "He was the one who liked to write."

Hugh had not thought he would have use for them either. But he had accepted them as a kind of duty, as one might agree to be guardian of something beloved by another.

Miranda murmured in her sleep. Hugh went and pulled the quilt over her shoulders. One of her hands lay on the pillow by her head, a smear of blue on the thumb. She had been painting. *Good*, Hugh thought, for painting had been her balm in the midst of the vacillations that had come upon her these last few months.

You know the mistress of late. Priscilla's words had truth in them.

They were small things, really. A change in mood, an excitability, an occasional watchfulness such as he'd seen that day in the garden. Her humors were in a state, Hattie had told him more than once, and they would no doubt come back into balance. But a catch in her words, felt more than heard, had given him pause. And now this latest incident, the scolding of James Martin.

The fire snapped and hissed. A sound his mother used to call the voice of the forest.

Desperate for sleep, Hugh pushed his thoughts away and changed into his nightshirt. Then he got into bed and kissed

Miranda's cheek.

"Un rêve d'amour," he whispered, thinking that a dream sometimes was troubled.

CHAPTER NINETEEN

On Thanksgiving, my guests arrived at five o'clock and eagerly began consuming hors d'oeuvres. Diana and I sipped our pear martinis in the kitchen as we worked to get dinner on the table. I liked a prompt six o'clock start for the holiday meal.

"Ah, the smell of a roasting turkey. If they could bottle that, it would be a close second to these martinis," Diana said, pouring homemade raisin sauce into a sauté pan where the kale was cooking.

I gave a stir to the pot of stuffing and reached for my cocktail. "Maybe," I replied. "But I have to say, these drinks are pretty yummy."

"It's the cinnamon. It adds a nice kick."

A moment later, as we joined forces to lift my sixteen-pound turkey out of the oven, Tara wandered in. She held up her empty pint glass. "Can I have another beer, Mom?" she asked.

"I guess it won't hurt."

After Tara poured her beer, Diana, already a little tipsy,

waved her off toward the living room. "Go back and amuse the menfolk." Then she turned to me. "Oh, wait. Did that sound inappropriate?"

We giggled over that in one of those warm, funny moments that we'd shared countless times before. And suddenly I was grateful for my friend all over again.

"So..." She turned to me, her fingernails shining a coppery rose against the yellowish liquid in her martini glass. "Tell me what's been happening here at the funhouse."

"Or not so fun," I said.

Scooping cranberry sauce into a bowl, I mixed in a few shots of Grand Marnier and told her about the return of the voice, the slamming door, and finally the diary page, a piece of living proof that even she couldn't deny.

"You know," she said, "a draft, even a small one, can slam a door. But are you sure you didn't close the door and just not remember?"

I shook my head. "I know what I did or didn't do."

"Okay, okay." She poured a slurry of flour and water into the roasting pan where she'd been stirring the gravy. "I'm just saying—"

"Need any help, ladies?" Mitch grinned at us from the doorway. Harry once joked that he married Robert Redford, and he wasn't far off. Sandy-haired and youthful at age sixty, Mitch bore more than a passing resemblance to the actor. He bowed and said, "At your service."

I pointed to the platter of turkey. "The king of the feast is ready."

He picked up the platter, said something about Norman Rockwell, and disappeared into the dining room.

"We better get the troops settled in," Diana said, pouring her finished concoction into a pitcher. "Gravy's only good when it's hot."

Dinner passed in pleasant rounds of potatoes and stuffing and Diana's Red Russian kale circling the table, along with refills of cabernet and friendly chatter about everything under the sun. Mitch regaled us with stories about his eccentric great-great uncle who once lost a Senate race in Kansas, and Cal brought us up to date on his latest canoe-building venture, a story that had Diana rolling her eyes.

"My husband has built three canoes, all of which are currently parked in our two-car garage," she said.

"Speaking of boats, here's a story for you," Harry said, and went on to recall a client he'd worked for early in his career who had taken more than a liking to him. "When I was done with her project, she kissed me full on the lips and asked if I'd sail up the Danube with her."

We all broke into laughter.

"That's because you are universally irresistible," I said.

As the laughter died down and I poured more wine, I thought, *here is a perfect Thanksgiving*. Friends, food, fun.

Perfect, if I could ignore the fact that my house was haunted and there was an empty space where Ray should be.

—

After the meal, Tara cleaned up the kitchen with Mitch while, in the dining room, Harry and Cal each ate a second piece of pie. I led Diana to the office to show her the diary page.

"This is it," I said, pulling it from the drawer.

She studied the page with a squint. "It does seem old, doesn't it?"

"There's a slash down here where a name should be, so I don't know who wrote it. But I'm pretty sure it was Hugh Peter Jones."

"So, you think this Jones guy left this for you to find?" she asked. She flashed a teasing grin. "At least he had good penmanship."

"Come on, Dee. Be serious, will you?"

"You know, it was probably upstairs all along, and you never noticed it before. Or maybe the cat dragged it out from somewhere. Or maybe, I don't know, this is just your—"

"My what?" A well of anger sent a flush to my cheeks. "My imagination? You don't believe me, do you? You haven't wanted to believe any of this since I first told you about it, which is completely unfair since—"

Diana held up a hand. "Settle down, girlfriend. You're asking me to believe there's a ghost in your house and that he's leaving you papers, and talking to you, and moving the furniture, and—"

"Yes! That's right! I want you to believe it because that's what friends do. They support each other, even if it's—"

"Enabling some kind of emotional..." She shook her head. "Look, I'm concerned about you, that's all—"

"Am I interrupting something?" Harry stared at us from the doorway, a hand in his pocket.

I waved him in, happy for the rescue. I didn't want to go on arguing with Diana, not on Thanksgiving, and I doubted it would do any good. Besides, my head was beginning to ache.

"Anything interesting?" he asked.

I held up the page. "That paper I was telling you about."

"The diary entry somebody wanted you to find, eh?"

Diana shot Harry an exasperated look. "Not you too."

"Harry doesn't think I'm crazy, Dee."

"I don't either, but really..." She shrugged and shook her head. "This is all pretty hard to swallow, and I don't think it's healthy for you to be—"

"We can all at least agree that this is real, and it came from somewhere," Harry said. He held out his hand for the page. "When will you be talking to the woman Penny's putting you in touch with, Lib?"

"What woman?" Diana asked.

"A Jones descendant, over in Brigham," I said in a dismissive tone, wounded by her disbelief. "I've only just found out about her."

Diana looked back to Harry, and for a moment something

seemed to pass between them. Some kind of alliance? Had Harry simply been humoring me? *No*, I thought. *Harry wouldn't do that.*

I took back the page and dropped it on the desk. "Anyway, let's get back to the others, shall we?"

Tension buzzed in the air as we trailed into the hallway.

"I think I'll corral Mitch, and we'll head out," Harry said. "I'm pretty bushed."

"I think Cal and I will do the same," Diana said.

One by one, my guests said goodnight and filed through the front doors. Diana turned to me before she exited.

"I just think you might need a rest," she said. "You've been going at it pretty hard here, and lately, I don't know." She forced a smile. "But it's your life. I'll be at the tree lighting Sunday, in case you're interested."

The tree lighting. In eleven years, Diana and I had missed only one, the Christmas before Ray died.

I shrugged. "I'll let you know."

CHAPTER TWENTY

Lighting the ceremonial blue spruce was taking longer than usual. The crowd seemed restless as they milled about the town green trying to keep warm, cups of mulled cider going cold in their hands.

"I think I better go light a fire under someone," Diana said. Then she trudged away from where we were huddling to find Bert Shuster, the keeper of the switch.

She had called me the day before to smooth things over, to say she hadn't meant for us to squabble, especially on Thanksgiving, and I'd accepted her apology and agreed to meet her here at two o'clock. So far, we'd avoided talk of what was happening in my house, but beneath our conversation about other casual matters, a current of friction hummed. Standing in the frosty air, I watched her disappear into the throng, hoping that sooner or later she would come around.

Then my eyes locked on a scene across the green. A dark-haired man in a navy jacket talking to a man in a parka. When a woman stepped up beside him carrying two cups of cider, he turned to her and reached for one. Keith Janus. He and the woman moved closer together, and he seemed to introduce her to the other man. After a shaking of hands, he curled his arm around her shoulders and drew her in.

I studied their easy familiarity. Could this be Alicia? Had she run back to him with the rugs and the furniture, looking for a fresh start? Would she veto our plans for warm and cozy?

The woman leaned casually into Keith, sipping her cider. I reconsidered. Maybe she wasn't Alicia, but someone new found on one of the online dating sites. Relationship retail, Ray used to call them. I tried to ignore the pang of...whatever that feeling was stirring inside me as I watched her fiddle with the blond knot on top of her head, her shoulder tucked so comfortably into Keith's. Was it annoyance, or a touch of— But what did I have to be jealous about? Someone else's happiness?

The lights on the spruce finally flickered to life, and everyone cheered and applauded. In the next instant, Diana materialized beside me, drawing my gaze away from Keith Janus and the mystery woman. When I looked back again to find them, they were gone.

—

Back home, I dropped a bag of peppermint herbal tea into a cup, doused it with steaming water, and held my face over the warm vapor to thaw my nose. The mint tingled as I drew it in, thinking about Keith and his unknown companion. Buck circled through the kitchen behind me. It would be pitch dark in an hour, and it looked like snow, so I quaffed the tea quickly.

The house had been so quiet since Thanksgiving—no voices in the dark, no objects moving around—and I hoped with each passing day that Hugh Peter Jones had drifted back to the ether forever.

I leashed Buck and led him out the front door. At the end of the driveway, we veered right and headed down the road. We hadn't gone far when a car door slammed up ahead. A silver sedan was idling in front of the Reardon School, the same car I had seen the other day while setting my table, and the same man in the same tweed cap was getting out of it. He made his way around to the passenger side and leaned into the open door to help someone out of the car. Emmeline, back from wherever she'd gone for the weekend.

Buck pulled on the leash, eager to investigate. The scene from Wednesday replayed itself in reverse, and soon the man was back behind the wheel, leaving Emmeline and her valise in the driveway. He smiled through the window at me as he motored by. I offered a friendly wave. Why hadn't he driven her up to the door?

But I could walk her there myself. "Emmeline!" I called, letting Buck tug me across the road. She hadn't moved from her spot on the driveway. "It's me, Libby Casey! Your neighbor. Remember?"

She turned her head as I stepped up beside her. "Yes, I thought that was you," she said in her English lilt. "Out for a walk?"

I thought that was you. The same thing she'd said that night I found her crumpled on the blacktop. "Yes, a walk. How are you? How was your Thanksgiving?"

"Quite well, as these things go." She stared blankly toward my face. "And you?"

"Very nice. It's always good to spend time with almost everyone who matters in your life."

"Almost everyone, yes. You were missing someone, I suppose. Someone who's left you." She offered the slightest of smiles. "That's always very hard."

She meant Ray, of course. But how could she have known about Ray? Had she been talking to someone I knew in Simms?

"I, yes, I lost my husband, going on two years ago. Did someone tell you?"

Buck reached his nose toward Emmeline's gloved hand and gauged its scent.

"No, no...I've always known things, you see." She offered her hand to Buck. "But here, I should go and let you be on your way. Get back to your nice warm house."

I've always known things.

I reached for her valise. "I'll walk you to your door."

We started down the driveway toward the big school in the distance, a few of its windows aglow in the dusk. Emmeline kept pace beside me, tapping her stick.

"Emmeline, what did you mean...about always knowing things? Do you mean to say you have a special gift? Like being psychic?"

Emmeline chuckled softly. "Everyone always wants to label me, ever since I was a girl. I suppose it's their way of making sense of things that make no sense at all."

"I didn't mean to label you. I—"

"Don't fret, dear. I'm quite used to it." A moment passed in which I wondered whether to press her further. Then she asked, "What was your husband's name?"

"Ray. Ray Meachum."

"So, tell me, what happened with your Ray?"

"He was ill for a long time. Cancer."

"Ah, poor man. And all of that is with you still."

"I suppose that kind of thing stays with you forever."

"Hmm, even when we've done all we can and done the things we must."

Those words pricked me. *Done the things we must.* Did she know, somehow?

Emmeline halted and pulled her stick to her side. "Well, here we are," she said, apparently sensing that we'd reached the end of the long drive.

In front of us, the blacktop curved around to form a large circle in front of a three-story edifice of pale limestone punctuated by high windows and tasteful architectural flourishes. One of those Gilded Age mansions built by some industrial robber baron, a little worn now with time, but still a fine example. A two-story stone cottage sat off to the right some ways behind it. An outbuilding of some sort, maybe a keeper's residence once.

"May I help you inside?" I asked.

"Not at all. You've been so very kind." She reached out her hand. "My valise?"

I pulled it toward her, Buck watching as she probed the air until she found the handle. "Have you lived here on the premises for a while?"

"Twenty-five years. It's been my life's work." She turned to me. "You must be frozen stiff by now, so you best not tarry. You and your dog. Buck, is it?"

"Yes, Buck. You have an excellent memory. Well, goodnight and take care. I'm across the road if you need anything." I was about to turn and go, but I paused, feeling in some vague way that we had more business between us. "Emmeline, would you like to come over for a visit one day? Maybe for lunch?"

"Oh, dear. I wouldn't want to put you to any trouble."

"None at all, I assure you. How can I reach you?"

She was already turning away from me with her valise. "Call the school and leave a message." Then off she went around the curve of the drive, tapping, tapping.

I led Buck back toward Chambers Road, revising my first impression of Emmeline, convinced now that she was not mentally confused. She was...something else. "She has always known things," I whispered to Buck.

As we reached the end of the driveway, I glanced back toward the school. The outline of its sturdy limestone had dissolved into the darkness. Emmeline was already gone.

—

The next day, I drove to my old neighborhood to meet with Laura Majewski, a mix of dread and anticipation churning inside me. I hadn't been back to Poplar Street since moving out a month ago. Was it too soon to go back?

I gripped the wheel of Ray's Malibu as if it might hold me steady and drew in the scent of leather seats, a Ray scent. And suddenly there he was, leaning over the engine in the driveway on a Sunday afternoon, tinkering, hands black with grease. We used to joke that he would be buried with the car. But that was when dying was an abstract and distant consideration.

My eyes met the iron signpost at the corner of Leland and Birch. *Welcome to the Historic Nash District.* My heart caught. *Yes*, I thought. *Still too soon.*

Two blocks down, Leland came to a dead-end at Poplar. I turned the corner. Walter Nash's big Victorian twins, built in the late nineteenth century after Simms became the county seat, lined either side of the wide street, some with wraparound porches, others with corner cupolas. Back when Ray bought Queenie, the neighborhood was "in transition," the real estate industry's polite term for "run-down with signs of hope." Even now, there were homes waiting to be rescued. But those were becoming the minority, especially at this end of the development.

My eyes swept over the familiar landscape. If it were spring, the azaleas and dogwoods would be in bloom. Was there any place on Earth that didn't look more beautiful with azaleas and dogwoods in bloom?

I parked one house down from Laura's, composed myself, and got out of the car. As I dodged pools of slush from last night's four-inch snow, I avoided looking up the block to where Queenie was and tried to ignore the voice in my head that said maybe I should have stayed there. For now, I would focus on Laura's kitchen renovation. Tin ceiling and farmhouse sink, beadboard pantry and fresh tile floor. Out with the old, in with the new—a happy transformation. Much easier to do with a kitchen than a life.

But an hour later, after my meeting with Laura, I found myself parked in front of 36 Poplar, staring through the windshield at the turned balusters on the porch, the burgundy wood trims, the green fish-scale siding on the second story that had taken Ray three months to restore. I swallowed back a knot of sorrow.

Eight good years and three abysmal ones.

Sometimes it felt like someone else's life, what happened here. The life we lived behind those walls. It was history now, something preserved in a jar, suspended in time. It was the end of that life that felt closest now, that threatened always to cut me. But the rest of it, those were the best years of my life.

We'd met in a way Harry would later describe as *cinematic*. I'd been taking a lamp into Farrell's Hardware for rewiring, a beautiful, one-of-a-kind 1920s reproduction, and as I reached the storefront, the door swung open and hit my arm. My precious lamp fell to the pavement and shattered.

"Why don't you watch where you're going?" I cried, looking down at my ruined lamp as if it were my heart. When I looked up again, I saw a man in jeans and a gray T-shirt, brown hair curling at his neck, slate-blue eyes.

He set down two big window screens, leaning them against the storefront. "I'm so sorry," he drawled, as he bent down to help me pick up the shards of my lamp.

"Not as sorry as I am," I said.

"Let me buy you another one. Please." He handed me the pieces he'd collected.

I shook my head. "It's a vintage one-of-a-kind."

He apologized again. "I'm Ray, by the way. Ray Meachum. I'd really like to make this up to you somehow."

When he asked for my email address, I hesitated. But he seemed so earnest, and his slate-blue eyes, well, they had captured me in some indescribable way.

When a week went by, I figured I wouldn't hear from Ray Meachum again. But then one day he emailed to say he had something for me. He arrived at my rented twin on Gable Street the next morning with a beautiful reproduction demilune table.

"I can't accept this," I said, admiring the inlay around the top and the brass fittings on the legs. "It's way too nice. And too expensive."

He shook his head. "I make furniture, and my client changed her mind when I was halfway through this piece. So now it's yours if you want it."

"I want it," I said, unable to hide a smile. "Thank you."

I invited him in for iced tea on the back patio and he ended up staying for lunch. Six months later, I moved into Queenie.

Life on Poplar Street was lazy Sunday mornings, getaways to Virginia to see Maddie at college, projects around the house. And that trip to Paris two years before Ray got sick. Somewhere, up on my third floor, was another photo album full of cathedrals and monuments and mansard roofs, gardens and bistros and boulevards. And Ray, leaning back against one of the ancient bridges that cross the Seine, the sunset behind him, his head tilted down. It was one of my favorite pictures of him. One that I'd always felt I could live in.

For our fifth anniversary, we decided we would share a gift. "Since havin' a baby isn't workin', how about a dog?" Ray said. At the rescue shelter, a shaggy, dark brown mutt with sparkling copper eyes walked right over and sat beside us as if he were the one choosing and not the other way around. Our beloved Buck.

I let my eyes linger on the house for one more moment and then pulled away from the curb. I still had Buck and Sugar Plum. I still had the Malibu. I still had my memories. But Ray was gone, and I would never get him back.

CHAPTER TWENTY-ONE

May 1760

"Do not move, Husband!"

Hugh had been sitting still as a post in the Windsor chair for an hour while Miranda perched on a stool ten feet away, half obscured by the easel and canvas in front of her. He was growing restless.

"I shall turn to stone very soon if you do not allow me to stretch my limbs," he said.

"Do you suppose Master Van Dyck permitted his subjects to stretch their limbs?"

He could not see the whole of his wife's face, but he could discern the teasing note in her voice, and it pleased him. She'd had a run of good weeks, the color back in her, her health regained, her keel seeming mostly even now. She'd returned to her books of verse and had even taken up her pen to write some of her own.

Hugh stretched a leg. "I know not of Master Van Dyck and

his subjects," he said. "But I feel certain he allowed them to use the privy, which I shall have to do quite soon."

"Just a bit longer. The light is still with us." Her hand went to the spattered table beside her, took up a brush, and touched it to the palette. "The more we accomplish today, the less need you will have to sit in the future." She peeked out from behind the big canvas and gave a flirtatious wink that belied the sharp intention in her eyes. "Besides, if I am to commit you to the ages, I must do it properly. Others will regard this canvas one day, and I want their eyes to see Hugh Jones for the man he was."

"Very well, my sweet. Your gesture touches me."

Hugh smiled and went back to trying to keep his arm still beside the goblet of sherry Miranda had placed on the pedestal table. A moment later, Alice toddled through the doorway, holding a pewter spoon smeared with something red.

"Bring that back!" Priscilla called from the hall. "Alice!"

Alice threw the spoon into the parlor, where it landed beside Miranda with a clink.

"Today, she is your daughter and yours only," Miranda said with a sigh. She set down her brush and wiped her hand on her paint-stained smock.

Hugh rose from the chair. "And I think she is telling us that the morning's session is over, hmm?" He went and picked up the spoon. Strawberry jam. Then he reached down and mussed Alice's dark curls.

Priscilla appeared in the doorway. "Pardon, but this one's a bit of a wild goose today." She took the spoon from Hugh.

"Do not fret," he said. "Every family must have its wild goose."

As Priscilla led Alice away, Hugh turned back to Miranda. She was standing in front of the easel.

"You must not peek," she said, eyes still sharp as a falcon's. "Not until it is done."

"I promise," Hugh said. "But you'd be best to put it

someplace safe so our little wild goose cannot assail it with a spoon full of jam. Now, I am off to find Sam. We need to move the table from the carriage house to the yard for our grand feast this afternoon."

"You do love your heathen feasts. But I confess that I love them too." Miranda bit her lip, a habit she had come into. She pushed him toward the doorway.

"That's because you have some of the heathen in you as well." Hugh loosened his cravat, eager to have done with it, and then feigned a bow. "As my mother used to say, we may forget all the holy days, but never Beltane."

—

Hugh watched the crop crew disappear into a deepening dusk as they trudged home to log dwellings on the other side of the estate, drowsy and full of ale. Miranda and Priscilla had cleared the remnants of their feast from the pinewood table and gone off to bed with the children. Only Sam was left, standing beside him. He had put away his pipe, but the scent of it lingered.

"I shall see you in the morning, and we'll make those deliveries," Hugh said. He looked up at the pinpoints of light beginning to wink in the sky. "Miranda says the stars will bless us with another good year."

"Let it be so," Sam said. "And now they will see me home."

"Ride Virgil back, why don't you? You can bring him in the morning."

With one last gaze into the starry sky, Hugh turned and made his way to the house, where he dropped to a kitchen chair and pulled off his boots.

"But what did you do with it?" Miranda's voice piped out of the darkness.

Where was she? He lit a lamp from the low flame in the fireplace and went to find her. She was in the hall, standing at the parlor door in her shift.

"You must tell me where it is," she said, looking into the

parlor.

"Where what is? Miranda?" Hugh stepped up beside her, and only then did she turn. He held up the lamp. "My sweet, what are you doing down here in the dark?"

She seemed to stare past him, the candle's flame flickering in her eyes. "The painting. They've taken it." She reached a hand to her forehead as if in a quandary.

"The painting? No one has taken it. It's upstairs in the lumber room. Remember?"

How could she have forgotten her debate that morning about what room would be best? The bustling up and down stairs with first the easel and then the canvas, Miranda insisting she be the one to carry it lest it be ruined, lest Hugh see it, and her admonition to the children not to go near it.

"No, they have taken it. They said so!"

"Who? Who said so?" A little storm brewed in Hugh's stomach as his wife's watchful eyes darted about the hall. "Miranda, please," he said. "Let us go up and I'll show you."

She ignored his entreaty and stepped into the parlor. "Whatever will I do?" she said. "I shall have to paint it all over again! Where are my paints?"

"Listen, Miranda!" Hugh went and took her arm. "You're speaking nonsense! You must go back to bed. We must both go to bed."

"Are you certain they haven't taken it?"

"Yes, of course. Now, come along."

Upstairs, Hugh held her back at the lumber room and raised the lamp. The painting faced away from them on the easel amid an array of other objects—the desk and the twins' cradles, the trunk with brass fittings and Priscilla's spinning wheel.

"You see," Hugh said with a calm note that he hoped would soothe her. "No one has taken it. It is quite safe."

Miranda looked up at him. "So it is, Husband. I do hope they don't return."

"They shan't," Hugh said, and this seemed to satisfy her.

"Now, it's off to bed."

A dose of Hattie's sleeping tonic was enough to make her fall quickly away. But sleep would not come for Hugh, who lay awake beside her, the mattress wheezing with each turn and toss he made.

She'd been faring so much better of late, and now this.

Was it possible she'd been ambulating in her sleep as Niall had done when he was a boy? Hugh would sometimes wake up and find his brother sitting on the floor of their bedchamber, trying in vain to pull on his boots, or spreading playing cards out on the little table by the window, all as if entranced, unaware of the time or the darkness. But never had he known Miranda to wander at night. She had always slept like a maid in clover.

But where had she gone that afternoon? She'd excused herself from the merriment around the table—the drink and song and conversation, the crop crew and Hattie and the children dancing to Sam's fiddle around the campfire—and when she returned a half hour later, her skirt muddy, its hem soaked, she had given no explanation for her long absence.

"Were you down at the stream?" Hugh had asked. And she'd bitten her lip and said, "Husband, do not worry."

When he asked what there was to worry about, she only sat down at the table and cut a piece of bread, leaning over for a word with Sam.

Hattie. He would have Priscilla ride out and bring her back soon. It would improve Miranda's spirits to see her. She could bring another tonic. But somewhere inside of him, Hugh worried that a tonic would not do.

He got out of bed, too far from sleep, and went to the lumber room with a lamp. Opening the desk drawer, he withdrew one of the diaries Mercy had given him. He sat down, opened it, and began to write.

CHAPTER TWENTY-TWO

Home from Poplar Street, I listened to a message on my landline. Penny Jenkins calling with a phone number for the Jones descendant in Brigham. Vivian, last name Seabrook. But I should wait until midweek to call her, Penny said.

I scribbled Vivian's name and number on a Post-it and stuck it to the counter, holding out hope that I wouldn't need it after all. The house had been strangely quiet, normal, for going on a week now. A good sign, I thought, but it wasn't time to celebrate yet.

After dinner, I took Buck for a walk. The moon, almost full, frosted everything in its glow. The night was cold and preternaturally still. As I passed the garden, I smelled again the sharp, floral scent I'd detected there before. I looked about at the desiccated beds and the withered shrubs that drooped against the fence. Impossible, and yet—

Back at the house, I sipped a glass of wine and then another half glass and went to bed pleasantly tipsy. *Be gone, Hugh Peter Jones. Be gone.* I drifted into a familiar dream, the man in the dark room, the glass with a twist in its stem glimmering with firelight, mesmerizing in its way. He drummed the table with his finger and looked up. "Are you waiting for something?" I asked. But he only turned back to the fire.

Then a phone rang in the distance.

I opened my eyes. The landline was trilling down in the kitchen. Or maybe it was the dream, because when I listened, all was quiet. The alarm clock read 6:00. Yes, the dream, for who would be calling at this hour? I threw back the quilt. Too early to get up, but too late to go back to sleep.

Downstairs, I fed Buck and Sugar Plum and poured myself some cereal. The message light on the landline was blinking. Not a dream, then. The ID log showed an incoming call at 5:59. *Unknown*. I tapped in the code but there was no message, only a faint static, like a glitch in the line.

As I hung up, an odd feeling came over me, like the air around me had stirred. Then a voice whispered my name.

Goddamn it.

He was back.

—

At the office, I saw evidence that Harry had already been there—a half-empty cup of coffee on his desk, his burgundy scarf thrown over a chair. Then I spied a note on my computer screen. *Mitch locked himself out, me to the rescue, then an errand to run.*

As soon as I settled in at my desk, the landline rang.

"Libby?" said a gravelly voice. "This is Keith Janus."

"Oh, yes, Keith. Hello." The scene at the tree lighting replayed in my head, the mystery woman who might have been Alicia. "You received the scope of work yesterday, right?"

"I looked it over last night. I have a few issues I'd like to discuss."

"We figured you might. If you hold on, I'll open my file."

"Actually, I thought we could discuss it in person. Would

you and Harry be free to meet for coffee? I do so much business over my devices. Sometimes it's nice to do things the old-fashioned way."

"I have tomorrow free," I said, still wondering whether the project was a go. "But Harry has to be out of the office all day. I can look at next week if that would work."

"Well, if you don't mind meeting me tomorrow without Harry. Unfortunately, I'll be out of town the rest of the week and busy the next."

"Sure. I'll bring my laptop, and we can go over the plans."

He suggested meeting at Cozy Cottage Café at ten. A small part of me—no, a large part—hoped Diana wouldn't be there. She and I needed a break to clear the air. I hung up, feeling something that might have been anticipation.

I made some tea and returned a few phone calls from potential clients, pleasantly surprised that inquiries were coming in so close to Christmas. Just as I hung up from one of them—a woman who was interested in restoring the first floor of her American Foursquare—Harry breezed through the door.

"Sorry about that," he said, tossing his coat over the upholstered chair beside his desk. "I think I need to start hanging Mitch's keys around his neck." He took his coffee cup from the desk and trailed off toward the dry sink. "Can I top you off with some hot?"

"No, thanks. Had enough."

When he returned to his desk with his lunch bag, I told him about my appointment the next day with Keith.

"So, he hasn't deserted us after all," he said, pulling a container of what looked like chicken salad out of the bag. "Your text last night had me wondering. How's everything else going? Did you ever get hold of the Jones descendant?"

"Vivian Seabrook. I'll be calling her tomorrow. She's elderly, so I'm not sure what to expect. If she can't give me some useful clues, maybe there's someone else who can. One of the recent owners. Actually, I think maybe I should consider that cleansing

Cassie mentioned."

"Let's start with the Seabrook woman and go from there. More information will help. How's the sleeping lately?"

"Okay," I fibbed.

Harry leaned back in his chair. "Remember, Lib, you have a choice. I know it's not your first choice, and you don't want to take a loss. But your mental health is important."

"Are you worried about that?"

He went back to his chicken salad. "Just think about it."

—

I got to Diana's at 9:55 the next morning and took a seat in my favorite booth. A few minutes later, Keith arrived.

"Thanks for agreeing to meet me at short notice," he said, tossing his jacket and scarf onto the bench opposite me.

We ordered our coffees and made small talk while we waited.

"I was down here the other day for the Simms tree lighting," he said. "Good crowd."

"Yes, I saw you there. You were with friends, and I didn't want to interrupt. Besides, my feet were frozen to the ground by then."

Rita delivered our mugs of coffee and headed back to the kitchen. The seductive smell of my mocha wafted up in a fume of dark chocolate and citrus.

"My kid sister, Jodie, was down from White Plains for Thanksgiving with her husband, and I thought it would be something fun to do," Keith said.

"Oh, so that was your sister." I hid my relief behind a neutral nod. Harry and I wouldn't lose the project after all. And Keith hadn't found a new woman—

"Her husband bailed on us at the last minute. He said it was too cold, so he stayed back at the house to watch a game. It was a nice event. I like those kinds of traditions. Morley doesn't do much of that, but luckily Simms isn't too far away."

"And you said you've lived in Morley for how long?"

"Almost four years. I never got down to Simms much until recently. I was caught up with business and Alicia was traveling a lot for work."

I dug a little more and found out he had a son, Spencer, in California, a junior in film school.

"He's a really focused kid. Almost too focused. He said he's been working day and night on this short film project for his directing class. I asked him, 'What are you doing for fun?' and he said, 'This is it.'"

When I inquired about his work in environmental law, he relaxed into a corner of the booth, hand on the table, and told me about the case he was working on, an effort to protect a large swath of old-growth forest out west. A shadow of whiskers played over his cheeks and jawline. His bronze eyes flickered. It was clear he had a passion for his work, and that passion brought a certain something to his pleasant features.

"What about you?" Keith was saying.

"Oh, me?" I asked. I'd lost track of the question.

"Yeah, what got you interested in interior design?"

Rita appeared at the booth, and we ordered more coffee.

I spun my empty mug in circles on the table. "I think it was all that rummaging around in thrift shops and consignment stores when I was furnishing my off-campus apartment as an undergrad. The old furniture and housewares and textiles—they grew on me. They seemed to have stories to tell."

"Like people. The older they get, the more stories they have, right?"

"If you decide you want to incorporate a few vintage items into the renovation, let me know," I said. "But tell me your concerns about the project. I have it right here on my laptop."

Over our fresh mugs of coffee, we discussed adding French doors on the entry-hall side of the office—something I had suggested while at his house but that he had declined—and replacing the slate floor in the hall with hardwood, then repurposing the slates elsewhere. I entered the notes in the file and reconfigured the draft for his approval.

As I closed my laptop, I noted the time. Eleven o'clock. If Diana was working the kitchen for lunch, she would be arriving any minute.

Outside on the pavement, Keith and I were shaking hands goodbye when she appeared up the street. She was walking at a good clip, as usual, and it was too late to avoid her. But Keith had already hurried off to Main Street by the time she reached me.

"Hey, you," she said, her gaze shifting from me to the retreating Keith, then back to me. "What's up?"

"Just coffee with a client. He wanted a review of his project."

Her eyes sparked with a question she didn't ask. "You should have told me you were coming by. I would have had Rita comp you a few scones or something."

"That's okay," I said. "I had breakfast. But I've got to go. I have a phone call to make before lunchtime."

"Oh, okay. Sorry we haven't had much chance to talk."

"Me too," I said. "I'll call you."

CHAPTER TWENTY-THREE

Vivian Seabrook answered her phone on the second ring. "Hello, Viv here," said the dry but friendly voice.

"Mrs. Seabrook. This is Libby Casey, over in Simms. I believe Penny Jenkins told you I would be calling."

A silence, then finally, "Oh, yes. I remember."

"I'm the one who moved into the Jones place. Your family's old property on Chambers Road? I was hoping to speak with you about it."

"Yes, well, as I said to the other girl, the one who called, I don't know what I could possibly tell you. I never lived there, of course." Another silence. "My grandmother called that place a heap of bones. I know that much. Let sleeping dogs lie, she used to say." She chuckled, an old woman's contralto.

Let sleeping dogs lie. What had her grandmother meant by that? "You don't have to think about it now," I said. "I could come by—"

A woman's voice piped up in the background. After a

muffled exchange with Vivian, the woman was on the line. "This is Carol Seabrook. I'm Vivian's daughter. May I help you?"

I explained myself again, and she said, "Well, I'm not sure what we could tell you. Is there something specific you're looking for?"

"No, I just have an interest in history—I do historical design for a living—and the house and its past seem so intriguing. Even if you just had some old documents or letters or a family story."

"Well, if my mother ever did have anything from the family, she probably would have thrown it out a long time ago. The Seabrook clan was never much for holding onto that kind of clutter. Except for Uncle Dan."

"Dan," I said. Here was someone useful, a family historian. "Maybe I could talk to him."

"Actually, he died ten years ago. Aunt Dot, his widow, might have something lying around. She told me once that Dan kept a stash of stuff in a closet under the cellar stairs. But I can't say what it was or whether it's still there."

In the background, Vivian piped up. "Why don't you tell her about Dan's mother, the chorus girl? You know the one."

Chorus girl. Maybe one of the sleeping dogs her grandmother had warned her about.

"Hush, Mother," Carol said. Then to me, "To tell you the truth, if you wanted whatever's there, it would suit me fine. Dot hasn't been well, and she'll be selling the house soon and moving here to where Mother is. I'll be the head honcho on that migration. So, the less junk to toss, the better, as far as I'm concerned."

"Well, if that's the case," I said, plowing on, "could you take a look the next time you're there and let me know? I'd be willing to take anything off your hands."

"It so happens I'll be seeing Dot in another day or two to get her signature on some papers. I guess I could check it out and get back to you. Right now, I've got to get Mother to a doctor's appointment."

—

With Harry out of the office for the day, I spent a quiet afternoon at my desk, happy to distract myself with filling out permit applications, ordering paint and fixtures, and revisiting American Foursquare style in the hopes that the woman who had called yesterday would take us on. The house was a fixer, she'd said, the woodwork damaged, the floors a wreck, the windows old and leaky. Just the kind of desperate project I loved to dig into, and a Foursquare didn't come around that often. I'd done design work in only one, and I had been ever eager to get my hands on another.

At five o'clock, I gathered my things to go home, my conversation with Carol Seabrook drifting back to me, her casual indifference to the *clutter* of her family history. I couldn't fault her for that. Except for Granny Eleanor on my father's side and a few aunts, uncles, and cousins on my mother's, my own history remained obscure to me. It had been my intention once to join one of those websites that promises to pull back the curtain on your ancestry. But somehow I'd never gotten around to it.

Maybe I should take the advice Vivian's grandmother gave to her, I thought. *Let sleeping dogs lie.* Which of us really knows what lurks back there in our bloodlines and whether it's best left alone? Then again, sometimes you can't avoid the past. Sometimes it comes looking for you and won't let you be. And sometimes it's not even yours.

—

That night, I woke with a start and found myself standing in the dark of the third-floor hallway. What was I doing here?

At the back of my mind, the sound of a door slamming and

the vague feeling that I didn't want to be up here alone.

I reached over and flipped the light switch at the top of the stairs. A dim glow washed over the hallway. The door to the west room was still open, just as Harry had left it that night I'd called him to come over. But on the floor in front of it lay something dark and coiled.

Buck huffed behind me. He walked over and lowered his nose to the coiled object, then wandered into the room.

I picked up the object and held it to the light. A tarnished silver chain studded on either side with what looked like small red gems. At the bottom, like a smile, hung a curve of filigree, and from that dangled an oval charm. A necklace.

Where on earth had it come from?

A scratching noise drew my attention to the open room. "Buck?" I peered in and saw his silhouette standing by the closet. "What are you doing?"

He looked my way. The scratching ceased.

"Come on!" I called, my nerves on edge. When he didn't move, I called to him again. "Let's go!"

Down in my room, the dog settled back into bed. I turned on the lamp and studied the necklace under better light. Its red stones were set about an inch apart on either side of the chain, four on one side but only three on the other, with an empty setting where the fourth should be. The oval charm at the bottom boasted a smooth milky pink stone ringed with tarnished silver beading. A locket?

I inserted my thumbnail into the groove to pry it open. It wouldn't budge. After fishing my nail file out of the bathroom vanity, I went back to work and finally the jaws released. With a little coaxing, the front pulled away from the back. The hinge was stiff, but I worked it gently until it opened all the way.

Inside was a clutch of dark strands pinched together with a thin piece of faded fabric. Grosgrain ribbon, flattened but still textured. I touched the dark strands. A lock of hair.

I flipped the hair onto the tabletop. Engraved into the silver of the locket were someone's initials, so tarnished it was hard to make them out. I would need some polish. I glanced at the clock. Almost 4:00. I would look for the polish tomorrow, although tomorrow was already well underway.

I returned the hair to the locket and eased it closed. Then I went out to the hallway, stood at the bottom of the stairs, and listened. All was quiet, but the memory of the scratching noise made me shudder.

Back in my room, I locked the door and crawled into bed beside Buck. I snapped a photo of the necklace with my phone and texted it to Diana. *Found this up on the third floor tonight!* The diary page hadn't gotten her attention. Maybe this would.

Before slipping the necklace into my night table, I took one last look at the little red jewels along the chain, the curve of filigree, the milky stone on the locket, the color of a pale pink tea rose. It was beautiful in the way things used to be beautiful when people made them by hand. And surely this necklace had been made by an expert hand, and in a time long gone.

Another piece of a puzzle. A glove, a diary page, and now this. *Who had it belonged to?* I wondered. Who had worn the locket of hair close to her heart?

CHAPTER TWENTY-FOUR

June 1760

"Ready?" Miranda flung open the kitchen door, and Hugh hurried out behind her.

Today was the day.

And a good day it was, Hugh thought, watching Miranda's skirt billow around her as she strode toward the barn. A fragrant, sunny June Sunday, although they would not be heading off to listen to Reverend Potter give the homily this morning.

At the barn, they climbed into the seat of the wagon. Hugh put a hand to the pocket of his frock, just to make sure it was still there. Yes, all safe and sound. Then he urged Virgil and Gwydion toward the lane heading west.

"You are quite mysterious, Mr. Jones," Miranda said, biting her lip. "Can you give me a hint as to our destination?"

"Aye, mysterious. And you shall have to wait and see."

They rode a while through the woods, the trees fully green

now, and then pulled onto a road that cut through Percival Cooper's wheat fields. Further on, it was more woods and then the Kent pasture with its post and rail fence and grazing cattle. At last, they came to a small lane that veered from the road and emptied onto an old towpath just wide enough for the wagon.

"Are we almost there?" Miranda asked above the bump and rattle. In a flurry of movement, her hands smoothed out her petticoat and then yanked on her weskit and then went back to her petticoat again. A moment later, she was tugging at a lock of hair that had come loose from its golden knot.

Hugh reached over and gripped one of her hands to still it. "Yes, we are almost there."

This restlessness had come upon her after Beltane and that odd incident with the painting. It was as if she sometimes didn't know what to do with her hands. Hugh would find her scrubbing and scrubbing a pair of James Martin's breeches or arranging over and over the red ware in the kitchen cupboard. It would come on suddenly, last for a few days, and then be gone. A week later, it would return.

He had urged her to work on the portrait, thinking it would help settle her. And for long sessions at a time, it did, as she sat and dabbed at her palette behind the easel in the parlor, looking from Hugh to the canvas and back to Hugh again, sometimes intent and silent, sometimes chattering like a magpie.

"What has happened to Mama?" James Martin asked one day after Miranda tutored him nearly to the point of exhaustion on his letters.

Hugh shoved the scene away, his son's questioning face, as he steered the wagon into a sunny clearing and reined in the horses. "And here we are," he said. "Shall we disembark?"

Gwydion snorted as Hugh and Miranda dropped from the wagon seat. Then he bowed his head to the tall grass, and Virgil did the same.

"So, this is it?" Miranda said, gazing about.

"Over there." Hugh pointed across the clearing. "Come."

He led Miranda through the grass and bracken to the edge of a gently sloping valley, green and dappled by the sun. Forty feet down, the waters of a narrow river rushed by with an unceasing *whoosh* as they flowed west toward Minton. Hugh's heart filled again with Wales.

"What do you think?" he asked.

Miranda looked out over the valley, her hands clasped in front of her. "Oh, Husband! I think—I think I must paint this." She turned and reached a hand to his cheek.

"Indeed, as soon as you finish painting me, hmm?"

He reached into his pocket and withdrew the leather pouch he had tucked there, gazed out over the valley once more, and knew he had made the right choice, and at the right time.

"And now, a little something else," he said, opening the pouch. "A gift for my sweet rose."

Hugh reached in and withdrew the fold of linen with his mother's necklace wrapped inside. With the excitement of a child, he pulled away the fabric. He'd been waiting a long time to do this. The necklace lay coiled in his hand, its silver chain gleaming and set on either side with four sparkling rubies. From a thin curve of open work at the bottom hung a locket, adorned with a polished rose quartz, milky and pink.

Miranda stared at the necklace and then looked up at Hugh. "What is the meaning of this? Have you robbed old Mr. Cuthbert the jeweler?" she said with another bite of her lip.

Hugh held up the necklace. Miranda, wide-eyed, tapped the locket with her finger.

"I have robbed no one. This necklace was my mother's."

"Your mother's? Truly?"

"As I stand before God."

On the day before he and Niall left Holywell for passage across the sea, his mother had taken him aside and pushed the necklace and a pair of matching jeweled earrings into his hands. Having no daughters, she'd been saving them for him, her eldest son. An inheritance from a second cousin who once did business in the English court. "Not even your father knows of it," she'd whispered. And when Hugh, incredulous, asked her what kind of business would garner such fine trinkets, she'd simply replied, "Never you mind, my boy."

The earrings he'd sold in Philadelphia in order to avoid taking a loan for the building of the house. A small sacrifice for a large return, although the money hadn't stretched quite as far as he had hoped. But he hadn't wasted a moment regretting it.

He opened the locket and pointed to the initials he'd had engraved inside. *MFJ*. "Now it is yours. You see? Shall I fasten it on?"

"I will throw you into that river right this minute if you don't."

With the necklace secured, Miranda pressed it against her flesh and pressed it again. "Perhaps I will never take it off." She turned and kissed him, a long, lingering kiss that set his desire aflame.

They stood a while, gazing out on the valley, listening to the river and the birds and the distant lowing of the Kents' cattle.

When at last they climbed back into the wagon and started for home, Hugh told Miranda the story of the necklace, for she was eager to hear it. Her hands lay settled in her lap as she listened. Only once did either of them move, when she reached up to fondle the silver chain. Yes, this had been the right time.

"You know what I think about the business your mother's relation had at court?" she said.

"Do tell."

"Courtesan." She glanced over at Hugh. "She pleased someone and gained his favor. How else would a woman come by such a thing? Unless she had married well, of course."

Courtesan. Hugh mulled that over for a moment. It would explain why his mother had been stingy with the details. "Well, you have gained *my* favor, hmm?"

Miranda's hand reached for the necklace again. "Am I your courtesan, then?" she teased.

"Aye, a very lovely one indeed, and with a talent to rival Master Van Dyck."

—

On Wednesday morning, Hugh settled at his desk in the lumber room. He removed his ledger from a drawer and set out the inkwell. He needed to enter the figures for their latest trade of rum. He would have preferred that Niall do the accounting, but his brother had little mind for numbers, so it had fallen to Hugh to record deliveries and payments.

He wanted to be quick about it. His head was beginning to ache. He and Miranda and Priscilla had sat up late with cups of ale, and he had indulged too freely. But no sooner did he take up the quill pen than a clamor arose downstairs.

"Mistress! Please! Mistress!" Priscilla shouted. Then came the thud of something heavy dropped on the floor, and then the yammer of a child. One of the twins.

He flew from the room and called down the stairs. "My dear ladies! What the devil?"

"Do not touch it!" Miranda.

A moment later, Hugh was in the kitchen. Priscilla and Miranda stood paces apart by the fireplace, like two wary cocks. A large iron pot lay toppled on the floorboards, a puddle of broth and onion and beans surrounding it. In the corner, Abby sat on a blanket, working herself into a wail.

Priscilla took a step toward Hugh. "Mr. Jones, sir, the mistress—"

"I told her not to touch it!" Miranda said, glancing down at the pot, her face stern and unyielding.

"But the babe..." Priscilla went to Abby and hoisted her from the floor to soothe her.

"What has happened here?" Hugh glanced from Miranda to Priscilla and back to Miranda again. The ache in his head was turning to a throb. "Must I attend to kitchen squabbles? For pity's sake, why is the pot on the floor?"

"I needed to take it from the fire, and she would not let me!" Miranda said.

"It was very hot, Mr. Jones, and she had no cloth for lifting it." Priscilla walked over to Hugh, Abby now calm in her arms. "Her hand. You will see for yourself."

Hugh reached for Miranda's hands. "My sweet, what have you done?"

Miranda resisted his attempt to pull up the hands for inspection as a child might do. "It was time to take the pot from the fire! She should not interfere."

"Please, let me see," Hugh said. "I do not have time for sport."

Miranda surrendered her hands to him. Across one palm flamed an angry red score.

"Do not look," she said, yanking her hands away. Her eyes darted from one side of the room to the other and came to rest on Hugh.

"Prissy, could you fetch the salve?" He reached for Abby. "I'll take her."

While Priscilla rummaged in the cupboard, Hugh turned back to his wife. "You must allow Prissy to dress that wound," he said. "If you get an infection, Hattie will give you the devil."

The mention of Hattie brightened Miranda's dour expression, but not as much as Hugh had hoped it would. "Yes, Hattie," she said. "When will she be here?"

Sooner rather than later, and with a tonic, Hugh prayed. He would have Sam ride out to get her this afternoon.

"I'll take Abby up to her chamber," he said. "It is time for her nap. Alice is already abed?"

When Priscilla nodded, Hugh left her and Miranda in the kitchen and climbed the stairs, wondering what had come over his wife. She knew better than to lift a pot from the pot arm with no cloth.

That unyielding look on her face. It was not like her at all.

Dear Miranda. What devil has gotten inside of you?

CHAPTER TWENTY-FIVE

M y phone chimed me from sleep. Diana.
"Oh, did I wake you?" she said, sounding surprised.

I looked over at the clock. 9:00. "Yeah, but that's okay. I must have slept through my alarm."

"You don't sound so hot. Not feeling well?"

"No, no. Just couldn't sleep last night."

"I gather. I got your text. Sorry, I was tied up this morning, Kenny-induced, long story, and just saw it a few minutes ago. What's this necklace all about?"

"Can I get back to you later? I need to call Harry and let him know I'll be late."

"Look, Lib. Maybe you ought to take the day off?"

"Maybe, I don't know."

"Rita's holding down the fort today at the café. I can come over with some day-old. You can tell me what's going on."

An olive branch. Diana was trying. "Okay, but only if you promise not to treat me like a mental patient."

Diana went quiet. "I promise."

I left a message with Harry to say I was sick. Not entirely a lie. My brain was foggy from the poor sleep, and the first pangs of a headache were hammering in my temple.

Buck appeared in the doorway, looking anxious. "Be right there," I said. I opened the night table drawer and was relieved to see the necklace still there. I tucked it into the pocket of my bathrobe.

Downstairs, I waited for coffee to brew and gulped down some aspirin. I pulled the necklace from my pocket. It must have been even more beautiful once, when the silver gleamed, and all the red stones were intact. Too beautiful to be lying in my third-floor hallway.

Not just anywhere in the hallway but in the doorway of the west room. And that scratching noise. It hadn't been Buck.

After breakfast, I texted Diana to ask her to pick up some silver polish. An hour later, she arrived with the polish and a white bakery bag.

"These might actually be two days old, I can't remember," she said, hoisting the bag. "Coffee smells good."

"I was just having another cup. Want some?"

"Talked me into it." She dropped the bag and polish to the kitchen table. "So this must be it," she said, eyeing the necklace. "Quite the piece. The only thing I found when we moved into Ashford Street was a dead mouse and the hose for an old vacuum cleaner."

"As you can see, it's very real, and not mine. And it wasn't here when I moved in." I set her mug of coffee firmly on the table to punctuate my point and opened the paper bag. Orange cranberry scones. Ray's favorite.

"I can see why you wanted the polish," she said. Her gaze shifted from the necklace to me. "So, this was just lying there in the hall, in the middle of the night?"

"And look at this," I said, lifting the necklace and laying the oval charm against my palm. "It's a locket." I pulled it open and tapped the contents with the tip of my finger. "Hair."

"Hmm," Diana murmured. She poured some cream into her coffee from the carton I'd left on the table and then poured a little more. "We may as well settle in and talk about this over the scones. I'll get us some plates."

Once we were seated, I recounted last night's experience from beginning to end.

"Whose hair do you think it is?" Diana asked.

I shrugged. "Hugh's, maybe? Although I don't know what color his hair was."

"Hugh. So, we're on a first-name basis now."

"Dee, please. My head hurts and I'm tired and you promised."

Diana tugged at her bangs. "Okay, but I don't like this, whatever it is. It's bad for you. You're already not sleeping." She buttered the last chunk of her scone and furrowed her brow. "Why would it be up on your third floor?"

Because there's something about the third floor.

"I haven't a clue. Anyway, I talked to that Jones descendant over in Brigham. Actually, her daughter."

"And?"

"She might have a few family items I can look at. She's going to get back to me. And I'll be heading over to the county historical society next week to see what else I can find."

"Maybe you shouldn't keep digging."

With my attention again on the necklace, I didn't reply right away.

"You know," Diana went on, "I saw a television show once about this woman who thought she was being haunted by a three-hundred-year-old pirate. She fell in love with him and married him in a civil ceremony, on board a ship, no less." She sipped her coffee and grinned. "You aren't going to pull a stunt like that, are you?"

I tried to laugh, for Diana's sake. I could see behind her teasing glance that she needed me to. "I'm not sure I'll ever fall in love with anyone again, if that answers your question. If I do, it won't be a pirate...I don't think."

"Hmm. So, who was the client yesterday, the one you were with at the café?"

The inevitable question. After giving her the bare bones of Keith, I told her Harry was taking the lead on his project and I didn't expect to see Keith again until February. Then I changed the subject.

"What was going on with Kenny this morning?"

"The usual. Too much Taylor and not enough school work. And Cal found pot in his room yesterday. He's got to start knuckling down, or he's going to find himself bussing tables at the café after graduation next year."

We chatted for a while longer, both of us trying to ignore the crack that had opened between us. Then Diana said, "I'd like to stick around to polish the silver, but I have to get going. Cal said he would make the meatloaf if I got the meat. Acme Markets, here I come."

At the door, her face grew serious. "All of this seems to be taking a toll on you. I wonder whether, well, you want to keep moving forward, right?"

"You said you wouldn't treat—"

"It's not about crazy. It's about getting past something. This ghost, or whatever it is, maybe it's coming from some sort of negative energy you're holding."

"Oh, so now it's my fault," I snapped, stung by her words. "How do you explain the necklace? And the glove and the diary page? Is that my negative energy, too?"

"I don't know. But ever since Ray died, there's been something down there inside you. I don't know what it is. And now since you moved in here—"

"Enough, Dee! I'm exhausted! If you don't want to help me with this, I'll do it myself."

She gave a quick shrug. "Have it your way. I'll try not to bother you anymore." Then she slipped on her sunglasses and went out the door without looking back.

As I cleaned up the kitchen, tears threatening to spill, I thought about what Diana said. *Something down there inside you.* She knew it wasn't just about my grief. She knew there was something else, something more troubling. But I needed her help, not her accusations.

Negative energy.

I pushed that thought away, opened the locket, and dropped the curl of hair into a glass leftovers container. Then I settled in at the table with a rag and started polishing. The tarnish was stubborn, and it took five minutes to clear even part of it away. The engraved initials would need more work, but if I held the locket at arm's length, I could just about make them out.

MFJ. J for Jones, of course. But which one?

I hurried down the hall to my office, took the Jones folder out of the desk drawer, and flipped through to the tree. *Miranda Jones 1734–1762.* The only woman on the tree with both *M* and *J* in her name. It must have been hers.

She didn't get to enjoy her beautiful bauble for very long. What had she died from at twenty-eight? An illness? Childbirth? The tree contained no record of a child born to Hugh and Miranda in 1762.

Hugh didn't die until 1792, thirty years later. Had he missed her all that time? I'd only lived for a year and a half beyond Ray's death, and already it felt like an eternity.

I tucked the tree away and went back to the kitchen. I could take the necklace to Moffitt's Jewelers in town and have Jenny Moffitt finish cleaning it. Jenny's business included restoring and selling vintage and antique jewelry. She could tell me whether it was as old as I suspected.

Buck wandered into the kitchen and began to pace. "Your turn now," I said, as I grabbed his leash and fastened it to his collar.

Outside, we trailed down the grassy shoulder of the road. A mountain of gray clouds had moved in, covering the sun. I hurried Buck along, chilly and tired, my thoughts swirling with

Hugh, Miranda, and the necklace. And Diana. As we were heading back up Chambers Road, a minivan with a Reardon School logo on the door turned into the school's driveway. As the van disappeared past the high wall of hedge, I remembered my promise to invite Emmeline to the house.

When I got back, I found the school's number and left her a message inviting her to lunch. She called back twenty minutes later.

"Libby Casey. Emmeline here. Have I got you at the right time?"

"Yes, this is fine." I repeated my invitation. "I'm planning to be a homebody this weekend. What about Saturday? Sorry for the short notice."

"I'm afraid I'm full up Saturday. Hairdresser in the morning. Then Ben's taking me to the market. The cupboard's quite bare."

"Of course," I said, wondering whether Ben was the driver of the silver Toyota. "But let's do it before Christmas. Oh! Can you do Saturday the twenty-first? I'm having an open house in the late afternoon for drinks and food, and I'd love for you to join us. Four o'clock. But come by an hour early so we can chat a bit over tea."

We hung up, and I pondered Emmeline. *I've always known things.* She was her own sort of mystery. Maybe she could become a friend. Right about now, I needed another friend.

—

That night I lay awake, thinking and tossing, Diana on my mind. Earlier, in the afternoon, I'd thought I might call her to try to smooth things over. But I'd changed my mind.

Don't give up on me, Dee.

From the very beginning, we'd clicked into place like tumblers on a safe. We were family right off the bat, Diana three years older and like a big sister to me. The sister I never had but always wanted. I'd been there for her through the café's lean early years and the tough times with Kenny, and that rough patch with Cal that almost ended their marriage. And she'd been my rock through the long ordeal with Ray.

Something down there inside you.

What if I told her what I'd done to Ray? Would that fix things between us? Or would it push us further apart?

I reached into the night table and shook out a pill. I didn't want to lie here, thinking, regretting. When finally I fell asleep, I found myself in the dark room with the man by the fire. He got up when he saw me and bowed from the shadows. Then he picked up the glass on the table and raised it to his lips. The twist in its stem flickered in the firelight.

"Please, come in," he said. "I've been waiting."

CHAPTER TWENTY-SIX

October 1760

Hugh handed Hattie the goblet of sherry and sank into the Windsor chair, weary to the bone. "Much obliged that you're staying," he said. A lamp sputtered on the table between them, hardly bright enough to fend off the dusk.

"I wish it were under more favorable circumstances," Hattie said. She held her goblet to the lamp. "These are quite beautiful. You said Mercy sent them out from the city?"

"Her son," Hugh said. "In April, just after she died. She had instructed him to send me the pair." He looked from his goblet to Hattie's, admiring the gracefully turned bowls and the glittering twists in the stems. "Miranda has painted one into my portrait." Hugh shook his head. "My poor, dear wife."

Hattie's eyes were all sympathy as she sipped her sherry and said, "You look much fatigued, dear man. This has become an ordeal for you."

"She is well for a brief while and then she fares poorly. There is no predicting it. Her mind when she is in the thick of these, these episodes, it moves about by fits and starts, going who knows where. You saw her tonight. If not for your poppy tea, well... Her humors are still quite askew, if indeed that is the problem."

Hattie fingered the feather trinket at her neck. "I'm going to ask Martha Little Cloud if she can make her some medicine. She could come out in a week or two if things don't improve."

"It pains me to say that I am losing hope for an improvement. And the children, they cannot comprehend." Hugh sighed with resignation. "Do you really think Martha can be of help?"

He knew little about Lenape medicine, only the modicum he had gleaned from Sam.

"I have as much faith in Martha as in my own remedies," Hattie said. "Let us try. I would find it preferable to having a physician let her blood."

Let her blood? Hugh shook his head. No, Miranda would never consent. Her mother had died not long after a bleeding, and it had made Miranda more than wary. He swallowed a generous gulp of sherry, its sweet tang a pleasure that felt lost on him now.

"Very well. Let us try Martha first. But tell me. If you were to wager on such a thing, Hattie, would you wager that this affliction can be cured?"

Hugh did not like the silence that followed or the uncertainty in Hattie's gaze.

"I do not wager, my friend. I pray. And I suggest you do the same. God might find a way where Martha and I cannot. I have seen hard cases turn for the better, prayer or none." Hattie tilted her head. "When I was down in the city once, I consulted with my friend, Portia Taggart, who had taken such a patient as Miranda into her care."

"And what did you conclude?"

"I thought it a nervous disorder. But I couldn't stay on as I had to get back to help Fanny Burns deliver her child."

"Very well," Hugh muttered, feeling done with talk of Miranda. His back ached from the long day spent clearing undergrowth in the orchard, and his mind was going dull with the sherry.

"I suggest she keep busy. She said she and Prissy have cabbages to crate up in the cellar and more beans to brine. If you have time, get her out in the wagon for some air while the weather holds. And get her back to that portrait."

"She is all but done with it, she says. I'll try to turn her to another subject soon."

With the lamp beginning to gutter, Hattie sipped the last of her drink and stood. "I cannot fight sleep any longer."

Hugh rose to see her out of the parlor. "Prissy has made up the chamber across from hers on the third floor. There is a pitcher there and some soap and a sponge."

With Hattie gone, Hugh took up the lamp, stared into the flame, and whispered a prayer to Arianrhod. Then he went upstairs to the lumber room, sat down, and took out his diary.

—

The next morning, when he reached the barn, Hugh found Sam Grey Feather already up on the seat board of the wagon.

"You are more reliable than the dawn," he said, climbing up beside him.

At his friend's feet sat the pipe pouch, pinched tight with a piece of twine laced through its neck. Apart from his blade, it was the only thing that Sam never traveled without.

"You do not mind driving?" Hugh asked. "I am not up to it."

Sam grinned from behind a drape of onyx hair. "The horses would not have it any other way." He steered the wagon toward the lane. "Your face wears trouble this morning."

"It's Miranda again. Hattie spent the night and has promised to stay on until we return. She hopes to speak to Martha about making some medicine."

"I regret your trouble, my friend." Sam made a clicking

noise with his tongue and then addressed the horses with a Lenape word, to which they nickered and picked up their pace. "Martha knows well how to cleanse a spirit. She did so for my cousin before he followed my father west."

Hugh's mood brightened at this bit of news. "And your cousin is well now?"

"I have not heard otherwise."

The autumn trees blazed orange and red against an overcast sky, and their laden wagon made a steady music as it thumped over roots and pits beneath its wheels. As he and Sam conversed about the work of the farm, Hugh drew in the damp air and picked out notes of earth and leaves and the rain that would surely come soon. Doing so helped him turn his mind from Miranda.

By the time they pulled into the Brown Pony for their last delivery, rain clouds had darkened the sky. Four horses idled at hitches in the dirt lot. A carriage sat on the cartway under the trees, another inside the two-bay coaching house.

"Henry is doing good business today," Hugh said as he and Sam dropped down from the wagon.

"Henry always does good business. He keeps his own *pau wau*." Sam grinned. When a hawk passed low overhead, he looked up, his grin falling flat, and murmured something else in his Lenape tongue.

Hugh could tell that the passing of the hawk had not pleased him.

At the inn's back door, he called into the kitchen. Hilda Wilkins, plump and red-faced, looked up from where she was stirring a pot at the fireplace. "I'll find my husband," she said, and a moment later, she returned with Henry.

"Hugh, Sam, just in time," he said, as always.

They unloaded the rum and then Henry bid them stay for an ale. The tavern was crowded with patrons. At least five parties of men sat at tables, pewter cups and dishes scattered in front of them, pipe smoke curling into the air amid a buzz of conversation. A ring on the finger of one man caught Hugh's eye. Thick silver band, large amber stone. The same ring he had seen before, here in this very inn.

"Sit," Henry said, then he went to fetch the ale.

Hugh and Sam settled at a table, and Sam set out his pouch. No sooner had Henry returned with their drinks than a voice called across the room.

"I didn't know you served savages in your establishment, Henry." An Englishman.

In Hugh's bowels, a little storm began to stir. He and Henry looked toward the voice, but Sam kept his eyes on the cup of ale in front of him.

"I serve whatever thirsty patron I please, Gideon Finch," Henry said.

"Even the ones who are killing our women and children out in the territories?" said Finch. He was a little older than Hugh and Sam, dressed in breeches, a frock and costly boots, and the big ring.

"The sooner we clear this land of them, the better!" said the other man seated at his table. A big puff guts of a Scot.

"Keep to your own business, sir," Hugh ordered to whichever of them might listen. "And we shall keep to ours."

The buzz of conversation died away. The patrons' eyes were now on the men in dispute.

"I'd say it's every bit my business," Finch said, pushing his chair back and rising. The Scot did the same.

"Gentlemen," Henry said. "Have a seat and I'll bring you a fresh round. On the house, what do you say?"

Hugh did not think more ale was advisable. The men seemed already full of drink.

"All the ale in the world wouldn't make this blasted rubbish..." Here Finch nodded toward Sam. "...any more welcome."

Sam rose and looked over at Finch and the Scot, his dark eyes aflame. "The drink gives you courage, pale men. I think it must be the only thing that gives you courage."

Hugh stood up too, just as Finch, stone-faced, took two steps across the room, joined by the Scot. When Henry tried to head them off, Finch shoved him away, and the old publican stumbled back.

What happened next felt to Hugh like some fantastical dream. The Scot's twisted snarl, the barrel of a pistol, Sam reaching to his buckskins, the bony arm of Gideon Finch suddenly within Hugh's grip, and then a shot and a flash and the stink of powder, and Sam's hand driving into the big Scot's belly.

With a garbled cry, the Scot dropped to the floor like a felled pine. "What the devil?" someone shouted. "Great gods!" yelled another.

Hugh looked down at the Scot, a red stain spreading over the man's linen shirt the last thing he saw as Henry shoved him and Sam toward the door, saying, "Get, boys! Get!"

CHAPTER TWENTY-SEVEN

I hurried up Main Street in the noonday chill. Harry and I had always counted ourselves lucky to have our business on this street, which combined the charms of turn-of-the-century village life with more modern updates and conveniences. This close to Christmas, it was busier than usual, with cars streaming by and holiday shoppers slipping in and out of storefronts.

I slowed down at Linden's Vintage when I spied an antique table lamp through the front window, a perfect Christmas gift for Maddie and her fiancé, Jeff, and I made a mental note to return soon to buy it. A moment later, I slowed down again when the door to Main Street Deli opened and out wafted the scent of chicken cutlet and provolone and smoked peppers, one of their specialty sandwiches. My stomach rumbled. Maybe when I was finished at Moffitt's, I would go in and get a sandwich. Harry was having lunch out today, so I would be on my own.

I rounded the corner and a few moments later pushed through the wooden door to Moffitt's. Bent down behind a glass case, Jenny looked up when she heard me enter. I had called her earlier, so she was expecting me.

We exchanged pleasantries, and I extracted the necklace from my satchel.

"This looks very interesting," she said in her usual sober tone. Everything about Jenny was sober. She stared down at the necklace with the slightest lift of her brow. "It's certainly silver. Let's have a look."

Donning an eyepiece, she laid the necklace out on a velvet pad and inspected it, moving the eyepiece from the chain to the curve of open work and finally to the locket.

"There are a couple of seed pearls mixed with this silver beading around the locket stone," she said. "They need some cleaning up." Then she zeroed in on the red gems. "Good rubies, and finely cut. One's missing, eh?"

Finally, she opened the locket and bent her nearly six-foot frame closer. Her gray bob fell forward over her fabric hairband, obscuring her face.

"I think the letters are *MFJ*," I said, trying to be helpful. "That's where I found the hair I told you about."

She straightened up and took off her eyepiece. "You found this necklace where?"

"Among some of my mother's things I had in a box."

After a moment's hesitation, she let the matter drop. Then she pushed the velvet pad toward me. "This open work is quite masterful," she said, touching the smile of filigree. "And you've got a fine rose quartz on the locket. All in all…" Here she paused as if considering. "…it has the hallmarks of an authentic eighteenth-century piece."

If Jenny was mystified or impressed by what she saw, I couldn't tell. But at least now I knew I was right. The necklace had surely been Miranda's.

"And the initials, what do you think?" I asked.

She bent over the locket again. "Could be *MFJ*, yes. If you don't mind, I can clean it up a bit. I'd like to get Horst's opinion on all of this." Horst was Jenny's partner in business as well as in life. She straightened up and stared across the counter. "If it's what I think it is, it's worth a pretty penny."

"How pretty?"

"Pretty enough that I'll be locking it in the safe if you feel comfortable leaving it for a few days. I'll get back to you about the particulars."

I agreed to her plan, and she disappeared into the back room with the necklace, asking me to wait while she printed out a receipt. My mind bounced back and forth between what she had said about the necklace and my now-ravenous hunger for a sandwich.

The shop door swept open behind me. When I turned, there was Keith Janus, amber scarf around his neck, navy jacket hanging open.

"Well, look who," he said, shutting the door behind him.

First the bookstore, now the jewelers. A coincidence or something else? I had been stalked once by a client, years ago when I was working for a firm in the city, and the experience of that had stayed with me.

"Are you following me?" I asked, only half in jest.

"I was going to ask you the same question," Keith said. "Actually, I came in to pick up something I got repaired for my mother. Doing some holiday shopping?"

"No, I need something appraised. I was just on my way out to pick up some lunch."

Keith nodded. "Okay, don't let me keep you. And I'm looking forward to the project."

Jenny returned from the back room and handed me the receipt, promising to call me soon. "Mr. Janus," she greeted Keith. "Be right back with your bracelet." Then she disappeared again into the back.

No, he probably wasn't stalking me. I bid him goodbye and started for the door.

"You know, I was going to head over to McGraw's for a

burger special," he said. "You want to join me, and we'll get a booth?"

He didn't *seem* like a stalker. Then again, they never do at first.

Regardless, he was a client, and business never mixes well with pleasure, even though I found myself suddenly wanting this pleasure. My stomach rumbled again. I was beginning to feel weak.

"All right," I heard myself say. "Let's do that."

—

McGraw's Pub was bustling with the lunch crowd. Keith and I chose a corner booth in the back dining room. As he slid in and tugged off his scarf, a pleasant, musky scent wafted across the table.

"Any plans for the holidays?" I asked.

"Spence is coming home from school for three weeks. We'll drive up to Jodie's for Christmas and stay over for five or six days. When we get back, we're heading into the city to check out a double feature he wants to see. I'm trying to get him to go visit Alicia on his way back to California in January. He says he doesn't like Arizona. Right now, I think he just doesn't like his mother."

"It will pass," I said. "I spent decades not liking my mother."

A young woman with a ring through her nose and a nametag that read "KATE" appeared at our booth. "Start you off with a drink?" she chirped. Keith ordered a pint of the special holiday lager, and I did the same. Just one wouldn't hurt.

"What about you?" Keith said. He was relaxing back into the booth with one hand on the table, the way he had at Diana's café. "For the holidays, I mean."

My eyes went to his hand for the briefest of moments and caught the gleam of a fingernail and the faintest wisp of dark brown hair. "Some friends are coming for an open house the weekend before Christmas. It's a tradition. We make an eggnog and cognac toast and eat a lot. I'll probably spend Christmas Day with my friend Diana and her family."

Probably. I wasn't sure Diana and I could hammer out a truce by then. Things had gone from bad to worse lately.

"So, it's just you?"

"Yep, just me."

"I'm sorry," he said when I didn't elaborate. "I don't mean to get up in your business."

The waitress delivered our pints, took our food order, and breezed away.

Keith sipped his lager. "You don't seem to wear a ring, so I figured you might be on your own." His eyes fell to his pint glass. I noticed then that they were the same bronze color as the beer.

"My husband died going on two years ago." I took a gulp of the cold brew, and then another. It quenched me in some indescribable way.

Keith swallowed his in kind. "What happened to him?"

In a few simple sentences, I told him about the lymphoma and Ray's long fight.

As we polished off our pints, Kate appeared with a burger and fries for Keith and a salad with crispy chicken for me. She placed the food on the table, looking from me to Keith. "Another lager?"

With my stomach empty, the beer had gone to my head. Would another pint be wise?

"Sure," I said, and Keith ordered one too.

He picked up his burger. "Best ones for miles around." He chomped down with evident relish.

I love the sight of a man enjoying his food. Annabelle from the kitchen in her netherworld.

I tossed my salad with my fork. Feeling loose with the lager, and against my better judgment, I dipped a toe into more personal waters. "So why doesn't your son like Alicia, if you don't mind my asking?"

"Not that long of a tale and not all that interesting," he said, and then he told me about how Alicia had traveled a lot for work, leaving him and Spencer alone much of the time, and how that had led to estrangement, separation, and finally divorce. "Pretty much end of story," he concluded.

"So, your son blames Alicia for the breakup?"

"Yeah, despite my telling him to let her off the hook." Keith sat up straighter and pierced a French fry with his fork. "What about your mother? You two didn't get along?"

"She was a librarian and liked a very ordered universe. Everything needed to be in its place, including me. Things got better after I moved out of the house."

"And your father?" He forked up another fry.

"He died when I was twelve. It left us feeling very alone. It had been just the three of us, and my father's sudden absence, well, he and I were like two peas in a pod." A warning flashed red in my mind. The conversation was growing uncomfortably close. But Keith Janus was a good listener, and it was hard to resist the quiet spaces he left for me to fill in. "Anyway, that is pretty much the end of *my* story."

"Fair enough," Keith said. "You mentioned at Moffitt's that you were having something appraised."

"Not exactly appraised. I just wanted Jenny to have a look at it. It's a necklace that someone…a relative left me. I mean, left my mother. I think it's quite old."

"How old?"

"Two hundred sixty years, give or take."

Keith narrowed his bronze eyes. "So, what, it was passed down in the family? That's quite a chain of custody."

He reached for his almost empty pint glass. Not Ray's hand, but still pleasant, a little wider and without the dusting of freckles on the back.

"Actually, I think it was acquired by a very distant relation a long time ago. I'm not sure how. But now it's mine."

"What does Jenny say?"

"She's going to get back to me. But what about you? You were picking up a bracelet for your mother."

"A family heirloom, like yours, but nowhere near as old. I should have showed you before I locked it in the glove compartment. It was her own mother's bracelet, and it means a lot to her. She wants to leave it to Jodie someday. I thought I'd get it repaired as a Christmas gift."

With my thumb, I rubbed the band of the emerald engagement ring I wore now on my right hand. *Chain of custody.* I had no daughter to leave the ring to, but I could leave it to Maddie.

Kate sidled up with the plastic check tray and the bill. "Will there be anything else?"

We declined, tossed our credit cards onto the tray, and Kate whisked it away.

Keith smiled across the table. "There's an old inn about halfway between here and Morley. The Brown Pony. I don't know whether you've ever heard of it. It dates back to the 1700s and still has the big tavern room and original fireplace. They do it up around the holidays with greens and candles, that sort of thing, and they always put a few old-fashioned dishes on the menu."

Oh, no. "It rings a distant bell. I think Harry might have eaten there once." Whether Harry had eaten there, I couldn't recall, but I needed to say something to dispel my discomfort. I was about to be asked on a date, and I didn't think I could accept.

"I thought you might enjoy it." Keith leaned back in the booth. "I mean, would you like to go with me next weekend, drink a little wassail? They bring a bowl right to your table with a ladle and recite some sort of colonial toast."

"That sounds like fun. But I don't read well, I try to keep my personal life and my work life separate, if you know what I mean."

Keith nodded and gazed down at his empty plate. "Sure, no

worries," he said.

"And to tell you the truth, I've got this new house I moved into recently, or actually an old house, and it's keeping me pretty busy and exhausted, and..."

My words came out sounding exactly like what they were—a bumbling excuse, a rejection. But somewhere inside me, refusing a date with Keith felt as wrong as accepting it.

He held up his palm. "I know what that's like," he said. "Well, we've both got work to do, so I'm going to find the men's room and then we can get going." He slid out of the booth. "Be right back."

CHAPTER TWENTY-EIGHT

At home that evening, I fed the animals and then took Buck for a walk. "Don't get lost!" I hollered as he bolted into the dark.

I clicked on my flashlight. Flurries drifted like confetti in the light. As I walked toward the woods, a voicemail Carol Seabrook had left me that afternoon played back in my head. *Found a few things that might interest you at Dot's.* But she hadn't had time to look through them, as her aunt had been admitted to the hospital. In the next breath, she said she was going out of town for a few days.

Carol Seabrook. A woman in perpetual motion. *Hasty*, Granny Eleanor would have called her.

My pace slowed as I reached the garden, my feet seeming to root to the ground. "Buck?" I called.

I sliced the darkness with my light, but there was only the falling snow. Where had he gotten to? Then I caught sight of two glimmering objects inside the garden. My dog's eyes. But how could he be inside the fence? He couldn't have opened—

The now-familiar scent hung in the air, and in that moment it finally came to me. *Lavender.*

A rustling sound pulled me back to the cold and the snow. I swept my beam over the garden. Buck was pawing at the ground against the far fence.

"What is it?" I asked, tripping on an old root as I hurried over to see. Under his paws was only hard earth and withered leaves. "There's nothing here," I said. Then I repeated it louder so the phantom of Hugh Peter Jones might hear me.

Back at the house, I opened my refrigerator to find the makings of an easy dinner, and my eyes landed on a jug of cider I'd bought, intending to mull it. *Wassail.* A bowl of wassail and a toast of good cheer brought right to your table. Good cheer felt so distant to me now.

Was there some place in time, some parallel universe, where I might have accepted Keith's invitation? Somehow my life had become a dark alley closed off by yellow tape that said *Do Not Enter*.

I didn't feel much like dinner, so I took a glass of cabernet to the living room, planning to distract myself with a movie. But when I settled on the sofa, with Sugar Plum dozing off beside me, I found I wasn't in the mood for entertainment. Resting my hand on the cat's back, I tried to absorb her calm. My emerald engagement ring sparkled against her tortoiseshell fur. Yes, I would leave it to Maddie. She would cherish it, just as Keith's sister would cherish their mother's bracelet. Then Maddie would pass it on to her daughter, if she had one, and so on.

An heirloom properly looked after.

Everyone had something to leave behind, some beloved piece of a life that would need proper looking after. A book, a chair, or a childhood toy. I recalled the afternoon I found Ray sitting on the floor in the TV room, sorting through his collection of baseball memorabilia. He was recovering from his second round of chemo, and sometimes he would settle in there with Buck to doze or watch a game.

I had opened the door to tell him dinner was ready but paused when I saw the items littered about. "What's all this?" I asked.

"Just goin' through some stuff," he said with a shrug.

Ray's collection meant a lot to him, and I knew why he was picking through it. He was trying to decide who might get what—the vintage trading cards his uncle had left him, the Stan Musial cleats, the Yogi Berra cap, the Ted Williams bat—when he was gone.

"You don't need to do that," I said. "None of that is going anywhere and neither are you."

We argued, and then I turned around and stomped downstairs and threw myself joylessly into putting dinner on the table. When Ray appeared in the kitchen a few minutes later, he came to me and took my hand.

"Who gets my stuff if and when I'm gone doesn't matter as much as who gets you," he said. "That's what really keeps me up at night. And whoever he is, I hate his guts in advance."

Sugar Plum stirred, dropping down from the sofa. I drained my glass of cabernet and debated with myself the merits of pouring another. In the end, Ray had set aside a few of the more valuable items in his collection for me, including the Ted Williams, as he called the bat, his sacred totem. "They'll bring a pretty penny in a pinch," he'd said.

Pretty penny. What Jenny said about the necklace. Another heirloom to be looked after.

—

I hurried up the walkway to the old Simms Elementary School at a near jog, late, having shut off my alarm and fallen back to sleep. I hadn't been able to talk myself out of that second glass of cabernet. A square of dark red brick with a rusty flagpole out front, the building had stopped functioning as a school forty years ago and now housed artists' studios and offices for community groups and non-profits.

A gray-haired woman named Betty, a volunteer for the Carroll County Historical Society, met me on the second floor and escorted me into an old classroom with an ancient blackboard at the front and a network of cubbies at the back. She'd set out a banker's box and a stack of three manila folders on a table. After beckoning me into a folding chair, she trailed away.

I looked at the box and envelopes with fading hope. Was this all they had? I yawned, took a few gulps of my takeout coffee, and then set it out of harm's way on the tabletop. At least it wouldn't take long.

In the first folder were paper copies of the photographs Susannah had shown me, along with a few originals I hadn't seen, including a portrait of a mustachioed young man in a Civil War uniform. Handsome, wearing a subdued smile, he stood erect in his high black boots, a saber dangling from his belt, his hand inserted into his Union coat Napoleon-style. I turned the paper over and saw a notation. *Capt. Jacob Denlinger, 97th Pennsylvania. Husband of Suzette Felicity Jones.*

The photo must have been taken before the war. A battle-weary Jacob might not have looked so composed, his uniform so perfect, when he returned home. *If* he returned. Maybe Suzette Felicity found herself widowed by the carnage at Gettysburg.

A hunt through the other two folders turned up some documents related to subdivisions of the property, a few handwritten invoices for the sale of farm equipment and cattle, and an 1873 commendation letter from the governor's office to John Carwyn Jones for his *exceptional dispatch and bravery* in helping put out a fire at the new county courthouse being built in town.

Another gulp of my coffee, now cold, and then it was on to the box. The morning was galloping forward. I removed the lid. Three manila envelopes sat atop a little bound book. I opened the first two envelopes and found land surveys, tax records, a drawing of the property as it looked in 1855, almost half of its acreage already sold off, and a copy of a letter, quite faded and dated in the 1890s.

In the third envelope were two thin yellowed pages. I removed them carefully and laid them on the table. *Kitchen Garden* was written at the top of one, and below that trailed a list of plants and flowers in faint but legible ink. Roses, yarrow, marigold, thyme, sage, parsley, carrots, Dutch brown, beans, tomatoes, onions, campion, poppy and, near the end, lavender. Yes, the lavender. Somehow, it had wafted through time to me. But why?

Bigger than the others. The second page was folded over. It was a garden plan drawn with eight rectangles inside a larger rectangle, outlined by a larger one still, the word *FENCE* penned vertically along one side. *My* garden, with its rotting bed frames and crusty pickets.

Inside the rectangles and along the fence were abbreviations, and in some cases, just a single letter. Notations for which plants grew where? In the place Buck had been digging last night was *PS*—parsley or purslane, maybe. I searched for an *L* for lavender, and there it was, repeated four times in one of the inside beds. I turned the page over. Down in one corner was a single faded word and a date. *Hattie 1755.*

I returned the papers to their envelopes and pushed them aside. I would ask Betty to make copies. Then I pulled the little book from the box. *A Brief History of the Jones Estate of Simms in Carroll County.* Under the title was a name, Edward Koch. The author, I presumed.

Did Susannah know about this book? She hadn't mentioned it. Inside, the title page bore a "thank you" to the Carroll County Historical Society for publishing it and the date of publication, 1910. The estate's sesquicentennial. I flipped the page to a miniature version of the photograph on the Simms Historical Society website and the heading "Introduction."

The Joneses of Holywell in Wales arrived on these shores

in 1750 and, two years later, purchased a verdant and well-situated property on the outskirts of the village of Simms some twelve miles north of Philadelphia. There the family remained for one hundred forty-five years, farming and running various enterprises that contributed to the ever more bustling life and vigor of Carroll County. Today, they are forever memorialized in the Georgian country home that still stands on Chambers Road in Simms Borough.

My watch pinged. I closed the book, a slim volume that numbered only about thirty pages, the print large at that. I hoped Betty would let me borrow it. I was more than eager to delve in.

CHAPTER TWENTY-NINE

November 1760

Hugh waved Sam into the kitchen and closed the door against the chill. He dropped a note he'd been reading onto the table.

"Good to see you," he said. "You make a timely visit."

Sam pulled off his napped leather coat, taking care as he slid his right arm from its sleeve. Near the top of the sleeve, a ragged hole, blackened around the edges, had been stitched closed with thick thread.

"Looks like that wound is still tender," Hugh said.

"Hattie and Martha have nursed me well. But I will not be able to help you cut the hay for a few more days."

"I am only grateful the Scot's ball did not find its way to your belly instead of your arm."

Hugh recalled again that calamitous day at the Brown Pony, their flight in the wagon as it began to rain, Sam's sleeve going damp with blood.

"A man who cannot hit his mark so close to his prey will go hungry," Sam said with a smile as he took a seat.

"Well said. But here is some sobering news." He pointed to the note on the table. "Henry has sent to say that the big Scot—Hamish Campbell was his name—is dead. You must continue to lie low at Hattie's. We don't yet know what sort of situation might arise."

Sam said something in his Lenape tongue.

Then Priscilla swept through the kitchen doorway. "Sam! Have you come for dinner?"

"No need for the dinner," Sam said.

"Of course there is." She smiled and stepped to the table, which was littered with various implements for cooking and the carcass of a freshly plucked hen. "A stewed chicken and some onion pudding. You mustn't go away hungry."

Priscilla offered Sam another warm smile, and he obliged her with his own. Hugh knew they had grown more than fond of each other. One day, he would plumb Sam's depth on the matter.

James Martin pattered in, bare of foot, blue stains on his breeches. "Sam Feather!" he called.

"*Mpilaechëm*," said Sam, pulling the boy in with his good arm.

"*Wink-a-lit*," James Martin replied, carefully sounding out each beat of the word. The boy already knew more of the Lenape tongue than Hugh was ever likely to.

He mussed the fair hair on his son's head. "Where are your shoes?"

"The mistress said they needed cleaning," Priscilla offered.

"And where *is* Miranda?" Sam asked.

James Martin gazed up at him. "Mama is sleeping."

"She started another portrait this morning and has rewarded herself with a nap." Hugh nodded down at his son. "By the look of those breeches, young man, you were her apprentice."

James Martin tapped Sam's knee. "Mama said she will paint you next. She said you have a fine counta...count..."

"Countenance," Priscilla said. "That's what it is. And a fine one indeed." She beamed again at Sam. "Shall I have a look at that wound?"

"Hattie dressed it yesterday."

"And no infection?"

Sam shook his head.

Just then, the chatter of a child sounded on the stairs. One of the twins. Alice, Hugh suspected, for Alice was always keen to rise from her nap early and run about the household. Their little wild goose.

"James Martin, go fetch your sister," Hugh said. "Before she wakes Mama."

James Martin stepped away from Sam. "Mama says Alice is a frightful harpy," he said, and he disappeared through the doorway.

A frightful harpy. Those words fell heavy on Hugh. He did not like them at all.

—

Two days later, the door knocker clanged with great force just as Hugh was tucking his crop ledger into the desk in the lumber room. He heard the door open and Priscilla offering a greeting, and the visitor, a man, offering one in return.

Then Priscilla called up to him in a hoarse whisper. "Mister Jones!"

Hugh went out to the hallway and looked down at her.

"It's the sheriff, sir." Her face was screwed into a look of concern.

"Blast it!" Hugh muttered to himself. There was only one reason the sheriff would come calling. He took a breath and descended the stairs, gathering his wits for what was to come.

In the center hall stood a man in a gray frock with a dusty bicorn in his hand. He was tall and thin, all nose and limbs.

"Thank you, Prissy," Hugh said. Priscilla paused with uncertainty before retreating to the kitchen.

"Mr. Jones. I'm Sheriff Phillip Gates," the man said. "I've come on a matter involving an incident at the Brown Pony Inn."

"Aye?" Hugh would offer no more than he had to.

"I'm given to understand that you and a companion created a disturbance that resulted in the dire injury of one Hamish Campbell."

Hugh paused as if thinking. "I know of no Hamish Campbell," he said.

"Whether you know him or not, he is dead, sir. And there are those who would like to bring the full weight of the law down upon you and the savage who attacked him. Henry Wilkins has not been helpful. I trust you will be more so."

"I have a number of friends and companions, Mr. Gates, but none of them are savages."

Gates narrowed his eyes. "But you were there, were you not? We have witnesses, one of whom is acquainted with you." Just then, his gaze was drawn to something down the hall.

Hugh turned and saw Miranda standing by the stairs, flour dusting the front of her dark weskit and skirt.

"Hugh Peter! Is there trouble?" She walked down the hall and looked up at Gates. "Who might you be, sir?"

Gates nodded. "The sheriff, madam. But your husband has the matter in hand, I'm sure."

"What matter?" Miranda looked from Gates to Hugh. "Has this to do with Sam?"

Hugh's heart sank.

"Sam," Gates said with a satisfied air. "So that is the perpetrator?"

"Perpetrator?" Miranda's eyes grew wide. "I do beg your—"

Hugh laid a hand to her arm. "Miranda, please. Prissy needs help in the kitchen."

"I do not like you, sir," she said, her eyes still on Gates. "Nor do I trust you. What right have you to come here? Who told you to—"

"Prissy!" Hugh called, and a moment later Priscilla was in the hall. "Could you take Miranda to the kitchen? There is dinner to prepare, is there not?"

Priscilla regarded Hugh knowingly and took Miranda by the arm. "Come, mistress. The rye dough, remember? It could use some more kneading, and you're best at it."

When Hugh turned back to Gates, the sheriff was watching the women depart with a look at once calculating and curious. "If you do not mind, Mr. Gates, I will see you out. There is nothing else I can tell you."

Gates set his hat on his head. "Very well. But this is not the end of it, Mr. Jones. You can be certain of that."

CHAPTER THIRTY

With the kitchen cleaned up for the night, I gathered my laptop and the things I'd brought home from the historical society and settled into my office. I took out the Jones family tree and set it side by side with the one in Edward Koch's *A Brief History*. They appeared identical, except that the tree in the book included an additional generation of the Joneses not contained in Susannah's. There at the bottom was John Carwyn Jones, next to his siblings, Malcolm, Cordelia, and Phillip Hugh. *Another Hugh.*

Jacob Denlinger, the Civil War veteran, was noted on both trees, in parentheses beside Suzette Felicity Jones, his wife. Suzette wasn't widowed by the war, after all. Jacob died in 1876, Suzette Felicity thirteen years later.

Felicity. One of those virtue names people were so fond of back then. Patience, Mercy, Chastity, Constance. "Fff-elicity," I whispered, lingering on that first push of air from between my lips. A light switched on in my head. *F*, the middle initial on the locket. *MFJ*. Miranda Felicity Jones?

I fell back in the chair. If I was right, that meant the hair in the locket had to be Hugh's. I thought of the little curl of dark brown strands I'd tucked into a leftovers container for safekeeping.

Another mystery solved.

Buck wandered in, looked my way, and then turned back toward the hall. "I know. Bedtime," I said.

Upstairs in bed, I opened the little history of the Jones estate and started in on the first chapter. Hugh Peter Jones and his brother Niall arriving from Wales in 1750, taking rooms in Philadelphia for a while until they acquired a property of one hundred eighty acres from a peach farmer, the brothers then moving into the farmer's small stucco house, now my kitchen and sided with clapboard, and adding flax fields in some moist acreage on the western side of the property.

They were nothing if not industrious, I thought. Determined to make a go of it in their new home. I closed my eyes and let my head fall back against the pillow, my mind swirling with Wales, the Jones brothers, and cash crops.

Suddenly, I was being pulled down to the bottom of a staircase where a woman stood with a book held to her chest. Jenny Moffitt. She beckoned me to follow as she turned and walked down a hallway, so quickly I couldn't keep up. "Wait! Wait!" I called, but she vanished, leaving me in the doorway of the familiar shadowy room, where the silhouette sat at his pedestal table, drinking from his glass, staring into the fire. "Hugh!" I called, and he looked up and said, "You've come back. Please. Stay."

Then a siren sounded in the distance.

—

I opened my eyes to the alarm beeping. 6:50. Buck was gone. Sitting up, I tossed back the quilt, accidentally knocking the history of the Jones estate to the floor. I leaned over and picked it up, trying to recall what I had read last night.

When my phone chirped with a text message, I jumped, my brain still sluggish. Carol Seabrook. I opened the message.

Meant to tell you about this the other night. Found it at Dot's. Thought you might be interested. At the end of the text, an attachment. I tapped it and an image of a painting in a gilt frame appeared. A partial image, snapped by hasty Carol. It appeared to be a portrait of a man sitting at a table, a fire behind him. Could this be—but no, how could it? I enlarged the photo and studied what I could see of the face, his dark hair pulled back, the spindle of a Windsor chair peeking out from behind his left arm. Yes, it was. It had to be the man in my dreams.

And this portrait—it must be the one Susannah mentioned that day at the historical society, the one she thought had hung in the house. Hugh.

I texted a "thank you" to Carol, my brain suddenly alert, and sent the attachment to my email. Then I rushed through a shower and yanked on jeans, a blouse, and a cardigan. What did it mean, Hugh Peter Jones coming to me in my dreams, and now this?

I hurried downstairs to my office and clicked the photo of Hugh into larger proportions on my laptop until more of the details could be seen.

His face was of an indistinct age but youngish, the hint of a smile on his full lips, and in the amber eyes as well. One curl of dark hair fell down across the top of his cheek. Had the hair in the locket been snipped from that curl?

I closed the image and texted Carol again. *Is it possible for me to see this in person?* Then I typed out an email to Diana and attached an image of the portrait. But at the last minute, I decided not to send it.

—

It was near the end of the day when Ellen Garcia, the woman who wanted work done in her Foursquare, called March & Casey.

"She hopes we can go look at her place before Christmas," I told Harry after hanging up the phone. "She's heading to Florida after the New Year and would like a proposal before she goes. Let's do what we can to make her happy. I really want to get my hands on that place."

"I figured." Harry winked across the office and stood up. "I'm feeling like some coffee with a splash of Rémy to end the day. Decaf, what do you think, kiddo? You can tell me more about that painting you mentioned."

When I turned up a thumb, he drifted off toward the dry sink. I sat, rethinking my decision not to send the email to Diana that morning. But what good would it have—

My cell chimed. Diana, as if on cue.

"Just calling to check in."

"You just want to see how my negative energy is going?"

Foul ball. Ray.

A moment passed. Then Diana said, "Actually, I was going to offer to bring over some Thai later. Cal's working late and I'm not going near a kitchen tonight."

Should I accept her invitation? Invite her over and keep the conversation to benign matters, like Mrs. Garcia's Foursquare? *No*, I thought. Avoiding the sticky subject of my haunting would feel like too much work.

"Well, I'm pretty bushed and I think I just want to go home and put my feet up," I said. "But thanks anyway."

"Oh, okay. You can play the avoidance game if you want. But it's not helping anything. I have to get going. Take care."

A second later, she was gone.

—

At home, I mindlessly spooned up lukewarm soup as I sat staring at the partial portrait of Hugh on my computer. Off to the left of the screen, just barely visible, was the rim of a glass. The goblet with the twist, no doubt. If only Carol had taken more care to include the whole scene.

But there would be pictures of eighteenth-century wine goblets somewhere online. I closed out of the portrait and quickly found a website with rows of ancient glasses and stemware. I clicked on a goblet that looked similar to the one in my dreams. A twist swirled through the stem like a glittering crystal helix. A beautiful creation shot through with the heart of its maker. Simple, elegant, a story in and of itself.

Weary yet wide awake, I settled into bed with Edward Koch's little history. In the next few chapters, he unspooled more of the story of the Jones estate—the construction of the house through 1760, Hugh's marriage to Miranda Prescott, and the birth of their children.

The family was regarded as somewhat Bohemian by their far-flung neighbors, Koch wrote. *But not much is known about the personal affairs of their household.*

Bohemian. What would qualify someone as Bohemian in the eighteenth century? Wearing reds and purples to church on Sunday? More importantly, did it have anything to do with what was happening in my house?

There is an account of an incident in 1760 that resulted in the bringing of an inquest, Koch continued. *A record of the final determination has not been found.*

An inquest? Had Hugh been involved in some kind of dispute or even a criminal matter? Had the rum trade led to—

Upstairs, the floorboards creaked. I held my breath. Maybe I'd imagined it.

Don't jump at every little noise.

Then a door slammed. "Not again!" I whispered, my heart galloping. Buck sprang to the floor and trotted into the hall. I tossed the book aside and got out of bed. What to do?

It was eleven o'clock. Too late to drag Harry out.

"Buck!" I called, inching into the hall. I went to the third-floor stairway and switched on the ceiling light. "Buck!"

Slam! The dog barked. Then came the creak of hinges.

I could run downstairs, throw on a coat and...no, where

would I go? And what about my animals? I couldn't leave them.

Gathering every nerve I could, I climbed to the landing and looked up to the third-floor hallway. Buck appeared and blinked down at me. Then he turned and walked back to where he'd come from, as if he wanted me to follow. I lifted my foot from the landing and began to climb. I had to face it down, whatever it was.

The hall was empty. A faint murmur drifted from the west room.

Be brave, Libby. Be brave!

I took in a cleansing breath and called into the room. "Who's there? What do you want? Please, just go away!"

The murmuring ceased.

"Buck?" His shaggy shadow stood beside the dark oblong of the open closet door. Harry had closed that door the night he'd come over, and I hadn't touched it since.

"Come here," I called to Buck. He turned, hesitated, and then padded to me at the doorway. I shouted into the room again. "I don't want you here! Go away!" The dog looked up, confused. "No, not you," I said, and I led him back downstairs.

Still shaken, I took a pill and locked my bedroom door. Fat lot of good that would do. A locked door wouldn't keep him out. But at the back of my mind, the question I'd been asking myself over and over. What did he want?

If he meant to do me harm, he had not yet done so. Why? What was he waiting for?

—

After breakfast the next morning, I went back to the third floor, feeling braver in the daylight. The closet door in the west room still stood ajar. I knew this was the door that had slammed last night. Slammed and then creaked open. Buck had known it too.

I pulled the door wide and yanked the chain hanging from a light bulb screwed into the ceiling. The same plaster walls and the same wood shelves, but there had to be something else. I scoured the interior, moving slowly from one side to the other, and found nothing unusual. I was just about to give up when my eyes caught on something down to the right of the door frame. A trail of nicks and scores carved into two of the pine planks, half obscured by a layer of dust. I bent down and wiped the dust away.

The marks didn't appear fresh—their edges weren't sharp as they would be if they'd just been made—but they did look deliberate. Slashes and lines, mostly, almost like hieroglyphics. But here and there was something that looked rounder, curvier, with a loop or a tail, like a letter in old-fashioned script. I wiped at the dust again. One of the letters appeared to be an *L*, another an *A*, and at the end of one trail were little figures that looked like…what were they? Wings?

The chime of the grandfather clock reminded me that I was running late for work. I closed the closet door and went downstairs. It was possible that long ago a child had made those marks, idling away a rainy day with a whittling knife. But somehow, I didn't think so.

Very soon, I would clear the rest of my belongings out of the west room and padlock it shut. Then I would call Cassie and get started on that cleansing.

CHAPTER THIRTY-ONE

I closed the door to Moffitt's and started down the street. Harry had gotten back from an appointment earlier than he expected, so I'd walked up to the jewelry store to retrieve the necklace. A genuine eighteenth-century Dobbs worth around eighty thousand dollars, Jenny had reported as I stared, speechless. "I imagine it could fetch even more at auction," she said.

I turned the corner at Main Street, feeling a little nervous with such a valuable object in my satchel. Jenny had given me a copy of Horst's appraisal and the name of a reputable insurance company that dealt in antique jewelry. Until the paperwork was completed, I would keep the necklace in my safe deposit box at the bank.

"Well, look who it is!"

Cassie Hughes was coming out of the deli, her hand raised in greeting. A perfect opportunity had just presented itself.

"Libby Casey," she said. She hoisted a paper deli bag. "Just getting some lunch. How's it going? How's that house coming along?"

"Actually, Cassie, you know the cleansing we talked about? I might want to get that number from you."

"Oh? What's going on?"

"I'm not sure. Some noises, like I said before, and just the feeling that maybe I'm not alone there. And I was thinking about what Ross Phillips told you."

A car horn honked on the street behind me, and for a moment Cassie's attention was drawn to the sound. She waved to whoever was driving by and then settled her eyes back on me. "Well, I myself have never used Sharon, of course. But I hear she's very good at this sort of thing. I'll find her number and call you."

"I'd appreciate it. I'd like to take care of this as soon as possible and then just move on, if you know what I mean. And Cassie, I'd like it if you kept this to yourself for now."

"Of course, Libby. Well, I've got to get back to the shop. This delicious sandwich is calling." She aimed a fond smile at the bag. "Reuben special with chips and a pickle. One of my favorites."

A Reuben sandwich with potato chips. Still not following doctor's orders. A stab of annoyance pricked me as I watched her turn the corner at Greenwood Street. Maybe it was time to have a talk with her. But not until I got Sharon's number.

I took out my phone and called Harry. "I'm outside the deli. Want anything?"

"What're the specials?" he asked.

"Reuben sandwich and…" I looked over at the chalkboard in the deli window. "…grilled chicken on Caesar and minestrone soup."

"Soup it is. In fact, pick up two, will you? I'll take one home for Mitch."

—

Back at the office, Harry and I talked about our mornings as we spooned in our minestrone. Harry's annual medical checkup, my encounter with Cassie, and finally Jenny's report on the necklace.

"I'll feel a lot better once it's locked in the bank," I said. "By the way, if a bus hits me tomorrow, let Maddie know where it is."

Harry took his last sip of soup, dropped the round paper carton into a trash can under his desk, and opened the wax bag holding a sandwich he'd brought from home. "So do I get a look at this award winner before that happens?"

"Oh! Of course," I said, reminded now that he had seen only a photo of the necklace. I dug the drawstring bag out of my satchel and removed a swath of navy-blue velvet. "Here it is." I laid the little packet on Harry's desk and pulled back its folds to reveal the now gleaming jewelry.

"My God, Lib, that's a real stunner." He leaned in to study it. "I'm seeing Cary Grant in a black turtleneck on the French Riviera."

"Cat burglar, right?"

Harry nodded. "This is the kind of thing he would have specialized in, before he started specializing in Grace Kelly."

I laid a finger to the curve of open work. "I can understand the impulse. It is beautiful, isn't it? Jenny said I could sell it at auction. But I'm leaning toward keeping it and replacing the missing ruby. What do you think?"

"Then you better wear it sometimes. Otherwise, what's the point?"

"True," I said, lifting the necklace from the velvet and letting it dangle from my fingers. "I'm wondering what the point is, period. I mean, what Hugh had in mind when he left me this, and why he didn't leave it to one of his daughters way back when."

"Still have the hair?"

I nodded. "Maybe we could have Hugh exhumed and compare it for DNA." This idea raised a question in my head.

Where was Hugh buried?

I laid the necklace back on the velvet. "Even if I did replace the ruby, what occasion would call for something this special?"

"We do have that fancy affair coming up in April that the historical society's planning."

"The fundraiser for the 1825 House, you mean?"

Harry leaned back in his chair. "Cassie told me it's going to be quite the event, formal, expensive, and all that. They'll need a lot of donations to add to that grant they've gotten."

The thought of attending a big affair in a room full of chatty people felt less appealing at this moment than being dragged behind a team of horses. "Not sure I'll attend. It's a long way off, and who knows?"

Harry nodded at the necklace. "If you wear that, I'll be your date."

"Okay, Mr. Grant. Deal."

I went back to my desk, tucked the necklace into the drawstring bag, and stowed it safely in my satchel. "I was just wondering a minute ago about where Hugh is buried."

"Sue Kunkel probably knows."

"Maybe he's under my floorboards," I said, only half in jest, thinking about the upstairs closet.

Should I tell him about that? I wondered. The door slamming again. The marks on the closet floor?

"Lib?" Harry was calling from across the office. I looked up. He narrowed his blue-green eyes. "Need anything?"

"Thanks, Harry. I'm good."

—

After leaving the bank, I stopped at the supermarket and made a quick round of the aisles, relieved that the necklace was now locked away.

A display of granola stopped me in my tracks. Bags of it lined up in a cardboard shipper, grouped in color-coded packages according to their flavors. The brand Ray used to eat, his favorite being the one with the red stripe on the label. Hazelnuts, dried apples, and cinnamon. He would come home from the store with three or four bags at a time, and within a few weeks they would be gone. "Where are you putting it all?" I once asked him. He grinned and laid a hand to his stomach and said, "The Meachum furnace, honey."

I took a bag from the shelf and dropped it into my cart, then stood looking down at it. Why had I done that? The last time Ray ate it, right after starting the clinical trial, he threw it back up, and he never ate it again.

The trial had ended a few weeks before Christmas. *Sorcery*, he'd called it. Our last resort. After it was over, he spent most days on the sofa with Buck, trying to recover. Behind him, in the corner, the big Douglas fir tree Cal had helped me wrestle into the house winked its white lights, lending an improbable note of cheer.

One evening, I was in the kitchen making dinner when a thud sounded overhead. I ran upstairs and found Ray lying on the bedroom floor. His eyes were closed.

"What happened?" I asked. "Ray!"

He opened his eyes and tried to focus. "Yeah, I'm here."

"I'm calling an ambulance." I reached for the phone on the night table.

"No, baby. Forget it, please. I'm okay. I just missed my step gettin' out of bed."

As I helped him up, I felt how weak he was, how shaky, like a newborn foal. "I don't know, Ray. Just let me call."

"I'm not goin' to the hospital!" he said, hoarse but emphatic, his eyes pleading. "We'll call Doc Hwang on Monday. I promise."

He got into bed, and I propped a pillow behind him. "She's going to be mad, you know. That you didn't go to the hospital. And she's not the only one."

"Two women mad at me at the same time," Ray said, trying for a smile that never quite broke. "That's the wrong kind of trouble."

"This is all the wrong kind of trouble," I said, and I went downstairs and cried.

Shoppers streamed around me as I stared down at the bag of granola in my shopping cart. Suddenly, I felt done with it. It was a relic from the past, and that's where I wanted it to stay. I took the bag out of my cart and put it back on the shelf.

CHAPTER THIRTY-TWO

December 1760

Sipping cold tea from a cracked cup, Hugh paced. The house was finally quiet, everyone abed. Night was closing in. Back and forth, back and forth. His boot heels echoed on the kitchen floorboards.

Martha Little Cloud had arrived with Hattie that afternoon and laid out a square of threadbare linen, three clay crocks, and a ragged eagle's plume. While Priscilla and Sam took the children out for a long ride through the orchard, Martha settled into the kitchen with Miranda and Hattie to commence her cure. Hugh had waited in the parlor, Martha's low incantations drifting down the hall like the strains of a sacred song. Like his mother's Welsh prayers that had sounded so much like music.

"Pray for us now, Mother," he whispered, swallowing the last of his tea. "Pray to all your pantheon of ancient spirits that Miranda will be healed. This is our very last chance."

The scent of burnt herbs still lingered. He lit a lamp from

the fire's embers, went upstairs to the lumber room, and took out his diary. Much of it was now filled, and he would soon be on to the other one.

He dipped his quill in the inkpot and recorded the day's events, concluding with a solemn wish that the Lord would bring Miranda the peace she was deserving of. Then he signed it with his usual *HPJ*.

The lamp flame sputtered and flared. Gods, he was weary. To his bones. A candle would burn, melt, and wink out. And so too would a life. But that was a melancholy thought, and tonight he would admit only hope.

In the bedchamber, he sponged the day's grit from his face, neck, and hands, dropped to the straw mattress, and fell quickly away. Miranda's voice woke him sometime later.

"Hugh Peter!"

Her place in the bed was empty. "Miranda?"

"Here!" She stood at the window, bathed in moonlight. "I am afraid," she whispered.

"Afraid?" Had she suffered some new torment? He got up and joined her.

"Something is terribly wrong, isn't it?" Her face was a map of worry in the silver light. "I am not me, am I?"

"Nonsense." Hugh brushed a lock of hair from her shoulder. "You are most certainly you. You are Miranda Felicity Jones, as fine and fair a woman as you always were."

"But I don't feel like it. Sometimes, I don't feel like it." Tears brimmed in her eyes.

Hugh took her hands in his. They were trembling. "Miranda, my sweet. You have had some troubling moods. And now we must see to it that your trouble ends."

"Martha is seeing to it, isn't she?"

"Aye, and she will return if we need her." Hugh gathered her in, his heart aching with pity but also lifted by hope, for this sudden presence of mind surely bode well. Perhaps Martha's cure had already taken hold.

"Please, Husband. You must keep me safe. And the children, the poor children. Have I been an inadequate mother?"

"No, and they love you, as do I. We will all keep you safe. Now, back to bed, shall we?"

Hugh settled Miranda under the quilt and slipped in beside her. Yes, with any good fortune, Martha's cure was taking hold.

—

Three days later, he was chopping the trunk of an old oak that had toppled beside the barn, thinking that the axe was not so sharp as it should be, when Priscilla called breathlessly behind him. "Mr. Jones! The sheriff! He's come back!"

"For the sake of Saint Peter," Hugh muttered, throwing down the axe. He'd hoped the bloody buzzard had given up. "Is he alone?"

"Yes, sir. But the mistress, she—"

A shot rang out. A musket report.

"What the blasted hell!" Hugh sped toward the house, Priscilla behind him, calling, "In the front!"

Hugh rounded the corner of the house. Gunpowder tanged the air, and the pinched voice of Sheriff Gates was squawking like a crow. "For the love of God, woman! Are you mad?"

Miranda stood outside the front door, the Brown Bess raised to her shoulder, her hair disheveled, half loose from its knot. James Martin cowered behind her, crying. Thirty feet away stood the sheriff.

"What the devil is going on?" Hugh pried the musket away from Miranda.

"Your wife is a lunatic, sir!" Gates shook a fist in the air. "She has fired upon me!"

"He is not welcome here!" Miranda whipped her head toward Hugh, her eyes wild in a way that chilled him. "Tell him he's not welcome."

Hugh felt a tug on his breeches. James Martin looked up, his face wet with tears. "I'm frightened, Daddy."

"Go with Prissy," Hugh said, urging his son toward Priscilla's outstretched hand in the doorway, and Priscilla led the boy away.

"Mr. Jones." The sheriff took a few steps closer and waved a scroll of paper in Hugh's direction. "This writ is for you, sir, and I mean to deliver it! And I can tell you it will not go well that your wife has made an attempt on the life of a king's officer."

"King's slattern is more like it," Miranda chided. "Foul devil." She turned to Hugh, again with that look like a cornered beast. "He means to harm us!"

"Miranda! Please! Go inside. I will deal with the sheriff."

"They told me to stop him," she whispered hoarsely. "For Sam! They told me to."

"And so, we shall," Hugh said. "I am sending him away this minute."

It was only as Miranda stepped into the house that Hugh noticed her feet were bare. Unshod feet on a December morning that had already turned the barrel of the Bess to ice.

"Mr. Jones!" Gates called. He threw the scroll of paper to the ground. "I shall come no further. Please see that you read that. It will inform you of an inquest to be held two weeks from next Tuesday at the Court." He turned and strode toward the horse tied to a post by the lane.

Hugh went and picked up the scroll, which was sealed with a circle of wax. A tiny wet flake settled onto it and then another landed on Hugh's hand. He watched the sheriff ride away, snow beginning to litter down. A knot tightened in his belly. Miranda's flashing eyes, her grip on the gun.

Lunatic. He shuddered.

CHAPTER THIRTY-THREE

I didn't think I would see Keith Janus again until the start of his project, and neither did I prepare for it. But fate had something else in mind when I woke up Wednesday morning to an unusually chilly house. I thought at first that the heat had gone out. But when I went downstairs, Buck trotting ahead, I discovered what had happened. The big pane of glass in the laundry room door had shattered and was now lying in shards on the linoleum floor. Frigid air washed in through the gaping hole.

"Now what?" I muttered to the dog, pulling my bathrobe tighter around me, regretting that I hadn't done something about the crack sooner.

A new door was out of the question anytime soon. It would need to be custom ordered to fit the ancient doorframe, which could mean weeks of waiting. I would just have to board it up. Or rather, someone would have to board it up for me. Who would be available to help? Cal, maybe? I thought about my last conversation with Diana. *Maybe not.* And not Harry, either, because he was spending the day with his mother.

I dialed a few of March & Casey's contractors but got no answer anywhere. No doubt they were all busy on job sites. Desperate, I called Keith. He once said he'd worked summer construction jobs while in college. Not that you needed to be very handy to nail a piece of plywood to a door. I would have done it myself if I could have handled the heavy slab of wood.

But how would it look, me asking him for help after turning down a date?

He answered on the second ring. I explained my dilemma. "But if you're busy in any way, please don't come," I said, giving him an escape hatch that I hoped he wouldn't use.

"No, just hang tight. I'll need to stop at the hardware store."

I cleaned up the glass rubble and taped a bedsheet over the hole, thankful that my pets hadn't gotten out and that a fox or raccoon hadn't gotten in. Then I shoved some frozen scones into the oven and put on some coffee, changed my clothes, and took Buck for a quick walk. Back at the house, I lit a blaze in the kitchen fireplace. Inside of me sparked a little flame of anticipation.

Thirty minutes later, Keith arrived with a toolbox and a hand-held saw. "Something smells good," he said. His hair looked newly cut. Under his brown winter jacket, he wore a sweatshirt that bore the words *Wild Thing* across the image of a green forest.

"Your consolation prize," I said. "Thanks for saving me."

"This is some place you've got here. When you told me it was old, I didn't imagine this."

"It's a 1760 Georgian. But don't let looks deceive you. It needs lots of work."

I led him back to the laundry room, where he pulled the sheet down from the door to examine the damage. "That is a pretty big hole," he said. "I can see why you wanted it taken care of right away. I'll go get the plywood out of my truck. Is there somewhere I can cut it down?"

"In the garage. You'll find a couple of old sawhorses and an outlet and light."

"Super," he said. He pulled a retractable metal tape measure from his jacket pocket.

Measure twice, cut once. Ray. He must have had four or five tape measures lying around his workshop at any given time. He was forever losing one and buying another.

When Keith finally finished boarding up the door, I dropped two more logs on the fire and we sat in the kitchen, sipping coffee and eating scones, Buck in his bed by the fireplace. *A comfortable arrangement*, as my father liked to say. And it was, perhaps *too* comfortable.

"Do you think you could show me around the place?" Keith asked after we finished our coffee. "I'd really like to see it."

How could I refuse? He had rescued me.

Leading him up to the third floor first, I resisted the temptation to take him into the west room to see the slash marks on the closet floor. I wondered whether Hugh Jones was spying on us from some dark corner there, plotting his next move.

"This place has fantastic character," Keith remarked as we drifted down to the second floor. "All this woodwork is pretty cool."

After a peek into the three bedrooms and the fourth, smaller room, Keith stopped to study the big photograph of Ray on the pitcher's mound. "Who's this?" he asked.

"That's Ray, my husband."

"Wow, you didn't mention that he played ball."

I shrugged. "Just didn't get around to it. Meachum was his name. Ray Meachum."

"No kidding. You were married to Ray Meachum?" Keith turned back to the photo. "My father practically cried when he had to give up the game."

We talked briefly about Ray's baseball career, and his second wind making furniture. I tapped the demilune table that sat against the wall under the photograph. "This reproduction is one of his pieces."

Keith shoved his hands into the pockets of his jeans. "He was a very talented guy." His look turned inward then, as if he was considering something. "I'm guessing that was his classic Chevy out in the garage?"

I nodded.

"Well, I guess I should let you get back to your day."

Downstairs, he thanked me for the coffee and scone, lifted his cup and plate from the table, and took them to the sink. *God loves a man who cleans up after himself.* My mother.

"Keith," I said as he pulled his jacket from a chair. I had no idea what I was going to say next. Then I said it. "Do you believe in ghosts?"

His bronze eyes met mine, the jacket held in mid-lift. "As in the haunting kind?"

"What other kinds are there?" I asked, trying to smile.

"So, are you saying this house is haunted?"

The fire gave a loud snap and a hiss. "Maybe. I mean, aren't all old houses haunted?" A supposition I hadn't until recently believed.

He set his jacket back over the chair. "Have you seen something?"

"I've heard things. It's hard to know whether it's the house settling or what." Half the truth was all I felt willing to tell.

"Well, I've never had the experience myself. But I believe others have. There have been too many stories to rule it out. Do you feel like it's a problem for you?"

"Oh, no, no. I'm good. I just have to get used to it, I think."

"Okay," he said with a skeptical tone. "Let me know if things change." He took up his jacket again and pulled it on, still seeming to ponder. "That plywood should hold pretty well for now. If it doesn't, give me a call."

At the front door, Keith thanked me for the tour. "You've got a real piece of history here," he said. "I hope the ghosts don't give you too much trouble."

He'd gone six feet down the walkway when I remembered the bag of scones I had packed for him. "Keith!" I called out, holding up a finger to signal him to wait.

When I returned from the kitchen, he was standing at the door.

"Tomorrow's breakfast," he said, taking the bag. After a pause, "I'm sorry about your husband. He sounds like a one-of-a-kind guy. I can tell you're still trying to get over the loss. Not that we ever really get over those things. I guess we just learn to move on."

If only he knew how much I wanted to move on.

I offered a modest little smile. "Yes, it takes time," I said. And as I closed the door behind him, I wondered whether, after what I'd done to Ray, all the time in the world would be enough.

CHAPTER THIRTY-FOUR

The next day, Harry and I did a walk-through at Mrs. Garcia's Foursquare. It had taken longer than we thought it would, so when we got back to the office late in the afternoon, we decided to call it quits. At home, I worked through a preliminary design for the project so we could quote her a price as quickly as she had requested. Fix rotting wood trims and porch boards, replace a dozen windows, refinish interior hardwoods and moldings, repair built-ins and paint the entire first floor in understated neutrals, but not gray—

Elizabeth!

I paused with my hands over the keyboard. Out of the corner of my eye, a shadow moved near the fireplace. I looked up, and it was gone. Buck continued dozing on the rug.

"Are you here?" I called.

Always here, Elizabeth!

I shut my laptop with a defiant snap, which made Buck raise his head. "Are you going to stay forever, Mr. Jones, skulking around my house, whispering and slamming doors? Stay away from the third floor! And stay away from me!" A linen drape on one of the front windows stirred. "This is a sick little game, and I am not your plaything! If you want something, for God's sake, spit it out."

I pictured myself packing up everything I owned, closing the door behind me, and dragging my tired bones to a new house that wasn't haunted and where I might sleep at night. I could do it if I had to. I could.

When he didn't speak again, I stood up and turned out the lamp. *Always here.* What did he mean by that?

Buck rose to all fours. "I still have you, my precious boy," I whispered. "Wherever we go, we're together. You, me, and Sugar Plum too."

In the morning, I pulled on my gray trouser suit and a good teal blouse. A little more formal than I felt, but I'd been neglecting the laundry, and my basket was nearly full of my more casual options. After breakfast and a walk with Buck, I packed my lunch and went to fetch my laptop. I tried to look ahead to the day, a little drugged from the sleeping pill I had taken. I kept relying too much on the pills, but I was desperate for rest.

Reaching to the desk for my laptop, I stopped when I saw a piece of paper next to the computer scrawled with old-fashioned cursive. *When there is naught to be done, who shall guide us?* Next to the paper lay Ray's Cross fountain pen, the cap beside it. Was Hugh taking a new tack? Writing to me now instead of speaking?

I read the message again. "This is a riddle!" I cried. "And I don't know what to do with it!"

Suddenly I thought of Emmeline. It sounded like something she might say, *who shall guide us*, or at least might understand. She would be coming over for the open house in a week. Maybe I ought to call and remind her. I dialed the school and left a voicemail that I packaged as a friendly request that she wasn't to bring anything but herself. Then I put the paper with Hugh's message in the desk drawer, packed up my things, and left for work.

—

As I pulled into the driveway that evening, my cell chimed. Carol Seabrook. I turned off the Prius and answered. In a breathless rush of words, she said she had returned to town and could bring me the painting from her aunt's house. "I've probably got a few other things you might like. Might bring them too. Aunt Dot won't miss them, and frankly, she's not doing well, poor thing. I'm her executor so... If Sunday works, I'm coming into Simms to visit friends."

"Yes, of course," I said. "I could make coffee, if you like."

"No, no, thank you. My husband will be with me, and I'll only have time to hand it off."

"I heard it used to hang here in the house a long time ago," I said.

"Yeah, Uncle Dan taped a note to the back of it. An ancestor of some sort, I think."

Of some sort, yes. I silently thanked Dan, the lone stalwart in a sea of familial indifference.

"Well, gotta run," Carol said. "See you around one on Sunday."

That night, a new energy coursed through me as I made dinner and walked the dog and finished up some work in the office. I would finally lay eyes on the portrait of Hugh Peter Jones. It was as close as I'd ever get to the flesh and blood of the man haunting my house, and I very much wanted to—*had* to—see him.

—

On Saturday morning, I finally got around to painting the hall bathroom. Then I ate a quick lunch and drove into town to get that lamp for Maddie and Jeff. Something for the new apartment they would be moving into together. Since it would soon be too late to find them something else, I was relieved to see the lamp was still there.

After a stop at the hardware store for a new string of tree lights, I drove back to Chambers Road in the waning winter sun. I hadn't yet managed to get a Christmas tree to *put* the lights on. But today would not be the day.

At home, I took the lamp from its box and set it on the dining room table. A real 1940s beauty, pale green with delicate gilt fern leaves floating down the round belly, and antique brass feet. I imagined a woman dusting it back in the day as she listened to news of the war on her RCA Victor radio. Maybe she had a husband or a son in France or the Pacific, and she left the lamp on at night like a beacon. That's what I would have done. A beacon to guide him home.

My cell phone chimed with a call. Diana. I paused. Would I regret answering?

"So, I haven't heard from you lately," she said by way of a greeting. "Any news about anything?"

"Quite a bit. But we can save it for later."

"Try me."

"I don't know."

Diana let a beat go by. The familiar tension buzzed. "I ran into Cassie yesterday."

Oh, no. How much had Cassie told her? Maybe she assumed Diana already knew about everything.

"She said you're going to get the house cleansed. To get rid of the spirits. It felt weird to get that kind of news about my best friend from a third party."

"I didn't think you'd be interested. And it's spirit, singular, as far as I know. Hugh, remember?"

"I'd like to forget. And not to put too fine a point on it, I think you should, too."

"Well, I can't, since this is my house, and I need to deal with it. I need to see it through." When she didn't respond, I said,

"Look, Dee, let's not run over old ground here. Believe what you want to believe. But I need to do something. Doors are slamming, he's leaving me messages, the necklace is insanely valuable. There's something wrong here, and I need to—"

"Whoa, sweetie! Slow down and take a breath! I'm beyond worried about you now."

"Then help me out and go with it, or just go on—"

"One of us has to have some sense here, and I guess it's me. And I'm telling you to get out of there!"

"And what? Live at a hotel? I have two animals and a mortgage."

"You can come here."

"Cal's allergic to cats, remember?"

Someone called Diana's name on the other end. "I have to go. Lucky you."

"Are you coming next week? To the open house?"

"Do you want me to?"

"Your choice." I hung up without saying goodbye. Then I stood in the kitchen and cried.

"I'm losing my best friend because of you!" I said to the phantom of Hugh Peter Jones, wherever he was. "I hope you're happy."

CHAPTER THIRTY-FIVE

Carol Seabrook had come and gone. Now I was alone in the center hall, looking down at the painting leaning against the wall, concealed behind the sheath of a large plastic trash bag. I tugged off the bag, tossed it to the floor, and took a deep breath.

There he was, sitting in his chair by the fire, one leg crossed over the other, his hand resting beside a goblet with a helix snaking through its stem.

I carried Hugh's portrait into my office and set it down in front of the bookcase by the window. It was about three feet tall and almost as wide, with a pale gilded wood frame. A daylight scene, not the shadowy dark of my dreams, everything clear and visible. The pedestal table, the goblet, the fire and carved green mantelpiece above it. I spun around with a sudden realization. *My* mantelpiece, except that it was now white. This was the room where the portrait had been painted.

Suddenly, I needed a drink. In the kitchen, I grabbed one of the quarts of Belgian ale I'd been saving for the open house and filled a pint glass. The first gulp of tangy brew sluiced down my throat in a cold, satisfying stream.

With pint in hand, I returned to the office and sipped as I studied the portrait's finely rendered details—the metallic glint of the shoe buckles, the slight sheen of the fingernails, Hugh's mysterious almost-smile, like the Mona Lisa's, and the keen amber of his eyes. Except for the stray sable curl falling over his cheek, his hair was held back in a ribbon, one end of it poking out from behind his earlobe, subtly textured, like the grosgrain pinched around the hair in the locket.

This portrait was as good as any that might hang in a museum. I scoured the canvas for a signature and found it tucked down in the right corner. A single word that made me feel woozy.

Miranda.

Hugh's wife had painted this. I gulped some ale. Miranda an artist? My eyes went back to Hugh with a new, more curious interest. The playful smile, almost coy, the invitation in his eyes, even the posture that was mannered yet relaxed. Hugh as Miranda saw him. I thought of my father's photographs of my mother, the intimate connection, the story behind the story.

Buck wandered in. "Now what?" I asked, finishing off the ale. He looked from the portrait to me and then back to the portrait again. "My thoughts exactly."

I would need to store the painting until Carol returned for it, but not in a closet. Locking Hugh away in a dark space didn't seem the proper thing to do. After all, he had been imprisoned in Dan and Dot Seabrook's basement for untold years.

"How long since you've seen the light of day?" I inquired, tipsy from the ale.

I gazed up to where the Wyeth hung above the fireplace and imagined the portrait there, where it might have hung once.

"Let's put you somewhere safe," I said. As I pulled the frame away from the bookcase, my eye caught on a dusty yellow Post-it stuck to the back. The note Carol told me about. I had completely forgotten. I peeled it off and read the big block letters. *HUGH JONES 1762?*

The question mark told me Dan wasn't certain about the date. But if he was correct, Hugh would have been thirty-one at the time, and Miranda would have been...in the last year or even months of her life.

I carried the painting to the living room, draped it with a throw from the sofa, and leaned it against the wall, backside out. I would figure out a better arrangement later.

Buck escorted me back to the kitchen and flopped down in his bed. I stood at the counter with a fresh pour of ale and stared out the big double window. Miranda dying in her prime, the painting lost for so long, Hugh—

Bonk, bonk, bonk. The door knocker.

I turned briskly and a tide of ale sloshed from my glass onto my shirt and jeans. "Coming," I called. Buck was already trotting through the dining room and into the hall.

I paused as I reached for the doorknob. What if Carol Seabrook had returned for some reason I couldn't immediately fathom? What would she think of me, tipsy at two o'clock in the afternoon, my clothes soaked with ale?

I opened the door to a blinding flare of sun. A box stood upright in front of me, asking to be let in, the UPS driver already pulling away. I dragged the box into the hall—a Christmas gift I'd ordered for Diana—and shoved it against the wall. I would worry about the gift and Diana later.

My stomach growled. Food. I needed food. Back in the kitchen, I mixed up some tuna salad, opened a jar of olives, and plucked two up with a thumb and finger. *Get a spoon, Elizabeth.* I pushed Annabelle's ghost down below the surface of my ale-soaked brain and held her there until she stopped breathing. I would eat my olives in peace.

I devoured the tuna and swallowed back the last of the glittering amber liquid in my glass. Time was, Ray and I could finish off two pints each of Chimay on a warm summer night.

Getting mellow, he called it.

My mind returned to the painting. Should I let Susannah know about it? Invite her over to see? Maybe not, for she might try to pry it away from Carol, thinking what a fine addition it would make to the historical society collection, how good it would look on the wall of the bungalow. No, it couldn't end up on the wall of the bungalow. Too chilly in there anyway.

I stood up, wobbling. Buck stirred in his bed and then rose to all fours, hopeful for a walk.

"Not right now," I said. "I need a nap." Then I found my way to the living room, flopped onto the sofa, and fell dead away.

—

The grandfather clock woke me with its chime. It was dark. I rolled over, my arm numb and heavy. I shook out the pins and needles. From somewhere in the room came my dog's soft huff. Switching on the lamp, I spotted him beside Hugh's portrait, his copper stare trained on me. The throw cover lay heaped on the floor.

Buck trudged over and nudged my hand. "I know, a walk," I said, still woozy. "Come on, sweet boy. Let's go. But you need to eat first."

The chilly night air revived me only a little, and by the time we returned to the house, fatigue was setting in, along with a pounding headache. I wasn't hungry for dinner, so I locked up the house and went upstairs. It was six thirty, but it felt like midnight.

Falling quickly to sleep, I found myself transported to a deserted street in an old city, vaguely European, the cafés and shops all closed. And suddenly there was Ray, walking ahead of me in his charcoal suit, the one he wore for our wedding, and when I called to him, he ignored me. Out of nowhere, an old woman stepped up beside me, and we both watched him disappear down the street.

"You've sent him away," she said, and in that moment, I

knew he was gone forever.

—

My cell phone rang, rousing me from sleep. Daylight was washing through the blinds and the linen drapes; I'd neglected to close them the night before. I let the call go to voicemail. My head ached, begging for some coffee and aspirin. I looked over at the clock. 9:30.

I sprang up and tossed back the covers. On my phone, a voicemail from Harry, short and to the point. He was concerned, said I should call as soon as I could. When he didn't answer his cell, I called the office. No answer there, either. I hoped he wasn't on his way over. I didn't want him to see me this way.

I shuffled to the bathroom, switched on the overhead light, and then switched it off. Maybe it was the hangover, but the shabby 1970s finishes seemed to have taken a turn for the worse overnight. I tried not to look at any one thing too closely as I gulped down a couple of extra-strength Bayer. Someday, the bathroom would be transformed—or maybe not if I followed my muddled instincts and moved out. Yes, if I moved out, it would become someone else's problem. This whole place would be someone else's problem.

And where was Cassie with that phone number, anyway?

After pulling on some sweats, I took the dog for a walk. A message from Harry was waiting when we got back to the house, so I put on some coffee and dialed him.

"I was ready to hire a posse," he said.

"Bad night...I mean day, or something. Too much to explain right now."

"Need reinforcements?"

"I'll let you know. I'm sorry about this morning. I think I need to work from home today."

"Well, it's pretty quiet here. Permits for Janus came in, by the way. So, there's some good news for you, in case you need some."

"I do and thank you. I'll check on those orders for the Jackson job. I think I can manage that much."

"Sure thing." He let a beat go by. "I heard from Diana this morning."

"And?"

"She's worried about you. And frankly, so am I."

"And Libby makes three. How about we talk tomorrow when my head is clear?"

"Lunch out?"

"Great idea, but not at the café. How about McGraw's?"

"Fair enough, but you two are going to have to straighten things out sooner or later."

"Right now, later sounds preferable. See you in the morning. And Harry..."

"Hmm?"

"Thanks for caring."

I nibbled some toast at the counter while coffee brewed, thinking of Harry's good news about the Janus permits. I hadn't seen Keith Janus since he boarded up my door. His sympathetic smile floated before me, the very last thing I'd seen of him as he turned to leave that day.

Then that smile rearranged itself into Ray's, the mouth going a little crooked, like the nose. I had seen that smile materialize thousands of times, a simple transformation that hitched up one side just a bit higher than the other. Yet as I stood trying to track it from beginning to end, to bring it to life once more, it, like his soft Virginia drawl, was becoming just a little more out of focus.

If I thought of the day we were married, that would help bring it back. Ray reciting the vows he'd written, his crooked smile beaming in the space between slate-blue eyes and the burgundy tie knotted at his throat. His charcoal suit—I still had it in the back of my closet. How beautiful he had looked in it. "Mind if I rip that off you later?" I'd said as we finished getting ready, the guests gathering in the backyard below. And he said,

"You better, baby."

I settled in at the kitchen table with a mug of coffee and the rest of my toast. The hammering in my head persisted. We hadn't wanted a big wedding, so we'd decided to have it at home. It was a fairy tale day, sky blue as Wedgewood, our apple tree by the back fence flowering white, the azaleas along the garage pink as cotton candy. Doc, Ray's best friend, retired from baseball and living in North Carolina, was best man. Diana was my matron of honor.

Diana. I should open that box and take out her gift. A vintage French dressing gown I'd found on Etsy. She had seen a similar one last year in a thrift store we were combing through one day. "I always wanted one of these," she said, declaring it *classy*. But in the end, she decided against buying it.

I let the box sit and instead made phone calls in my office while Sugar Plum dozed on the upholstered chair. At eleven o'clock, I headed to the kitchen to refuel with another cup of coffee.

In the hall, I stopped mid-stride, my attention suddenly drawn to the blank pale wall to my right. I had thought I might fill that space one day with a piece of art. But I was waiting for the right... I hurried to the kitchen, took one of Ray's metal tape measures and a pencil from a drawer. Then I went to the living room to get the portrait of Hugh. In an inspired flurry of activity, I fetched the stepladder, measured for the center of the wall between two sconces, and then tapped in a big picture hook.

Maybe I shouldn't do it, hang the portrait here as if it were mine. But I couldn't have stopped myself if I tried, and it would only be here a little while. And once Carol took it back, I would already have a hook in the wall for my next piece.

The portrait was unwieldy to hang, but I finally managed to settle its wire into the picture hook. I stepped down to the floor, adjusted the frame, and watched him, the man who once stood where I stood now, whose bootheels once echoed in this very hallway, who once was Miranda's coy muse.

"Is this what you want?" I whispered. "To hang on my wall?"

No. Hugh Peter Jones wanted something else, and whatever it was, there was trouble in it.

CHAPTER THIRTY-SIX

January 1761

Hugh steered Virgil toward the road and settled himself for the ride home from the village. Gray clouds loomed. The smell of snow was in the air.

Hanging from his saddle, the Brown Bess jumped with each step of the horse. He would need to put it back in the lumber room when he got home. He had kept it hidden there under a floorboard—with the old trunk on top of it—ever since that day Miranda fired on the sheriff. Only Priscilla and Sam knew where it was.

But what would it be next? The days were becoming more and more unpredictable. Miranda blustering about, shooing the children, speaking nonsense, or withdrawing to their bedchamber for days, silent and spent. Thanks be to God for Hattie, who had come more than once to calm her with a strong poppy tea or a decoction.

"It's a bloody ordeal that only gets worse," Hugh had said

one evening as he sat with her over cups of beer. "And there seems to be nothing to do about it."

Hattie curled her hand around his and said, "There isn't, Hugh. But you might think about hiring in a girl to help you keep order around here. Priscilla has her hands full with the children and the cooking, and frankly, she is beginning to look a bit—"

"Knackered, aye. I see it too. I'm afraid we are all done up with it. Me, the children..."

A tiny fleck settled on Virgil's mane, and then another and another. By the time they reached home, the ground was covered with white powder. Hugh stabled the horse with some hay and then hurried to the house with the gun and a new iron file he'd bought from John Lester's smithy. Finally, the axe would get a sharpening.

The smell of stewed hen met him at the back door. Suddenly, he was famished.

Sam looked up from where he was buttering a piece of bread at the table. "Your gods brought you home just in time." He gazed out the window. "The snow will fall for many hours yet. Prissy has taken James Martin out to see it."

Hugh stowed his haversack on a hook in the corner. "And how fares the rest of the household?"

"Miranda is in her bed this morning. And the twins as well."

"No incidents?"

Sam shook his head.

"It was good of you to come," Hugh said. At the sound of Priscilla's voice outside the door, he smiled at Sam. "You and Prissy getting along?"

Sam returned Hugh's smile. "As we always will. I am thinking of a marriage. She has the heart of a proud, young doe. Strong and true. But tell me, did the inquest go in our favor?"

"Aye, thanks be to God. Henry and one of his patrons told all the truth of it, word for word, the same. There will be no further action."

"I am much obliged to you, my friend." Sam offered a nod that held more than mere gratitude. "You risked much to protect me."

"And I would do so again." Hugh shook his head. "Will the day ever come when imperious men cease their persecutions?"

The back door opened, and Sam went to welcome Priscilla and James Martin in.

Hugh moved to the fire to warm himself, taking in the scent of hen and beans simmering in the pot, enjoying the blessed peace of the moment.

—

Over the next week, Miranda drifted about the house like a phantom in her shabbiest day gown, hair unkempt around her shoulders. Hugh tried to make a great ceremony of hanging the finished portrait over the parlor mantelpiece, thinking it would cheer her. But once it was hung, she gave it only a glancing look and wandered away.

One morning, he came upon her in the children's parlor. She was curled on the windowsill, pointing toward the yard, saying, "Isn't that curious? Isn't that so curious?" But when Hugh went to the window, nothing was there.

"Miranda," he whispered, putting a hand to her shoulder. "Shall we go out for a while? Some air will do you good."

She looked up at him, pale and confused. "Out? What is the month?"

"Today is the first of February."

"You go. Take those children. They are much too noisy here."

Those children. She said that as if she had no claim on them. "I think I shall," Hugh said. "Priscilla is here if you need her."

He turned to go, but she only went on staring out the window. Then she said, "Who is that other girl, the one who comes here sometimes?"

"Molly. Prissy's friend from the village, remember?" But of course, she didn't remember.

"I do not care for her. She doesn't belong here."

"It is only twice a week. You must accept her, for Prissy's sake."

Outside, Hugh bundled Abby, Alice, and James Martin into the wagon bed with a blanket. They chattered happily, excited for an adventure. His beautiful children, growing so quickly. The twins, past two years old now, and James Martin, a full-fledged boy, with a boy's curiosity about the world. The very picture of Miranda, with his honey hair and hazel eyes and merry countenance. A cruelty, if Hugh thought too long on it. For looking upon his son was too much like looking at his wife as she used to be.

He steered the wagon toward the lane. Were his children to be abandoned by the mother who had fed them at her breast and declared them to be "*God's own*"? Would they have from her no more goodnight kisses? No more adoring smiles?

His eyes stung with tears. He hadn't cried since he left Wales. He brushed his mitted hand against his cheek to wipe one away. The happy life he'd thought possible here felt distant to him now, like a memory, or a lost treasure never to be reclaimed.

—

Through late winter and spring, their household sank deeper into disorder. More and more, Miranda's behavior alarmed the children. The outbursts and agitations, the sullen silences.

"Please make Mama stop!" James Martin cried one afternoon as she paced in a fury up and down the hall, talking to someone unseen, saying, "Not now! Not now! Will you give me no peace?"

Angry, impatient, the work of the fields falling behind, Hugh had taken her by the arm and escorted her to her easel and the landscape she'd left smeared and abandoned in the children's parlor. "For the sake of Christ, Miranda, sit!" he ordered. "Paint!"

She turned like a rabbit and sped from the room. Hugh followed her as far as the kitchen, where she rushed past Priscilla and the tearful James Martin, and fled out the door.

"Miranda!" Hugh called after her. But she was gone.

"Shall I go find her?" Priscilla asked.

"No, let us wait a while."

It was not the first time Miranda had fled into the woods, nor was it likely to be the last. Sometimes it was the garden. Hugh once found her crouching over a bed, yanking up the lavender. She always returned.

But with supper eaten and night closing in, and Miranda still gone, Hugh saddled Gwydion, lit a lantern, and rode out to find her. After a long and fruitless search, he steered the horse to the footpath that led back to the house. He would fetch another lantern, ride to Sam, and ask for his assistance.

In front of the springhouse, Gwydion halted and struck the ground with his hoof. Hugh lowered the lantern. A shoe lay on the dirt, the horse's hoof flattening one side of it. Miranda's slipper.

He dropped down and picked it up. "Miranda! Where are you? Miranda!"

A sound like weeping drifted from the springhouse. Hugh held up his lantern and saw the door was open. He stepped inside. Miranda sat hunched on one of the stone ledges, beside jugs of milk Priscilla had left there that morning. Her face was wet with tears, her hands pinching at her linen skirt.

Hugh's heart twisted with pity. "Miranda, my sweet." He sat down and put his arm around her shoulder. "You must come home now."

"Home?" she said with a sniff. "I have no home, sir. They have taken it from me."

Hugh pulled her up and walked her to the door. An echo of that long-ago day came back to him, Miranda's sighs at his ear, her hair falling against his cheek. Their shameless pleasure in Eden.

But now a serpent was coiled around their tree.

CHAPTER THIRTY-SEVEN

McGraw's was quiet when Harry and I arrived. We slid into a booth in the dining room and shrugged off our coats. Harry blew on his hands.

"If it snows tonight as much as they're predicting," I said, "I'm not sure I'll get out of my driveway in the morning. I haven't gotten around to finding someone to plow."

Harry pushed his porcelain mug closer to the edge of the table, as if that would summon the waitress with the coffee sooner. "That winter I lived in New Hampshire. I almost forgot what my driveway looked like."

We talked about bad winters and snowfall records and how his mother had taken him sledding when he was a boy. "She got a real kick out of it," he said. "She was a big kid at heart."

The waitress arrived, took our order for coffee, and hurried away.

"And how *is* Helen?" I asked.

"Not speaking much anymore. When Mitch and I were in to see her last week, she looked pretty lost. But I guess that's how it goes when you don't know who anyone is anymore, or where you are."

"I'm sorry, Harry. I know how close you two always were. It might not feel like much consolation, but you've done the very best you can for her and that means a lot."

"The darn thing is, I keep wondering at the back of my mind whether that's the way I'll end up myself." He gave a little grimace of discontent.

"So far, you're the same sharp tack you always were," I assured him.

The waitress returned and poured our coffee. "Ready to order?"

We hadn't even looked at our menus, but we hardly needed to since we knew them almost by heart. I stared across at Harry. "How about some comfort food? A platter of McGraw's famous chicken nachos? And a couple bowls of tortilla soup? It feels like that kind of day."

"I'm in." Harry grinned up at the waitress. "We're going for broke today."

With the waitress gone, he returned to the subject of his mother. "I'm beginning to think it would be a mercy if she just died in her sleep one night. Why go on living when your life as you knew it is over? But none of us are in charge of that department."

On the rare occasion, we might be in charge, I thought. Or someone could be in charge for us. Should I say that now? Confess my crime?

"But tell me about the other day," he said. "The painting and all that."

"I know I shouldn't have, but I hung it in the center hall. I wanted to see how it would look there."

Harry eyed me for longer than a moment. "Guess I'll see it Saturday. Diana still coming?"

"I left it up to her. I haven't heard much from her lately. We're on a hiatus."

"Still set on the open house, with everything that's going on?"

"Yes, I still want to go through with it. It's tradition, and it feels like...normal. I need a dose of normal right now."

Harry nodded and sipped his coffee. "I get it. And as far as Diana's concerned, things are bound to get better."

"She's dug in, Harry. She's convinced I'm losing my grip, even though occasionally she makes the effort to humor me. Sometimes I wonder if there's more going on there, some reason she's so reluctant to believe me. Something more...I don't know...complicated."

The waitress arrived with two steaming bowls. As I spooned into my soup, Harry leaned back against the booth.

"We all have our complications, and sometimes it's hard for others to understand them," he said. "Diana's heart is in the right place. She's just hoping...you'll be okay. You have to admit that ever since you moved into the new house, you've lost a little ground."

"That's what Diana thinks."

He reached his hand across the table to mine. "Maybe it's time to take a breath and finally decide what the house means to you. If you still want to stay, we'll figure out what to do next."

With that, Harry began eating his soup. Having made his point, he wouldn't belabor it.

—

Fat flurries were falling as I pulled into my driveway that evening and eased the Prius into the garage beside the Malibu. So far, the weather forecast had been right on the nose about when the snow would start. Just in case a blizzard did happen, I had set the office phones to forward any calls that might come in the next day.

I hurried into the house and fed the animals. Ten minutes later, Buck was rocketing out the back door and into the dark. He chased about the yard beneath the light of the motion detector, snapping at flurries. Then he galloped off toward the woods.

I turned on my flashlight. When I caught up with him at the garden gate, he was nosing at something on the ground. "What is it?" I asked. I shone my beam down to an object on the dirt.

I picked it up and held it to the light. A little glass bottle, about six inches high and grimed with dirt. An old bottle, by the look of it.

Wind stirred and whipped around me. A storm gathering its power.

I shoved the bottle into my pocket. "Come on," I said. "We better get going."

When we got back, I stripped off my coat and gloves and examined the bottle under the ceiling lights. It was pale green, slim and rectangular, with a narrow neck that opened to a wider mouth, the rim tilting just a bit lower on one side than the other. The kind of imperfection that occurred when glass was blown by hand.

I washed it off at the sink. No imprint or label. Just a smooth glass surface with tiny bubbles encased here and there. A new puzzle piece to add to my collection. But where did it fit? I set it on the counter and tried not to think about it. My brain was done computing for the day. I opened the refrigerator. McGraw's nachos had ruined my appetite for dinner, but the big jug of cider stared out from between a milk carton and a bottle of chardonnay. Wassail.

I took out a pot, poured in the cider, and added some orange juice and spices. Then I set it on the stove. That's when I noticed the landline light blinking. Two messages. The first was from Tom Barrett, letting me know he plowed properties in the winter, and given the forecast, he could come plow mine tomorrow. The second was from Cassie with the number for Sharon Straub, the cleanser.

I called Sharon first. After asking me some questions about what was happening in my house, she said, "I'm positively certain I can help you." But she wasn't free until the first week of January, if that would be okay. I assured her it was, and we made the appointment.

Finally, I thought, feeling my mood lighten just a bit. I would get rid of Hugh Peter Jones.

I went and pressed my face against the Dutch door's window. Snow swirled like glitter in sweeping gusts of wind. Yes, I would need to be plowed. I called Tom back and accepted his offer.

I took my mulled cider to the living room, settled on the couch with Sugar Plum, and watched *A Christmas Carol* on TV. If Ebenezer Scrooge could banish his ghosts, so could I. Before going up to bed, I opened the back door to check on the storm's progress. The wind was whirring, blowing white dust everywhere. A half foot of snow had already accumulated. Ordinarily, Diana would call me during a snowstorm like this, or I would call her, and we would joke about needing a dog sled or warmer underwear or a plane ticket to Maui. But I knew Diana wouldn't call this night, and I wouldn't call her either.

A moment later, I found myself in the hall, staring up at the portrait of Hugh.

"I don't care about your little green bottle," I said. "In fact, I just might smash it to pieces. And then you and I are going to part ways."

Buck wandered into the hall. I turned out the light, and together we went upstairs, the sound of the wind keening all around us.

—

When I woke the next morning, a blinding white snow blanketed everything. I emptied two pills out of the aspirin jar in the bathroom, swallowed them back with a gulp of warm water, and let gravity pull me downstairs. Another headache. Maybe it was a nacho hangover. Harry and I had nearly cleaned the platter.

With the animals fed, I put some French roast on to brew

and lit a fire. Then I went and looked out the back door. Eighteen inches at least.

After breakfast, Buck fought his way out into the snow while I tried to sweep a path with the broom. A few minutes later, he was back, tracking white fluff through the kitchen. Then he shook himself and flopped onto his bed by the fire.

I tried to avoid the green bottle sitting on the counter but finally surrendered to its pull. Maybe I wouldn't smash it after all.

"Let's get this over with," I grumbled, then I poured a second cup of coffee, grabbed the bottle, and went to my office.

I set the bottle on my desk. An everyday jar made for practical uses. Without threads for capping, it would have been stoppered and set on a shelf. I turned on my laptop and searched for eighteenth-century bottles that resembled this one. After ten minutes of combing through websites, I decided that I had a common apothecary bottle.

A rumbling sound out in the driveway drew me to the window. Tom Barrett had arrived with his plow.

—

In the afternoon, I gave in to a sudden urge to clean out the pantry. Then I finished up one last piece of paperwork for the company insuring the necklace. At three o'clock, my landline rang.

"Oh, hey...Libby?" said Keith Janus, sounding startled to hear me.

"Yes, this is Libby. Keith?"

"Sorry, I didn't expect anyone to answer, given the state of the world. I figured I would just leave a message. How did you get into the office? Snowmobile?"

"I'm at home. I'm having our calls forwarded today. Is everything all right?"

"Yes and no," Keith said. "We survived the blizzard, but the deck didn't. At least, most of it didn't."

We. I wondered about that as he said, "I just thought someone might want to come out and look at the damage once the roads get cleared. Since the deck is part of the project, I wasn't sure if this was going to change the scope of work."

I told him I would try to get one of our crew to pay a visit by the end of the week, although the chances of that were slim.

"No hurry," Keith said. "How's that door holding up?"

"Just fine," I assured him, and then we said goodbye.

—

That night, another dream of Hugh. He waved me into the dark, fire-lit parlor, got up from his Windsor chair, and pulled out another on the other side of the table.

"Please," he said, waving me into the chair. I thought I should leave, that I didn't belong there in that shadowy place that seemed to be his private domain. "When there is naught to be done, who shall guide us?" he said with his Welsh lilt. Then he turned to me with a sad smile. "Elizabeth, who will guide us?"

A deep rumbling outside the dark room made me look away...

It was morning. A plow was scraping down Chambers Road. I got up and opened the blinds just in time to watch the tail end of it disappear toward the Reardon School, leaving a swath of packed snow in its wake. The last embers of the dream glowed in my head. I had gone into Hugh's room and sat down at his table, which I'd never done before. I had joined him.

When there is naught to be done, who shall guide us?

"A good question," I whispered. And one to which I had no answer.

CHAPTER THIRTY-EIGHT

By Friday, two days of sun had left the roads slushy and passable. With Harry off at a job site and no one else available to survey the damage to Keith Janus's deck, I set out for Morley.

"Thanks for coming out so soon," Keith said, answering the door in jeans and a sweatshirt. He waved me into the front hallway. Something was baking, filling the house with a spicy aroma.

"Better to get this done now," I said. "If we need to file a revised permit, I'll want to do it before the borough offices shut down for the holidays."

I followed Keith into the living space. Sun washed through the windows looking out over the back of the property.

"And Spence and I won't be around after tomorrow because we're heading up to Jodie's on Sunday," Keith said.

A clatter to our left drew my attention toward the kitchen, and I looked over to see a young man with dark hair lifting a baking pan out of the oven.

"This is Spence," Keith said, gesturing toward his son. "Spence, this is Libby Casey."

The mystery of the *we* he'd mentioned on the phone the other day had now been solved.

Spence, dressed in a black long-sleeved T-shirt and jeans, set down the pan and waved in that noncommittal way young people have with strangers. "Hi there," he said.

"Spence is the chief baker around here at Christmas," Keith said.

"Want a cookie?" Spence pointed a metal spatula at the baking pan.

"Maybe later," I said.

As Spence cut up whatever was in the pan, Keith and I stepped over to the windows. "Here it is," he said.

I gazed out to the blank space where the deck had stood. A few boards that ran closest to the house were still in place, but the rest had either fallen to the ground or dangled in splinters from posts on either side.

"Looks like Mother Nature has done some of our work for us," I said. "Mind if we take a closer look?"

"Sure thing." He swung open one of the French doors. "But be careful."

I leaned out over the wreckage. It looked worse than it really was. Most importantly, the back wall of the house appeared intact. "I doubt we'll need to revise the permit," I said. "I'll just need a few photos to show Harry." I rummaged in my purse for my phone.

"Want me to do that?" Keith asked, watching closely as I angled into the doorway.

I declined his help and snapped my photos. Then, as I moved further out over the edge of the doorjamb to take the last one, my head suddenly went light, and I felt myself falter. The next thing I knew, Keith had wrapped an arm around me and was pulling me back with a tug. I felt my phone leave my hand. Both of us stood still for a long moment, looking down to where the phone had tumbled through space, Keith's arm still around me, my heart racing at this brush with calamity.

"Oh, no," I heard myself say.

We moved away from the door, and Keith let his arm fall away.

"I'll go get it," said Spence, who had stepped up to join us, and then he stuffed a cookie into his mouth.

"No, I'll do it. I don't want you down there," Keith said.

"I'm sorry," I said. "I don't know what came over me. Let *me* go. It's my phone."

Keith shook his head. "You're safer here. It'll just take me a few minutes."

He disappeared into the hallway that led to the master suite behind the kitchen. I stood at the French doors, both of them now closed, trying to pick my phone's blue case out of the collage of snow and mangled deck boards below.

"Don't worry," Spence piped up. "My dad will get it."

This admiring confidence in his father touched me, for it was the same confidence I once had in my own father. "I'm sure he will," I said.

Keith reappeared in the living room clad in a jacket and boots. "Sit tight," he said, and he hurried out the front door.

"Want a cookie now?" Spence frowned a little, as if he wasn't sure what the moment called for.

When I assented, he took the plate of little squares from the kitchen counter and held it out to me.

"I smelled spice when I came in," I said. "What kind are they?"

"Ginger bars. We make them every year." He set down the plate.

I bit into the tender cookie crust swirled with a buttery ginger concoction. "This is delicious. Are you sure you shouldn't be in culinary school?"

He smiled his father's smile. "Everybody always likes those."

I devoured the rest of the ginger bar, my gaze drawn to the front of his shirt where the plump face of a man was outlined in white brushstrokes, the word *Hitch* scrawled under it. "What got you interested in film?"

"Hitchcock, mostly." He pulled at the front of his shirt. "And John Huston. I like the old auteurs. They knew how to create scenes."

The adoring words of a neophyte. I couldn't help but smile. They reminded me of my own days as a neophyte infatuated with classic architectural styles. Not that I'd ever stopped being infatuated.

"Who doesn't love Hitchcock?" I asked, sensing he would welcome more discussion on the topic. "Ever see *Notorious*? That might be my favorite movie of all."

"Yeah, I've seen that one like five times. It's awesome. Everybody talks about *Psycho*, but I don't think it's his best work."

The front door opened. Keith stamped snow from his boots, advanced into the living room, and held up my phone. "Not even cracked," he said, thrusting it out to me. "The snow saved it."

"I told you he'd find it," Spence said. At the sound of a ping, he reached into his back pocket and drew out his own phone. Tapping the screen, he walked toward the stairs, waved without looking back, and started to climb.

I thanked Keith and clicked on my phone. "Still working."

"So, what happened there? I mean, when you were taking the pictures." Keith shrugged off his jacket and tossed it onto one of the two chairs Alicia hadn't taken. "You looked a little pale. Are you okay?"

I opened my mouth to reply, but I couldn't muster the words. That one little question had just knocked the wind from me because, no, I wasn't okay. *I am not okay.* I felt myself fighting for breath.

"Hey, look, why don't you sit down?" Keith gestured toward

the empty chair and watched as I lowered myself into it. "I'll get us both a cup of coffee. I made a fresh pot not long before you got here."

Should I make some excuse and hurry away? No, that would be rude, especially to a client I needed to impress—although impressing him wasn't exactly what I was doing at the moment—and to the man who had so kindly boarded up my back door.

"Cream and sugar?" he called over from the kitchen.

"Just cream," I said, hoping he wouldn't pry further with questions about my condition.

He returned, balancing two cups and a plate with ginger bars that he set on a table between the chairs. Tossing his jacket to the floor, he sat down and propped one leg over the other, his calf at a right angle to the opposite knee, boot dripping onto the bare floorboards.

I reached for a cup of coffee, craving the first hot sip, and at the same time a little worried about those floorboards. They shouldn't get too—

"If you want to talk a little more about anything, I'm pretty good at listening, despite being a lawyer." He smiled and bit into a ginger bar.

"That's kind of you, but I'm not sure I could even tell you why that happened." I took another sip of coffee. A cleansing sip. "I think I'm just coping with a lot right now. Please understand," I added quickly, "it's nothing to do with work. So don't worry about that. I mean, about your—"

"No need to explain that you're human," Keith said. "And I have complete faith in you and Harry." He finished off the ginger bar. "So, does that ghost have anything to do with how you're feeling? I'm not sure you gave me the whole story that day."

"I didn't, but the whole story is complicated. I'll take you up on your offer to listen another time."

As we finished our coffee, we made conversation about his

sister and my animals and the upcoming spring gala for the 1825 House. Finally, I said I had to be going. I grabbed a ginger bar from the plate. "Mind if I take one of these? Tell Spence I want his recipe."

At the door, I turned to Keith, the idea of wassail at the Brown Pony returning from some corner of my brain. "The holiday open house I told you I do every year? It's tomorrow," I said. "Would you like to come and bring Spence?" The wrong sort of impulse, but I couldn't take it back. "It's last minute, I know, and if you're too busy getting ready for your trip to your sister's…"

"Actually, that sounds great," he said. "I might have to work on Spence. Most kids are glued to their video games, but with Spence, it's the classic movie marathons I have to pry him away from."

"My friend is bringing her son, Kenny, who's almost eighteen. And Harry is a complete movie buff. I'm sure he'd love to compare notes with Spence."

"Say no more." Keith smiled. "We'll be there."

—

Home from work, I set down a bag of last-minute groceries for the open house. The office would be closed for the next twelve days. That happy fact made me sigh with relief. I ignored the little green bottle that I'd left on the counter and put away the food.

Harry had been in his usual good spirits when I returned to the office that afternoon, and when I told him about my impulsive invitation to Keith, he'd simply shrugged and smiled. I uncorked a bottle of red zinfandel. I hadn't told him how I'd almost tumbled out Keith's French doors. That would be my and Keith's little secret. I poured the wine into a stemmed glass and admired its rich claret color. Keith Janus and I shared a secret, something only the two of us knew. How oddly intimate that felt.

After dinner and a walk, I mixed up some batter for pumpkin bread, filled two loaf pans, and slid them into the oven. Should I text Diana? We were still on hiatus, and I was as doubtful as ever that she would show up for the open house. In eight years, she hadn't missed it, but in those eight years we had not fallen out. Not once.

No text, I decided. Then I threw myself into setting the dining table buffet-style while the rich aroma of pumpkin and spice filled the house. I thought the elegant holiday touches—holly napkins and Granny's china, good silverware and brass candlesticks—would cheer me. But when I stepped back to admire my work, I felt only empty. My first Christmas in this house and possibly my last. Not exactly cause for celebration.

What Harry said about finally deciding on the next step had been rattling around in my mind all day. Should I cancel Sharon and call the realtor to feel her out about selling? If I had to take a loss on the place, so be it. Maybe getting away from here was the best way to fix my life.

That night, Hugh pulled me from a fitful dream where he'd reached across his table and grabbed my arm.

Elizabeth! Elizabeth! His voice echoed through the bedroom. *Help me! Please. You are the one.*

"Help you?" I shouted. I sat up. "How can I help you? I don't know what you want!" Buck rolled over and reached out his paw. "What about me? Did you ever think about me? That I'm the one who needs help? Because I do! I...need...help!"

I drew in a stuttering gulp of air, and some fuse inside me sparked. "You aren't going to make me leave! You know that? This isn't your house anymore. It's mine. If anyone is going to leave, you are!"

CHAPTER THIRTY-NINE

On Saturday, Emmeline arrived at the stroke of three. When I opened the front door, she was waiting on the stoop with a poinsettia in her hand. Behind her, the man in the tweed cap retreated toward his silver Toyota.

"I told Ben to find the nicest one," she said, holding out the flower. "Followed my orders, did he?"

"Perfectly." I looked back to the man. "Emmeline, do you mind if I meet your driver?"

Emmeline swiveled her head toward the driveway. "Ben!" she called. "Come back! Libby is keen to meet you."

Ben turned and strode back. A white fringe of hair poked out from under his cap. As he drew up beside us, Emmeline said, "She thinks you're my driver, Bennie."

"I suppose she's right about that," Ben said with a chuckle. He had the same English accent as Emmeline's and the same bright blue eyes. "I also do duty as her big brother." He held out his hand. "Benedict Caldwell, and of course you're Libby. Em has told me about you."

"Nice to meet you, Benedict." I took his chilly hand in mine.

"Just Ben will do," he said. He looked up at the house behind me. "Fine old place you've got here. Working out for you, is it?"

"Still lots to do."

"Well, then, I ought to be going. A pleasure to meet you, Libby. Em, girl, be back for you later."

"Ben," I said, before he could spring away. "You're invited as well, if you like."

He tugged once at the bill of his tweed cap. "Much obliged. But I'm on a mission to the shops and then to fetch a tree." And off he went.

Inside, Buck padded over to Emmeline. "Good chap," she said, letting him sniff her hand. "Ben has been at me to get a guide dog. But my flat over at the school seems a bit too cramped." She surrendered her woolen trench coat, and I took it to the closet. "We'll see come January. I'm up for head of school. If it works out, I'll get the cottage."

"Is it that stone building behind the school?" When I turned back to her, Emmeline had her hand pressed against the wall near Hugh's portrait.

She let it drop when she heard me approach. "Ben is so fond of your Georgian here," she said. "They're all around back home, of course. A penny a bushel."

"This one's 1760," I said, wondering about her hand on the wall. "Cup of tea?"

"Yes, grand."

In the kitchen, Emmeline settled in at the table and leaned her stick against the end of it. Her white hair was pulled back in a low ponytail, and she was dressed simply in black trousers, a red sweater, and gray-and-white sneakers.

"Is black tea okay?" I asked. "I have some Earl Grey, if you'd prefer that."

"The world thinks we English are all mad for the Earl Grey," Emmeline said with a chuckle. "I'll take the black tea, thank you."

I set our steaming teacups on the table. "There's milk and sugar right in front of you. I can help."

"I'll manage," she said. After fixing her tea, she paused as if she'd heard something or had a sudden thought. "Got all your holiday business done, have you?"

"Almost."

"My mother used to spend a week preparing all the food. The gingerbread, that was my favorite." Emmeline sipped her tea and set the cup back in its saucer with remarkable accuracy. "All that lovely spice."

"Exactly," I said. "Spice makes the world go round. So that must have been back in England?"

"A little village north of London. We had a cottage and a lovely small garden, but a few years after Daddy died, Mum moved Ben and me to America so we could live with Auntie Harriet. I had lost my eyesight by then, and Mum was at sixes and sevens and needed help, you see."

She told me about the disease of the retina that had stricken her when she was ten and left her unable to see anything but vague shadows. Then we moved on to talk about her family and mine as we finished our tea. I poured us each a second cup.

"You've no children," Emmeline said. A statement more than a question.

"Ray and I tried for a while. He had a daughter from his first marriage. Maddie. She's become like a daughter to me, too. What about you?"

"I wouldn't have been good at children, I'm afraid. At any rate, they got crossed off the list after Horace left. My husband," she explained, lifting the fresh cup of tea from its saucer. "After two years of marriage, he nicked the small savings I'd put aside from tutoring and flew the coop. A dodgy bit of business, he was."

"How terrible."

"Better to know that sooner rather than later, dear." Below

us, the heater rumbled to life, and Emmeline tilted her head. "I do wonder about your house," she said.

"To tell you the truth, so do I. I'm afraid I've been wondering ever since I moved in."

"You found it already occupied, did you?"

"Can you sense that?"

"Unfinished business. It keeps all of us stuck in places we might not want to be, living and dead alike."

I wanted to tell her I knew all too well about being stuck. "His name is Hugh Jones. He was a Welshman," I said. "He built this house, and for some reason, he's still here. I've...heard him. Hugh speaks to me sometimes. In fact, just last night."

"Hugh. You've become acquainted, then."

"He leaves me things. And I dream of him. I can't explain it, but—"

"No need, dear. This life is full of things that can't be explained, hmm?" She sipped the last of her tea. "I would say that this house, this Hugh, needs you and you need him."

"Go on. Please, tell me."

"There are always reconciliations to be made."

"Reconciliations?"

"The reason you moved here," Emmeline said, her unblinking eyes staring across the table, seeming to burrow down into my secret truths. "Here to your Georgian."

"It felt like mine, in the beginning. Like a new start, a place I'd been called to. But now I think I should have stayed where I was."

"Except you didn't, did you? Your unfinished business was calling. One day soon, you will find a way to finish it."

"I... It's a long story. But I've contacted a woman who does cleansings. She's coming after the New Year. I'm hoping that will finish it."

Emmeline smiled. "Yes, cleansings. Sometimes they're just parlor tricks, mind you."

"You don't think it'll work?"

"If Mr. Jones has been here all these years, he might not be inclined to leave because of a little smoke and abracadabra."

"Then *I* will. That's my plan. I'll move out."

"Hmm, but your business is bound to follow you, isn't it?"

The grandfather clock began to strike the hour. Emmeline pushed out her chair. "I had better find the loo before your other guests thunder in."

CHAPTER FORTY

September 1761

Hugh entered the kitchen, sweaty from harvesting peaches with the crop crew all afternoon. A supper of cold chicken, bread, and cheese had been set out on the table. Molly would have gone home to the village by now. Priscilla and the children were nowhere to be seen.

He wiped his face with a rag, sat down, and took off his boots. His sore feet needed to breathe.

A great, startling scream rang from somewhere in the house.

"Prissy?" he called.

Then came another, like that of a strangled animal. Miranda.

Hugh flew to the hall. "Prissy!" High above him, a loud dispute was brewing. He sped up the stairs.

"Daddy!" James Martin called from his bedchamber. Up on the third floor, Priscilla was saying, "Give it to me, mistress!

This minute!"

"Daddy, Daddy!" Not just James Martin, but the twins crying out as well. He rushed to his son's chamber and saw the three of them huddled in the farthest corner, Abby and Alice sobbing, James Martin out in front as if to shield them from harm.

"Get out! Get out!" Miranda screamed overhead.

"James Martin, you must be my strong boy," Hugh said. "Stay with your sisters. Keep the door closed. I shall go to Mama."

"Mr. Jones! Mr. Jones!" Priscilla shouted. "Please, she's got a knife!"

Hugh bounded up the stairs and found Priscilla and Miranda in the west chamber.

"I tried to take it from her," Priscilla said, looking over at Miranda, who stood near the single bed with a paring knife, her hair in disarray, her eyes flashing with menace, the jeweled necklace dangling from her neck. For a week they had tried to take it from her, for fear she would rip it off in a fit and ruin it, but she wouldn't let them.

"Are you here to help me?" Miranda asked. "Tell her to get out!"

"Miranda!" Hugh said. "Prissy does not wish you to be harmed. And neither do I."

Miranda raised the knife as he approached and then turned her head to address someone unseen. "No, shh, quiet!" she whispered. She turned back to Hugh. "This is your doing!"

"Prissy, could you go check on the children?" Hugh said, dread coursing through him. "And then fetch Hattie's sleeping potion and some wine."

Priscilla hurried away. Hugh took another step toward Miranda. "My sweet, you must relinquish the knife and then we shall talk."

"Talk about what? Time's winged chariot? Time's winged chariot! Time's winged chariot!"

"Yes, poetry and Mr. Marvell, if you like." Hugh held out his hand. "Now, turn over that knife or I shall wrestle it from you."

"A chariot with wings, wings. I've put them in the floor," Miranda murmured. She regarded his hand for a long moment and then dropped the knife into it. "Do not let the other one have it." She looked up at him, her eyes now distant, and cold as stones.

Hugh's heart seized at the sight of those eyes so bereft of warmth or fondness. It was all he could do not to turn away. "Sit," he said, gesturing toward the bed.

Miranda gazed over at the closet. "You mustn't look in there. It's not for you." Then she dropped to the mattress, whispering, "Chariot hurrying near. It's coming, isn't it?"

"Mr. Jones." Priscilla had returned with a cup of wine and a small, pale green bottle. "I have already mixed it." She set the wine on a little bedside table and held up the bottle. "The laudanum Mistress Hathaway left. It might take hold faster than the potion."

"Send her away," Miranda said. "Can't you send her away?"

"In a moment," Hugh said. He nodded at Priscilla, who removed the stopper and tipped three drops into the wine. "Thank you, Prissy. Gather the children for supper. I will be down presently."

At the door, Priscilla turned. "She was in the closet with the knife, Mr. Jones. I thought it not safe."

"Very well. You acted with prudence." With Priscilla gone, Hugh handed the cup to Miranda. "Some wine, my sweet. It will improve your spirits."

Miranda eyed the cup with suspicion but took it and gulped it down.

"Lie back and have a nap," Hugh said.

She lay back on the pillow, her lips moving silently, one bare foot sweeping back and forth like a pendulum.

Hugh reached down and brushed back her wayward hair. His heart howled inside of him like a great wounded beast. His beautiful, dear Miranda. His Venus, his charm.

—

October came in with all its array of red and gold, and the harvest was finally done, but Hugh could take no pleasure in any of it.

"The children are refusing to be anywhere near her," he said to Sam one night as they sat drinking ale in the kitchen. "She has taken to closing herself in on the third floor, preferring the closet, it seems. If not for the fact that poor Prissy has taken the brunt of her tenancy up there, I would consider it a blessing."

"Prissy has told me." Sam puffed at his pipe and grew thoughtful. "Martha says Miranda's spirit must be free to be at peace."

"And how does it get free, my friend?" Hugh swallowed the last of his ale and poured more from the redware pitcher. He lifted his cup in Sam's direction. "Has she told you that as well? Has she told you what's to be done when no physician might help? When the case has become hopeless?"

Hopeless cases. His aunt's words long ago. She'd been telling him about that hospital in London, Bethlem, that they called Bedlam. How a pedestrian walking by at any hour might hear the screeching of the lunatics imprisoned there and the rattling of their manacles, that it was bad luck to get too close, for the ills of the hopeless cases might spill out and—

"What are you thinking, Hugh Jones?"

Hugh looked across the table to his friend's searching eyes. "I don't want Miranda to suffer indignities, to lose all that she is, or was. I don't want her locked away. But what other choice presents itself?"

"I will tell you more of Martha's wisdom, if you would like to hear it." Sam laid down his pipe.

"Yes," Hugh said with a nod. "Please tell me."

CHAPTER FORTY-ONE

Harry and Mitch arrived to the open house shortly after four o'clock, followed by Keith and Spence ten minutes later. At four thirty, still no Diana. I plated the hors d'oeuvres as my guests' voices drifted from the living room. Finally, the knocker clanged again, and someone, probably Harry, went to answer it.

The front door opened, followed by the muffled sound of Harry's greeting and then the crack of Diana's laughter. I didn't go to welcome her. Let her come find me.

As a bustle of activity at the coat closet died away, she appeared in the kitchen. "Hey, girlfriend," she said, stepping up to where I was fixing a cheese board at the counter. "Long time, no speak."

"Long time, yes. I'm glad you made it."

"I was tempted to drop my son off at an undisclosed location and drive away, but Cal talked me out of it."

She was trying to make nice. I should too.

"Things no better with Kenny?" I set a wedge of brie on the board, cut a sliver off the end, and held it out to her. An olive branch.

She slid the cheese into her mouth. "Hmm, brie, the food of the gods. I'm working on a poor man's cheese tart for the café, by the way. You can be my guinea pig."

After adding a block of cheddar and an assortment of crackers, I pronounced the cheese board done and hoisted it from the counter. "My hungry guests are waiting," I said.

"Here." Diana reached for the board. "Let me."

She hadn't seen Keith and Spence yet, so I was half-expecting her to boomerang back to me after she dropped the food off in the living room. She would have questions. But a few minutes later, she'd still not shown up. The ice might have cracked, but it hadn't completely broken. I added a few more spinach puffs to the plate of hors d'oeuvres and shuttled it to my guests.

Everyone had settled in nicely, Emmeline on the sofa between Harry and Mitch, Keith and Cal in the easy chairs, Spence and Kenny cross-legged on the area rug, with Buck crouched in front of them. No Diana.

"Eat up," I said. "Eggnog and cognac coming soon."

On my way back to the kitchen, I found Diana in the hall, standing in front of Hugh's portrait. I realized then that I should have taken it down for the evening, but it was too late now.

"There you are," I said. "I was wondering where you'd gotten to."

"Let me guess. This is your ghost?" Her eyes remained on the portrait. "Where'd it come from?"

"Vivian Seabrook's daughter found it in her uncle's basement. She offered to let me see it."

"So, you hung it up. Won't she want it back?"

"After the New Year. I figured it was best to hang it to keep it away from the animals."

She shrugged and turned to face me. "That makes sense, I guess." Diana was straining for equilibrium, I could tell.

"Actually, I'm looking for something else to fill that spot for was just lying there?"

I nodded. "I know how that sounds, and I'm sorry I didn't tell you the truth. But it's not the kind of thing, well...it's all gotten very confusing."

Keith tipped the eggnog into a glass. "Confusing enough to make you almost fall out of my deck door yesterday?"

"Maybe even a little more. There have been—"

Diana breezed through the doorway. She looked first at me and then at Keith. "Oh, I'm sorry. Am I interrupting something?"

"No, of course not," I said. "We were just fixing the eggnog."

"Can I help?" She came over to the counter and looked down at the serving tray.

"Nope. Almost done," I said.

Keith turned to go. "I'll leave it to you two now."

"He's helpful," Diana said when he was gone. "I like that in a man. Another check in the pro column."

"Oh? I didn't know we were keeping score." I reached for the tray.

"Come on. Don't be coy, Libby Casey. He's a person of interest."

The same thing she once said about Ray. We'd been chatting over coffee the morning after I first introduced him to her, and we got giddy the way girlfriends do about such things. The memory stabbed me with regret now that—

"Or is that something else I'm not supposed to know?" Diana's voice pulled me from my thoughts.

"It's not like that," I said, letting her remark pass. "It can't be, not right now. Anyway, let's go before the mob comes for us."

—

At 6:30, Ben arrived for Emmeline with a Douglas fir tree in tow. "Em called and said she thought you could do with this," he said, maneuvering it through the door.

"That's so kind, but how did you know I didn't—?"

"Perfect timing." Harry. He came up behind me and helped Ben haul in the tree.

I looked from Harry to Ben and back to Harry. "This sounds like a conspiracy."

Harry answered with a wink.

Five minutes later, the tree was in its stand in front of the living room bookcase, and Emmeline and Ben were saying goodbye at the door.

I leaned in to hug Emmeline. "Thank you for the tree, and everything else," I said.

"I'm only doing what I was meant to, Libby. And so must you. Do ring me up if you need me. Or any old time."

Mitch and Harry left a short time later, along with Diana, Cal, and Kenny.

"We're still on for Christmas, aren't we?" Diana asked, pulling on her coat, a plea in her hazel eyes.

I offered a smile in return. "Yep, if you'll have me. Casserole in hand."

Closing the door, I followed the sound of voices to the kitchen and found Keith and Spence cleaning up. When I tried to wave them off, Spence said, "It's faster with three people."

For the next few minutes, we put the leftovers away, loaded the dishwasher, and took out the trash. Buck sat by the fireplace, watching us.

"Your dog's really cool," Spence said. "So is your house. It would make a great movie set."

"You're welcome to use it someday," I said, glancing from Spence to Keith. "And thanks, both of you, for helping with the mess. I'm sure you want to be on your way, though. You have a drive ahead of you tomorrow."

"Aren't you going to decorate your tree?" Spence plucked a ginger bar out of the plastic container he and Keith had brought and shoved it whole into his mouth.

"Maybe Libby wants the house to herself now," Keith said.

Spence gave his half-frown. "Sure thing."

"You know, I never did like stringing the lights. Maybe you could help me with that," I offered.

Twenty minutes later, my new white lights were twinkling on the tree.

"Excellent ambiance," I said. "Thank you."

After a moment of quiet appreciation, Keith and Spence gathered their coats to go. At the door, Keith handed his son a set of keys. "You want to get the car started?" he said.

As soon as Spence ran off, he turned to me. "Have any plans for your ghost problem?"

"I've called someone about doing a cleansing. I've decided not to go down without a fight."

Keith nodded. "All right. If you need backup, let me know. I'll be home from Jodie's next Friday."

I watched him disappear down the walkway, considering his offer. No point in dragging a client any further into my troubles than I had to, although he felt like more than a client now.

I closed the door on that thought and went to turn off my office lamp. Sugar Plum was half asleep on the upholstered chair, her refuge from the evening's noise and bustle. A piece of paper lay on the floor.

"Have you been knocking things off my desk again?" I asked, snatching it up. It was a reminder I'd written to track a package due to arrive any day now. As I dropped it to the desk, the light hit it in such a way that I could see the shadow of something dark on the other side. I turned it over.

My apologies. HPJ.

"It's a little late for that," I said. "Apologies not accepted."

If what Emmeline said was true, that Hugh and I needed each other, I hadn't the slightest idea why, and I didn't care to find out.

CHAPTER FORTY-TWO

For most of Sunday, I lay on the sofa watching heartwarming holiday movies, Sugar Plum tucked beside me and Buck dozing on the floor. I didn't feel like fixing meals, so I nibbled at leftovers from the open house. In the afternoon, I decorated the Christmas tree while my curious animals looked on.

There had been no more sign of Hugh, no more notes, no more whispers, no slamming doors. *My apologies.* As if that could make up for everything.

At four o'clock, as Buck and I headed out the front door for a walk on Chambers Road, I spied a package beside the stoop. Another UPS delivery. But when had it arrived? Yesterday, after the open house?

I looked at the return address on the small box. Carol Seabrook.

Suddenly revived, I hurried Buck through his walk. Then I took the box to the kitchen and sliced through the packaging tape. Inside was a shoebox, with a note taped to the top: *Libby*, it read. *Had some holiday shipping to do so I thought I would* send these along. Those things I told you about from Aunt Dot's. Unfortunately she died a few days after I came by your place and we had her cremated. Carol*

Tucked inside the shoebox were two identical books, very old, about the size of a trade paperback but thinner in volume, with plain leather covers. I took them out and set them on the table. Touching them gave me a feeling I couldn't quite name.

I sat down and opened one. My heart ticked.

The Diary of HP Jones, containing herein his thoughts and ruminations.

The paper I found upstairs. This must be the diary it was torn from.

Turning the page, I inspected the inside binding and knew for sure when I saw a frayed track down the length of it. I began to read:

18 May 1760

Miranda once again anxious. Her hands always busy. I am perplexed by this turn in her deportment and I continue to worry over it. Sherry and a tonic at night help her sleep.

The next few entries had to do mostly with work on the farm and Hugh's interactions with a man named Sam, with whom he seemed to be friends. But always there was a mention of Miranda. She was restless and then she was calm and then she was restless again.

In late June, an entry confirmed my suspicions about the necklace:

M has receiv'd my gift with much gratitude and celebration and she looks a rare sight with it around her neck and with the locket hanging down on her bosom. She has already clipped a piece of my hair to put inside it.

It seemed to bring a welcome diversion. Dear girl.

But a few days later:

Another turn in M's behaviour this morning. Prissy bore the brunt of it and had to clean up the spilt soup. And poor dear Abby sent into a wail over the whole affair. My heart was heavy all day with the thought of it. M bearing no resemblance to herself and making such rebuff to Prissy. Hattie, thanks be to God, arriv'd at four o'clock with another tonic.

Hattie. The name on the garden plan at the county historical society. An herbalist or a midwife. And Prissy, a housemaid or servant?

The next few pages, dated the end of June, had to do with crop work again, deliveries of rum Hugh made with his friend Sam, and his concerns about being away from home for too long.

An entry in August referred to the portrait:

I have encourag'd M to take up her brushes as frequently as she can for painting seems to focus her mind. She tells me she has nearly finish'd the portrait. I have view'd it in secret against her admonitions and found it to be a superb rendering. I was however dispirit'd to wonder whether she might ever put her considerable skills to making another.

August 1760. Dan had been wrong about the date. I set the diary aside and went to the hall and stared up at Hugh. Here was a mere moment in time, a man sitting at a table in his parlor, warmed by a fire. But behind that moment was a complicated world not visible to the eye.

A superb rendering. Yes, despite the troubles residing there, it was superb. But had it really been the last thing Miranda ever painted? Had it been the only thing?

Back in the kitchen, I fed the animals and made a sandwich. Then I took Buck for a walk. When we returned to the house, I poured some decaf and went back to the diary. Miranda, Hattie, poppy teas and tonics, and in October…what was this? An incident at the Brown Pony Inn, an altercation in which Hugh's friend Sam was shot and wounded, his attacker dying soon after from a knife wound Sam inflicted.

Had this incident prompted the inquest Edward Koch mentioned in his history of the Jones estate? A far cry from wassail and a toast of good cheer.

Hugh ended the entry:

A curse on the blasted devils for one of my gauntlets fell lost as we fled. But we were fortunate indeed not to have lost our lives.

The glove he'd left me. It must be the mate to the lost one. I slid my phone from across the table and dialed.

"Libby?" Keith answered. In the background, the sound of conversation and laughter.

"I'm sorry if I've gotten you away from something."

"We were having cocktails with some friends. No worries. Is everything okay?"

"I just, well, I've gotten hold of Hugh Peter Jones's diaries, if you can believe it, and—"

"The Hugh Jones who built your house?"

"Yes, him. My ghost. Anyway, he mentions the Brown Pony Inn, funny enough, and I thought…"

What had I thought?

"What does he say?" Keith asked.

"He and his friend Sam were having a drink, and two men picked a fight with them because Sam was Indigenous."

I reported to Keith the rest of what Hugh had written about the incident—Sam stabbing the man who'd shot at them, Hugh and Sam fleeing in the wagon.

"Wow, I didn't realize the place was an eighteenth-century crime scene," he said, his interest evidently piqued. "That's pretty heavy stuff."

"I think it might have become a court case, or something. But according to a book about Simms I read recently, the records might be gone. I guess it's another mystery for me to try to solve." Someone called Keith's name in the background. "I should let you get back to your party."

"It's just food being served. Listen, we'll talk when I get back. Maybe we can solve the mystery together."

"Please, don't worry about it, and Merry Christmas. Tell Spence I said hello."

"Same to you. And Libby?"

"Yes?"

A silence. "Nothing. Not important. Take care."

It was seven o'clock. I took a cup of warm wassail and two of Spence's ginger bars to the living room, switched on the Christmas tree lights, and sat on the sofa to read the rest of the diary. There was another entry about the Brown Pony incident, a sheriff coming to question Hugh, and Hugh sending him away.

In December, there was some sort of ritual performed on Miranda by an Indigenous woman named Martha Little Cloud. Maybe a friend of Sam's?

Dear God, do not let it fail. Else we shall find no other to save her.

How well I knew the feeling. They were desperate for a cure, so they went with their last hope, their version of an eighteenth-century clinical trial. *The sorcery*, as Ray had called it. But Miranda didn't get better, and when the sheriff returned a few days later, she shot at him with a musket, and Hugh had to hide the gun thereafter to keep it away from her.

The bulk of the following entries told of Miranda's decline, her behavior more erratic, the children frightened, the house in chaos. The more I read, the more I understood what had been happening in the Jones household.

Hallucinations, voices, conversations with people who weren't there. How hard that must have been in a time when no one had the slightest inkling what mental illness was. What did they do to people like Miranda back then? They locked them in a room or chained them to a wall.

Though it was late, and I was tired, I read a little more before going up to bed. Miranda ranting and raving, refusing to change her clothes or comb her hair, throwing a jar of lavender oil across the bedchamber at someone unseen, cracking a window.

Lavender. The scent in the garden. Had it been Miranda out there all this time and not Hugh? Did I have two ghosts?

With only a few pages left, I continued to the last entry:

8 January 1761

I find no satisfaction in the death of the Scot Hamish Campbell but thanks be to God that the court saw fit to release me from all responsibility in that regard, and that Sam will not swing from a rope.

Mystery solved.

I closed the diary, led Buck upstairs, and got ready for bed, thinking about something else Edward Koch had written in his little history.

But not much is known about the personal affairs of their

household.

Once upon a time, someone must have known something about the affairs of the Jones household. Someone who had read the diaries, whether it was Dan Seabrook or another person. A diary by its very nature begs to be read. Wouldn't at least one family member have been curious enough? Vivian's grandmother, maybe. These could be the sleeping dogs she had advised Vivian to let lie. Mental illness, no matter how far back in the bloodlines, wasn't something you talked about in Vivian's day, or even now.

I lay awake and thought about Hugh. So helpless in the face of Miranda's illness, a scourge that couldn't be stopped. Our common ground.

Elizabeth!

Did I imagine that? I rolled over and opened my mouth, but I couldn't find words to answer.

CHAPTER FORTY-THREE

Harry called in the morning. "Need anything?" he asked.
Yes, but I don't know what. "All good for now, thanks." I would tell him about the diaries later. At the moment, they seemed too complicated a topic, and I wanted to finish reading them first.

"You still planning to spend Christmas with Diana and Cal?"

"I have to. I'm bringing the crowd favorite, and I can't let them down."

"Sweet potato casserole? I'm jealous. But all's forgiven if you're bringing Sloane's meatloaf and mashed potatoes tomorrow for Christmas Eve."

"I've already got the order in."

"Music to my ears. Mitch will make the salad. We'll wash it down with a stellar cabernet he found the other day. You'll love it. Anyway, I gotta go. We're heading up to Katie's for lunch."

With a cup of French roast in hand, I was about to dive into the second diary when my landline rang. Cassie.

"Libby, I've been meaning to get back to you about Sharon

and how all that went. But I ended up in the hospital for a few days. Blood sugar too high."

Of course it was. "Is everything okay now?"

"The doctor told me that if I didn't bring down my levels, I could start losing toes, or worse. Goodness sakes."

"The good thing is, there are lots of options out there for diabetes, Cassie." I was on the verge of telling her how lucky she was to have those options, but I bit my tongue. "Just follow the doctor's orders and you and your toes will be fine."

"Yeah, I've been getting told a lot lately about what's best for me." An awkward moment of silence passed. Had I upset her even with that benign bit of advice? Eventually, Cassie blew out a sigh. "Sometimes you just need a little time to figure things out yourself."

"I know what you mean," I said, thinking about Diana and my own annoyance with unwanted advice.

"So, tell me. Have you called Sharon?"

I told her about the appointment I'd set up. "Maybe you can come out before then for coffee. You wanted to see the house, right?"

"I'd love to. I'll check my calendar and get back to you."

After hanging up, I took the second diary and my mug to the living room, put my feet up on Ray's coffee table, and started in. Month by month, the whole of 1761 was a downward spiral, Miranda disappearing into the woods or the garden, growing thin, shutting herself away in one of the rooms on the third floor.

The third floor. Miranda. Had she been the one who carved mysterious markings into the floorboards? Had her ghost been the one slamming the door?

In December, Hugh wrote:

The children refuse to see M or even venture close to her. I count the days she spends locked away on the third floor as a blessing for their sakes. There is no light in her eyes for them or for me. And daily I wonder whether to put a lock on the door to that room so she might be confine'd there with her demons and leave us alone. I have consider'd what Martha told Sam and it weighs heavy upon me. Hattie says time will be my tutor. What will be its lesson?

When there is naught to be done, who shall guide us?

Hugh's words to me not so long ago. I knew now what he meant.

This diary wasn't filled to the end as the other one was, and there were only a handful of pages left. I wasn't sure I had the heart to read them, to hear the chronicle of misery and despair that surely would follow, so I skipped ahead to the last few entries dated March 1762:

Oh, how can I keep a steady hand to write this?

Miranda is gone from me forever. My good, my gentle and dear Miranda. My heart!

I took in a sudden breath. Miranda dead? Had she done away with herself? Flung herself from a third-floor window? Yes, of course. 1762.

Hattie arrived in the morning and mix'd the deadly contents in the cup. But it was I who offer'd it to M and bid her drink. I alone shall bear the black mark for this act and shall carry it with me all my days. I shall wander through this life like a lost and wretched pilgrim.

But my children. All that I do now must be for them.

"Hugh," I whispered, tears rising in my eyes. "Oh, Hugh!" I wrapped my arms around my middle and rocked back and forth. The diary fell to the floor. "You know about Ray. Somehow, you know."

In the next moment, all my guilt and sorrow welled up into a flood of choking sobs. I wasn't sure whether I was crying for Hugh or myself, for Miranda or Ray. I could only sit there, rocking and sobbing, feeling his pain and my own.

Buck came in, wandered over, and laid his head on my knee. I put my cheek to his brow and felt his consoling warmth. "Thank you, boy. Thank you," I whispered, sniffing back the tears.

I sat up, wiped a trail of slime from under my nose with my sleeve, and picked up the diary. One last entry.

I have hidden the green jar at the back of my dresser drawer like a relic. It was M's transport to Heaven and that is where she shall always dwell. Hattie says I will join her there one day.

But where will I find forgiveness? Who will understand what I have done?

"I forgive you," I said. "I understand. You and I are the same."

I closed the diary and set it on the coffee table and cried all over again. Hugh had been waiting for me, waiting and waiting through the centuries, and finally I had come. I had found him.

There are always reconciliations to be made.

Was it possible that Hugh and I could finally find peace together?

CHAPTER FORTY-FOUR

May 1762

Sunlight streamed down from a cloudless sky as Hugh pushed the wheelbarrow through the trees. The headstone thumped and his shovel rattled against the barrow's wooden bottom, making a dark, low note to accompany the twitter of birds overhead.

It was a grim task ahead of him. But at least the earth would be good and soft. That hadn't been the case two months ago, when he and Sam had given up trying to dig Miranda's grave out of the frozen ground. For a month, his wife had lain in the barn, nailed into her coffin, awaiting her burial. He had spread an old horse blanket over the box, thinking improbably that it might keep her warm. But perhaps the truth of it was that he hadn't wanted to see the coffin there as he went about the work of the farm.

And so, he had prayed for spring and an early thaw. As soon as the earth loosened in April, he and Sam had gone back to digging. Then Johann and his sons came to help them lower Miranda into her grave.

Hugh pushed into the clearing and set the wheelbarrow back on its legs. Then he took the shovel and dug a trench at the head of the still freshly turned patch of earth. He thought of their wedding night, how they had buried the paper under the garden gate. How long ago that time felt now. How like some other life.

Throwing down his shovel, he pulled the thin slab of stone from the wheelbarrow, straining with its weight, and lowered the bottom into the trench. After filling earth in around it, he shored it up with a few rocks so that the headstone could settle into place for a while. He would need to discourage trees and other growth from invading the clearing. He, too, would be buried here someday, beside Miranda. Laid to rest, as it was called. But no, he wouldn't rest. He didn't deserve to rest.

He tossed the shovel into the wheelbarrow, said a silent prayer to Arianrhod, and headed toward home.

—

The next day, he took the children back to the clearing. Abby and Alice toddled on either side of him in their grubby little gowns and soft shoes while James Martin walked ahead, gripping a clutch of lavender tied with string. Priscilla had offered to accompany them, but Hugh wanted to bring his children here alone, this being the first time they would set eyes on Miranda's grave.

"And here we are," he said as they reached their destination.

James Martin pointed to the patch of turned earth. "Is that where Mama is?"

"Aye, she's there," Hugh said, reining in Alice, who'd become distracted by a squirrel. He then pulled Abby in and held each of the girls by the hand. "Shall we say a prayer? Our Father, which art in Heaven..." Hugh started, and James Martin joined him. Miranda had taught their son the prayer, and he knew it by heart. The twins chattered aimlessly along.

"Would you like to lay Mama's lavender on now?" Hugh said when the prayer was done. The very word *lavender* filled him with sorrow. Who would love it now? How could he catch the scent of it and not feel an ache in his heart?

James Martin bent and laid the purple bundle on her grave. "Here are your flowers, Mama," he said. He rose and turned to Hugh. "Can Mama hear me?"

It was all Hugh could do to utter a reply. "Aye, she can. Up in Heaven. And you may speak to her whenever you like." He pointed to the headstone. "And that is how you will know where her grave is."

James Martin went and kneeled down beside the stone. "Something happened to Mama. I didn't like it."

Abby and Alice pulled away from Hugh's grip and went to join their brother.

"Nor did I," Hugh said. "But I will remember her for all her goodness, and you must do the same."

As they all trailed back to the house, Hugh thought of his children going on without Miranda, not remembering her as he would, never knowing the full light of her worth. But he would make certain their lives were as fine as they could be. It was all that was left to him now.

"You will see Mama again," he said. "She will be waiting for all of you in the grace of God."

But would *he* see Miranda again? Hugh shoved that question as far into the distance as he could.

"Un rêve d'amour," he whispered. A moment later, when he began to cry, he wiped away his tears quickly so the children wouldn't see.

CHAPTER FORTY-FIVE

I called Diana first thing in the morning. Christmas Eve.

"I know you're probably busy getting the house ready for company," I said, "but I need to talk to you."

Silence, then a sigh. "Look, sweetie. I think you'll just have to work this out on—"

"No, Dee, listen. I really need to talk about…everything."

There was a long pause. "Okay," she said finally. "Ten o'clock. I'll make coffee."

"I'll bring bagels," I said.

Coffee and bagels had been one of our rituals through the years.

When Diana answered the door, she studied my face as if she might discern some clue as to what I was about to tell her. Then she took the bakery bag from my hand and inspected the logo. "Good. I wasn't going to let you in unless they were from Bannerman's."

We settled in at her kitchen table, but suddenly I wasn't hungry. I was too nervous to be hungry. I had to get everything out first.

And so, I did, telling her, beginning to end, about the night I took Ray's life. Tears washed my face as I made my confession. The lethal dose of morphine, the harrowing silence that followed, my collapse onto the bed where I lay beside him one last time before calling an ambulance. "I felt empty. My whole being felt empty," I said, swallowing back a sob with a sip of coffee. "I had taken Ray out of the world and silenced him forever."

I leaned back in my chair. "So that's it," I said, looking into Diana's composed face.

She reached her hand across to grab mine. "All you had to do was tell me this before. I mean, why didn't you tell me? It explains a lot."

"I thought…I thought you wouldn't understand. That no one would. And it's a crime, you know, eutha…putting someone out of their misery, even though it's really a mercy. Don't you think it was a mercy?"

"Oh, Lib," Diana whispered, getting up and coming around the table. She pulled me up for a hug. "Of course it was." She plucked a tissue from a box on the counter and handed it to me. "You loved Ray, and no one could blame you for what you did. If it had been Cal, well, I can't say I wouldn't have done the same thing."

"But I promised to stand by him and do what we needed to…to keep him alive. And I gave up and let him down. I let everyone down." I dabbed at my eyes.

"You let him go. That's what you did. You gave him peace, which he must have wanted."

"I tried so many times to tell you, and Harry, and I just couldn't get the words out. And then, well, Hugh… I know this sounds crazy, but I think he was helping me, that he brought me to that house so we could both find a way to move on."

I told her everything about the diaries and Hugh's confession about Miranda, and then I told her what Emmeline had said. *I would say that this house, this Hugh, needs you and you need him. There are always reconciliations to be made.*

Diana shook her head, her hazel eyes lit with curiosity. "I have to admit that it all has a crazy logic to it now, doesn't it? And I'm sorry, sweetie. I really am. But you seemed to be sliding into another bad place, and that felt wrong."

"I feel like I'm done sliding now, so try not to worry anymore. Oh, wait," I said, feigning a thoughtful look. "Diana Pruett not worrying about something. I don't know if that's possible."

"Too funny, girlfriend." Diana flashed a smile that held both relief and affection. "Now you sound like my husband."

When we finally said goodbye, I walked out her door and down her front steps, feeling like Scrooge redeemed.

—

At home, I took Buck for a walk. "Not that way," I said when he started down the path for the springhouse. "Let's go somewhere else."

I led him through a grove of trees toward the western part of the property. I had taken a quick walk through the area before moving in and hadn't been back since. Now, feeling freed of a terrible burden and in the mood for something new, I wanted to go back and explore.

In a small clearing about two hundred yards from the house, Buck stopped and sniffed around the ground. Then he barked and bounded off again.

I went over to what he'd been sniffing at. A rectangular slab of stone about twenty-five inches high lay in the dirt, half hidden by withered weeds. This wasn't a random piece of granite that had seized out of the ground, but a stone cut deliberately, with squared edges and a rounded top. A headstone.

Its surface was pocked and chipped and grimed black. I bent down for a better look. The engraving was impossible to read, and my attempts to brush away the grime proved useless. Whose headstone was it? I thought back to what I'd said to Harry about finding Hugh's grave. Maybe this was it.

I had never liked seeing a headstone toppled—it always looked so bereft, so undignified—so I took the top of the stone in both hands and lifted it to test its weight. No, too much. I would need to bring Harry back to help me. The two of us could stand it upright and dig the bottom back into the earth.

I whistled to Buck, and a moment later, he charged out of the tree line. "Come on," I said. "I have something I need to do."

Back at the house, I dug my pruners from a kitchen drawer, found some red ribbon amongst my Christmas gift wrap, and went back outside, where I snipped some stems from an evergreen and tied them into a bundle. Then I walked back to the clearing and laid it on the headstone. A tribute to whoever was in the ground beneath.

On my way back in, Carol Seabrook texted. *Libby: Keep the painting. My Christmas gift to you. Enjoy!* I texted a "thank you," went to the hallway, and looked up at Hugh with a new fondness.

"I guess we're stuck with each other now," I said.

The grandfather clock chimed. Time to get moving. Harry and Mitch were waiting for dinner. I packed the meatloaf and mashed potatoes into a bag, and at the last minute added a bottle of Rémy Martin. Then I texted Harry. *Christmas Eve feast coming right up.*

After we ate, I took Harry aside and told him the whole truth about Ray's death, just as I had with Diana. He listened attentively, but I couldn't tell what he was thinking behind his calm blue-green eyes, so when I finally finished, I asked, only half joking, "Still want to be my business partner?"

His gaze softened. "In this life and the next," he said. Then he gave me a hug and poured me a cognac.

As we sipped, I told him about the headstone. We decided that on New Year's Day we would gather at my house with Mitch and Diana and Cal and light candles for Ray and Miranda. Maybe I would invite Emmeline too. She was as much a part of this now as they were. She deserved to be there.

—

On Christmas night, I came home from Diana's and lay on the sofa with a glass of cabernet, watching the tree lights glimmer. Hugh had said he would wander through his life like a wretched pilgrim. Would he continue to wander even now? Or would he finally be at rest? And Miranda, was she still here? Had she ever been here?

The house had stayed quiet and still since I read Hugh's diaries. Not a sound, not a thing out of place. Nothing.

The diaries. Where had I put them? I went to the kitchen and found them on the counter. Gathering them up, I took the diaries to my office and tucked them into a drawer. I had tidied my desk before Christmas, but now something lay right in the middle of it. A pebble. I picked it up and held it to the light. It was red and faceted. A ruby.

Of course. The missing ruby from the necklace.

"Thank you, Hugh," I said. "But I'm afraid I have nothing to leave you."

The next morning, when I took Buck back to the western side of the property, the bundle of evergreens I'd placed on the headstone was gone.

CHAPTER FORTY-SIX

Keith Janus called two days later. "In the mood for a cup of coffee?" he asked. "We could talk about those diaries."

"Sure. Diana's?"

"Mind if Spence comes along? I told him about the ghost. Hope you don't mind, and he can't wait to hear about it."

In a booth at Cozy Cottage Café, the three of us spent two hours chatting over lattes. Hugh, Miranda, the diaries.

"And that missing ruby from the necklace?" I said. "I found it on my desk Christmas night."

"No way," Spence said, leaning forward with a glimmer in his eye. "That is so awesome. It's like Hitchcock meets del Toro."

We moved on to other matters, Keith and Spence sharing the kind of easy rapport I imagined my father and I might have had if he'd lived long enough. And Keith, well, I realized all over again how smart and warm he was, and how satisfied I felt when he looked my way.

By the time we all said goodbye, I knew I wanted to see them both again.

"How about you gentlemen come over for Libby Casey's famous cheese lasagna one night? Sunday, perhaps?"

"Awesome! I can't wait to see your dog," Spence said.

"And there's something else you might like." I explained about the old headstone. "Be sure to come over while it's still light. Maybe we can do a rubbing of the stone."

Two days later, as I waited for them to arrive, I went upstairs and took a photograph of Ray from on top of my dresser and stared into the face I had lost.

"You were the love of my life, and you always will be." I kissed the photograph. "And if I could have you back, I'd give everything I own. But I can't, and now I need to move on. Or at least I need to try."

Keith and Spence arrived at four o'clock, and together we went out to the clearing with a few pieces of paper, a few pencils, and a small scrub brush. After scrubbing away as much dirt from the stone as we could, we made the pencil rubbing. *Miranda F Jones, Beloved Wife of Hugh P Jones*, the engraving read. Under it were her dates. *1734–1762.*

"I was so sure it was Hugh's," I said.

Spence reached into his pocket. "I'll take a picture." He snapped a shot with his phone and then turned to Buck, who was nudging his arm.

"If you want, Spence and I can come back and get the stone upright," Keith said.

"Hey! Look what I found!" Spence was crouched on the ground a few feet behind us. "I think it's another headstone."

Keith and I went over to join him. "I think you're right," Keith said, lowering himself beside his son. "It's really down there in the dirt."

The two of them brushed at the soil encasing it and pulled at the weeds.

"We'll have to dig it out with a shovel," Spence said.

Keith scrubbed the top with the brush. Then I bent down

and placed a paper over it and rubbed with a pencil. *Hugh P Jones, Devoted Husband of Miranda*, it read. His dates were underneath. *1730–1792.*

"The two of them together. Of course," I said. "This could have been a family plot." I thought then of James Martin, who died at Germantown. How that loss must have been yet another stab to Hugh's heart. Was his grave somewhere nearby? "But it's getting dark, and lasagna is waiting. We can look another time."

—

On New Year's Day, we all gathered in the clearing. Harry and Mitch, Diana and Cal, Keith and I. Spence had gone back to California to spend the holiday with his friends, but before he went, he and Keith had set Miranda's and Hugh's headstones upright again.

"Emmeline not coming?" Harry asked.

"She's with family," I said. "She'll be over next week."

I passed out electric candles and poured cognac into the paper cups I'd given everyone.

"This truly is a new year and a new chapter in my life," I said. "Thanks to all of you for helping me make that happen." I raised my cup. "Happy New Year, my friends."

Everyone raised their cups and added in "Hear, hear!" or "Sláinte."

Then I raised my cup again. "And here's to Miranda and Ray, and to Hugh. May they rest in peace."

Back at the house, we feasted on homemade soup, French bread, cheese, and wine. After everyone else had gone, Keith helped me clean up the kitchen.

"So how are you feeling now that things are becoming normal around here?" he asked.

"Pretty good. But there's one thing that would make it even better."

"What's that?"

"A bowl of wassail and a toast of good cheer."

"The Brown Pony." Keith smiled. "I think all that ends on New Year's. How about we go a week from Saturday and make our own toast?" He grabbed my hand and brought it to his lips. "What should we toast to?"

"Let's start with new beginnings and go from there."

ACKNOWLEDGMENTS

Thank you to everyone who made this book possible. My wonderful writing partners—you know who you are—for their astute and intelligent insights. Barbara Kyle and Greg Frost for their editing on early drafts of this story, and Mark Spencer for his invaluable editing and mentorship in the later stages. My publisher, Literary Wanderlust, for seeing merit in this story and taking it on, and the mighty Jennica Dotson, my editor at LW, for her keen and thoughtful eye that made the story stronger in every way. My family and friends for their support in all my endeavors.

My husband, Jim, for his quiet grace and tireless courage that inspire me every day to do and be better.

ABOUT THE AUTHOR

C.J. McGroarty grew up in a small town outside Philadelphia, PA, where history was around every corner. She knew she was a writer early on and made it her life's work. A former reporter for *The Philadelphia Inquirer* with an MFA in Creative Writing, she has also taught English and writing at the college level.

Her fiction and nonfiction has been published in journals and magazines that include *The MacGuffin, BloodLotus, Newtopia, The Schuylkill Valley Journal, Dark City Mystery Magazine, Rathalla Review*, and *Toasted Cheese*, among others. Her short story "The Dying Season" was nominated for a Pushcart Prize.

C.J.'s debut novel, *Clara in a Time of War*, was published in 2022 by Atmosphere Press. Set in Pennsylvania during the American Revolution, the story features an earthy and determined heroine as well as some of C.J.'s favorite themes, including love, loss, friendship, and courage. When she isn't writing, C.J. enjoys reading, gardening, and scratching her history itch as a tour guide at Historic Waynesborough, the lifelong home of celebrated Revolutionary War General Anthony Wayne. She lives in Chester County with her wonderful husband, Jim, and their indomitable tortoiseshell tabby, Lily

www.ingramcontent.com/pod-product-compliance
Lightning Source LLC
LaVergne TN
LVHW090925260825
819208LV00008B/93